One

A woman entered the church behind me and dipped a finger in the stoup. She was slender, not unattractive and about forty years of age, so she and I had age and at least one characteristic in common. Her brown hair was short and thin and a touch greasy, it was frayed at the edges and curled slightly at the back, and beads of water were taking shape on her brow, but then it was a hot day and even duchesses sweat. She moved elegantly in a flower-patterned ankle-length skirt and a blazer-type jacket. She carried her affluence effortlessly, complacently even, as if she were born to it and had never had to rub her padded shoulders with anyone beneath her station. She possessed a pair of legs that would not have disgraced a model on a Versace catwalk.

Watching people was a hobby of mine, the one for which I was paid. In my line of work, it paid to be observant. Anything and everything that one could see might prove to be useful. One simply never knew.

The woman shot me a glance. It was not a friendly face that she showed me. The last time that I had seen such a look was when I was a detective constable and had just asked a detective chief-superintendent out on a date. I watched as she made her way to a pew about halfway down the church, to the right of the aisle, her heels clicking on the marble floor as she went and resounding amid the vaults and colonnades. She genuflected, artful as a ballerina, and took her place at the left end of the pew. She put her hands together and focussed lovingly on the Sanctuary. Before starting her prayer, she looked over her left shoulder and saw that I was still watching her. I wondered what she was praying for. Some people were praying for fine weather, as there was some kind of fair in town that week, but I doubted that she was praying for that.

As I was starting to enjoy the silence, a man in black emerged from the shadows, his cassock flapping as he walked towards me.

"Hello…" he said.

"Hello, Father…" I replied.

"I've seen you in church a couple of times," the priest returned, speaking gently and with humility, "but you've never ventured beyond the stoup."

It seemed that *I* was being watched now.

"I'm something of a coward in churches," I confessed, "especially in Catholic churches."

"You're not a Catholic, I trust."

"I'm a private detective."

"Are you in trouble?"

"Trouble is my business."

"You look troubled."

The priest was standing three feet away from me, by the stoup, oozing fatherly concern for my welfare, though he did not know me from Adam, his hands clasped together in prayerful supplication. I listened for sounds coming from Woodstock Road, but came there none, for this was a place of peace, a refuge from the clamour without, tranquil as the grave. We were gazing at each other. I blinked first. I heard myself doing so. I had no idea what to say to him. I had no idea why I was there. Eventually, I spoke.

"Since I'm here, I should light a candle."

The priest's near-inscrutable features betrayed the anguish of a man who had spent a lifetime carrying the weight of human sin on his narrow shoulders, and who now compounded his pain by shouldering mine. However, I was not prepared to let him suffer for my sake; rather, I wished to suffer for his, and more; so we stood facing each other in mutual expiation. The church was arousing in me feelings of which I did not approve. I had to get out of there, but not before I had confided in this gentle, humble man.

"Today, apart from my birthday, is the one day of the year that I dread."

The priest nodded, slowly, as if to coax more information from me. It was then that I realised that the man did everything slowly. He walked slowly. He talked slowly, extending his words, his vowels leaving his

Sailing By

Sailing By

Darren John Wilson

Code Unknown
http://codeunknown.co.uk

First published in Great Britain 2014

Copyright © Darren John Wilson 2014
The moral right of the author has been asserted

Code Unknown, 74 West Way, Oxford OX2 9JT
http://www.codeunknown.co.uk

ISBN 978-0-9931089-0-7

Designed and typeset by Fridolin Wild (Code Unknown)
Cover design by Fridolin Wild (Code Unknown)

mouth in a languid stroll, as if they had nowhere to go and were in no hurry to get there. He was hearing my disclosure, slowly, so much so that if I did not hurry it along then I would find myself having become a Catholic by osmosis.

"Today is my mum's birthday," I continued. "If she's alive, she'll be fifty-eight years old."

The priest remained silent. He just looked at me, slowly.

"Today's also the thirty-second anniversary of my dad's death. On my mum's twenty-sixth birthday, my dad died, aged twenty-seven. What a bitter-sweet day that was."

"What happened to your mother?"

"Two months after my dad died, my mum went to a parents' evening at my school…but didn't come home."

"And you haven't seen her since?"

I shook my head. "She vanished in a puff of smoke, and I didn't even see the smoke."

"You know, we priests are exposed to the gamut of human folly. You wouldn't believe what we hear in the confessional. We don't believe it ourselves half the time. But the years have taught me one lesson: that people try their best in trying circumstances; and that people rarely act without good reason."

That sounded to me like two lessons.

"So bear that in mind as you wonder, as you must, why your mother took her leave of you, apparently without cause."

The priest's words were kind and designed to reassure. They filled the church with their wisdom, and they swirled in my head, where they mingled with memories of a time so long ago that it seemed like the setting for a fantasy, a fable, a tale of lore. Except that the day that Roseanne left might have been yesterday.

"If ever you're here and need to talk, ask for me, won't you? I'm here more often than not."

"I will do that, Father, thank you."

"I'm Father Gregory Sansom, bachelor of this parish."

"I'm Daniel Winter, likewise."

7

"I'll be seeing you, Daniel."

"You probably will be, Father."

The priest signed himself with consecrated water from the stoup. He genuflected. He left the church. His footsteps tapped on the tarmac as he crossed the courtyard on his return to the Oratory House.

When my phone rang, I retrieved it hastily from my jacket pocket. The number showing on the screen was a new one. I was being pursued by a prospective client. He or she – hopefully, she – would have to wait. I silenced the phone. The woman at prayer looked over her shoulder again at me, scornfully, as if she wished to chastise me, a punishment to which I would gladly have submitted. I whispered "sorry" in her direction, though she was not the sort of woman readily to be appeased.

A single flame atop the candelabrum beckoned me. Having obeyed its call, I took a second candle and lit it with the flame of the first. The candles were now placed side by side. They burned together, until a draught – from nowhere – threatened to blow them out, but, after a flicker from both, the flames soared, they surged, blazing audibly in the hush of the church. I was wary of signs, or of what appeared to be signs. People were apt to project meaning onto random occurrences. There were co-incidences, accidental and incidental convergences in time and space, and there were signs, portents from the beyond. People believed in one or the other. I drive a rare car – there are probably no more than ten of them left in the world – yet one passed me on the Oxford ring road two days prior to that Monday in August. That it did so meant nothing. What was simply was, what is simply is, and what will be simply will be.

Yet there I was, in a Catholic church, lighting a candle.

Two

The last person I wanted to see was Gabriel Tolpuddle. I didn't mind his inherited wealth, nor had I the least objection to his leisure. His relative youth – he was twenty-five years old – vexed me only insofar as he paid scant respect to someone fifteen years his senior; someone, moreover, who had given several years of his life keeping the streets safe enough for moneyed people like him to walk on.

"Well, if it isn't Daniel Winter!"

"Hello, Gabriel…"

We intercepted each other. Gabriel regarded the Oratory curiously, as if he were at a wedding reception and had come across a relative whom he didn't quite recognise.

"I didn't know you were a papist," he said, gleefully, for now he had yet another stick with which to beat me.

"I'm not."

"I guess there's a lot that we two don't know about each other."

"Shall we keep it that way?"

"If we keep meeting like this then we're going to get to know each other rather well, aren't we?"

"Rather too well for my liking…" To suggest to him that I had been joking, I proffered a smile so false that it would have exercised a lie-detector. "Would you like a lift home?" The insincerity of the offer was so cunningly disguised that if fooled even me.

"You might be a man of humble proletarian origins, Winter, with the likes of whom someone from a family as distinguished as mine should not associate, but you are very nearly a gentleman with it."

"Was that a 'yes'?"

"Let's say that my acceptance of your offer is heavily qualified with a sense of noblesse oblige."

"Naturally, I'm humbled by your acceptance."

"Lead the way."

I led him the twenty yards to my car. He carried on walking for a short time after I'd stopped, doubtless because he never imagined that such a distinguished vehicle could possibly have belonged to me; upon seeing me open the door on the driver's side, he seemed prepared to countenance the possibility that I was not committing theft. He regarded the car from his distant perspective, before approaching the rear and casting a critical eye over it, as if he were assessing a girl being offered for his delectation in a brothel.

At last, he passed judgement. "I say, old man, this is a tasty bit of steel."

"It gets me from here to there."

"Where did you find it?"

"Someone owed me."

"And he repaid you with this?"

"He still owes me."

"What did you do, save his life?"

"I did more than that."

Gabriel nodded at the stereo. "What's this shit?"

"The Fall…"

"You're a fool for listening to it."

"This is one of The Fall's best albums, *The Infotainment Scan*, and this track is one of their best. It's called *A Past Gone Mad*. And hasn't it just?"

"I've never heard of them."

"In May, nineteen-ninety-three, the year this album came out, I went to see The Fall at The Grand, at Clapham Junction. I'd lost the tail of the thief I was tracking, so I went to the gig. I didn't have a ticket, but I got in by showing the bouncer my warrant card and saying that I had someone present under surveillance. And who did I see in The Grand?"

"The thief you were supposed to be tracking?"

"The very same," I replied, nodding. "When I nicked him, I complimented him on his music taste. Before I interviewed him, back at the station, we compared notes on Fall gigs that we'd been to. It turned out that we'd been going to the same gigs for years. He told me that he knew someone who knew Mark E. Smith, The Fall's leading man, and that he was meeting the band at a party after their gig at the Victoria Rooms, in Bristol, four days later, and that he could get me an invitation to the party. So I got him off."

"You didn't charge him?"

"He'd stolen a few handbags – expensive, but empty, from shops – and a bit of jewellery, but he was small-time, not worth pursuing when we had bigger fish to fry. I signed the paperwork and out he walked, promising never to steal again. Because of him, I got to meet Mark E. Smith. He was smoking some queer stuff as well – Mark E. Smith, at the party – but I didn't nick him."

"Were you one of those bent coppers?"

"Is there any other sort?"

We were cruising down Banbury Road towards Summertown, an hour before the city's offices began to spew out people. We stopped at a pedestrian crossing. An old man with a stoop took an age to pass before us, so that, by the time he reached the other side of the road, rush-hour was not such a distant prospect.

"I've a confession to make."

My passenger was suffering a bout of contrition, but I suspected that he had the strength of character to overcome it.

"I can put you in touch with a priest," I replied.

"I read that book of yours…the one you wrote…"

"Then it's a shrink that you need."

The old man reached the pavement. Watching him had been like contemplating a snail in hot pursuit of a tortoise. I hoped for his sake that he didn't have much further to walk.

"I wanted to see what all the fuss was about."

"I wasn't aware that there'd been a fuss."

"Enough people bought the book to enable you to live in bourgeois splendour in North Oxford."

"I'll never be bourgeois, and I wouldn't call my flat splendid, though I'm happy enough with it."

My fixation with the old man, as he made sclerotic progress towards an all-too-distant destination, promised to overtake me, as did the beeping car behind. I put my car into gear and into motion.

"I've another confession to make."

"It sounds like you're going to need a year's supply of sackcloth and ashes."

"Reading your book changed my life."

My antagonist deserved an Oscar, so masterful was his disguise of the Gabriel Tolpuddle that I knew.

"Have you undergone a personality transplant?"

"It made me give up using prostitutes."

For a second, I had no idea what to say. The second became two seconds.

"I liked the book's sensibility." Gabriel was holding out his hand like a priest giving a sermon. "It seems to me that your book is a plea for compassion in a broken world."

"That's an interesting interpretation."

"One of the characters in the book is a prostitute. You described how she came to work in a brothel. You traced her life from childhood. It made me see that working girls are not mere chattels existing solely for my pleasure. They are people, with feelings, family, friends, hopes and dreams. Your book made me feel ashamed of my life of self-indulgence."

Refreshingly disconcerting though it was to meet the new Gabriel, I wasn't hearing the voice of the penitent. I was hearing the voice of someone who had changed his mind, having been persuaded of the merits of another's argument. Still, I was pleased that Gabriel had seen the need to mend his ways, and wished to express my pleasure in a fitting tone. Wishing not to sound pious, then, I opted for a touch of flippancy.

"Gabriel by name…angelic by nature…Who would have thought it?"

We had got stuck at the lights by Marston Ferry Road.

"Don't you disapprove?" Gabriel returned.

"Of what?"

"Of my having frequented brothels..."

"I don't disapprove of your grammar."

"Have you never gone with a prostitute?"

"I've nicked a few."

"The upshot of my newfound sense of virtue is that I'm going to use my leisure for the good of society."

"I can't disapprove of that."

"So, among other good deeds, I've agreed to fund the campaign against the building of the leisure centre at Middlemarch Farm."

"Would that be the leisure centre that Dane Goldman wants to build?"

"It would."

"Good luck with that," I joked.

"The man's a crook. The police should have nicked him years ago."

"He's one of those slippery characters: every copper's worst nightmare."

"It's his money that's slippery. It keeps slipping into the pockets of policemen."

The comment was so horribly close to the mark that I pretended not to have heard it.

"I bet he'll be there tonight," my passenger continued, "down at the lodge, with some of Oxford's finest boys in blue, their silver buttons nice and shiny, vodkas and tonic and funny handshakes all round…"

"Will your dad be there?"

"That depends on which lodge we're talking about."

The car behind me, the same one as before, discharged a volley of mechanical expletives.

"Why are people so impatient?" I wondered aloud.

"My dad made millions by being impatient."

As I drove straight ahead, I searched the rear-view mirror and watched with relief as the car behind me turned right into Marston Ferry Road.

"Would you like to join our campaign?"

"That's a most tempting offer, but I'm rather busy at the moment."

"The environment is the Big Issue, old man, because, when it's in ruins, we will all of us be homeless."

"Have you ever considered a career in advertising?"

"There isn't a career that I haven't considered."

"Do you mind if I let you out here?"

Gabriel watched helplessly as I turned left into a space in the slip road by the shops.

"Here's perfect," he replied, "as I fancy a couple of jars in the Dew Drop."

Facing Gabriel, I told him that, as always, seeing him had been a pleasure, whereupon a commotion was heard. We both looked right, over the half-open window on my side of the car, at the group of girls spilling out of the Dew Drop. There were six of them. They divided into two equal groups and formed battle lines.

"You leave my man alone, d'you 'ear?" the leader of the one group yelled.

"I'd rather sit on me finger than go wiv 'im!" the leader of the other cried back.

As the two leaders made a move for each other, brightly-coloured earrings, necklaces and bangles shaking manically with the shifting cellulite, their respective comrades pulled them apart and struggled to keep them apart.

"Poor bloke, whoever he is, being fought over by those two…" Gabriel said.

"No two women have ever fought over me, hard though you'll find that to believe."

"I'm telling you, old man," Gabriel went on, depressed, "civilisation's doomed."

"I wouldn't give up on it just yet."

"The high-water mark of civilisation has been reached. Mankind is sinking back into the abyss."

"It's just a row between a few people who've had too much to drink."

"At four o'clock on a Monday afternoon?"

"At least they're not lying on their backs, servicing the moneyed and leisured likes of you."

"I wouldn't go with any of them if *they* paid *me*."

We were talking calmly, as if we were discussing the prospects for economic growth in the final quarter.

"People like them blight the lives of people like us," Gabriel resumed.

"It's 'people like *us*' now, is it?"

"Their kind is breeding like rabbits. They shall inherit the earth. God help us."

As the circus across the road moved on, Gabriel and I sat facing straight ahead, morosely, like two bored policemen on surveillance.

Gabriel broke the silence. "Listen, I might need to seek your advice."

"You, a modern-day aristocrat, want advice from a lowlife like me?"

"I need a purpose in life."

"I thought you'd found one."

"That's just a start. I need to do something that defines me, that tells the world who I am…that tells *me* who I am."

"Can't you work for your dad?"

"He's retired. Anyway, I wouldn't want to be one of his placemen. I want to be my own man."

My wallet was taken from my black Harrington jacket, and my business card produced. It was plucked from my hand.

"Call me," I said.

"'Daniel Winter…Private Detective…'" Gabriel read. "So, you couldn't leave the detective work alone, eh?"

"Except that I'm the Lone Ranger now…"

"Do you need a Tonto?"

"When I do, you'll be the first to know."

"Have you any cases on the go?"

"Someone has been trying to call me."

"You'd better return that call then."

"I will…when I get a chance."

Gabriel acknowledged the hint with a mournful smile. "I've given you a hard time down the years," he said. "I'm sorry."

"I've enjoyed the banter."

"If truth be told, I look up to you."

"I'm not sure that I can cope with your being nice to me. It makes me suspect that I've strayed into a parallel universe."

"You are the man that I want to be."

My search for a reply was very nearly fruitless. "We all want to be someone else."

"I *will* make amends. I *will* be a good man."

Embroiled in a curious situation, one that was becoming more curious by the second, I sighed. "You're talking to me as if I'm some kind of moral exemplar."

"I needed to tell someone, and you're here, and you're a good man."

"Just take one step at a time. Don't try to become Saint Francis of Assisi overnight. It won't work."

"It's all right for you. You're naturally virtuous."

"I think you're confusing me with someone else."

"For years, I've been whoring my way around the Thames Valley. I'm surprised that I haven't dropped dead with exhaustion."

"As you've just said, you plan to harness that energy to a better purpose."

"Are you taking the piss?"

"As if I would…"

"You're wondering how long the reinvented Gabriel Tolpuddle will last, aren't you?"

"It had crossed my mind."

"I'll show you."

"You have nothing to prove to *me*."

Deep in thought, Gabriel continued to stare into space. He had the air of the penitent now. He looked like a man who had condemned himself to a lifetime of virtue and self-denial. It was not often that a man suffered an epiphany in the passenger seat of my car. I was about to hint that it was time for him to leave and get on with being virtuous, when my phone rang.

"Thanks for the lift, old man," Gabriel said as he bundled himself onto the pavement. He showed me an approving and hopeful thumb, which made a change from being shown a disdainful and dismissive finger. He slammed the door shut.

This prospective client was persistent and persistent clients were the sort that I liked.

Three

Climbing the four flights of stairs to my flat was like ascending one of planet earth's smaller mountains, even a man fifteen years my junior would have found it so, and an Olympic athlete would have reached the summit feeling like his workout was done for the day. Breathless I was, then, when my next-door neighbour apprehended me.

"Here you are, dear!" As she waddled towards me, like a duck in a desperate hurry, she brandished that day's edition of the *Oxford Mail*. Though I kept telling her that I was quite happy to buy my own copy, she would insist on handing me her dog-eared remnant at about this time every day.

"Thank you, Maureen," I said as the paper passed from hand to hand.

"The lift's not working again," she moaned.

"You're still a young woman, Maureen," I lied. "You can manage a few stairs."

Maureen blushed. "You do flatter me," she returned.

"There should be a man in your life to flatter you." My reply was heart-felt. "We can't have a fine-looking woman like you going to waste."

Maureen's cheeks turned a deep shade of crimson as she adjusted hair that was lacquered so thoroughly that it resembled a bowl of overset jelly. "Another murder…" she said, pointing at the newspaper, though for a second I thought she was referring to her latest hairdo. "What is the world coming to?"

My key was in the door when I glanced at the headline. "Dead Man Weds" would have made me laugh, but "Dead Man Identified" had me sighing with resignation at the evil that men do. Before I had one foot inside the flat, I knew that my unwanted guest was still with me. I could smell her. She had turned my bathroom into her private spa and my spare bedroom into a veritable boudoir.

"Hi, Daniel…"

"Kendal, you're still here." I went into the kitchen and dropped the newspaper on the table. "Why am I not surprised?"

Kendal followed me. She stood before me. A lightweight red top was clasped to her burgeoning chest; it had no sleeves to speak of and failed to cover her waist. Her belly-button, protruding amid an expanse of flesh, was pierced by a golden stud. Below her waist, a short black skirt hugged curves that coalesced with unspoilt legs, legs that increased, with seductive abandon, to flat green shoes and the grey-tiled floor.

"Put some clothes on, will you?"

Kendal looked down at her person to check that she hadn't lost her modesty entirely. "I *am* wearing clothes," she protested.

"I've seen more material on a bandaged thumb," I replied.

Kendal scowled at me as I went to the kettle.

"Cup of tea?"

The girl considered the question as if I had just asked her to explain the theory of relativity. She had an endearing countenance when faced with situations outside her limited experience of life. At such times she was stripped of bravado, she was the girl trying to come to terms with the world around her, the child struggling to counter the threat of lost innocence.

"I baked you a cake." Kendal tended to answer a different question to the one that was asked her.

"What?"

"Are you deaf?"

"I've never thought of you as the cake-baking type." I would not have been more surprised if she *had* just explained to me the theory of relativity. "Anyway, I didn't know that I had the ingredients in the house to bake a cake."

"You didn't. I bought them."

"With what?"

"With the tenner you owe me."

"But *you* owe *me* a tenner."

19

"Then I used that."

"Don't pick at it," Kendal urged, "eat it."

"What is it?"

"It's carrot cake topped with marzipan."

"What are you trying to do, poison me?"

"I'll cook you dinner tonight."

"I have to go out tonight."

"Where?"

"To the Dew Drop…"

"Who with?"

"Sabrina…"

Kendal glared across the table at me, her displeasure palpable. "You're seeing *her* again?"

"I've put her off twice. If I put her off again, she'll kick me into touch."

"So, let her."

"I like her."

"Is she your girlfriend?"

"No…"

"Will you bring her home with you afterwards?"

"How long's this interview going to last?"

"Will you?"

"No…"

Watching Kendal eat her cake made me feel guilty, because the piece that she had given me was fast becoming a fossil. I raised my cup to my mouth and drank some tea. When Kendal copied my movements, I suspected that she was playing one of her games. Up went the mug to her mouth, where it lingered longer than was necessary, before being lowered, with exaggerated finesse, to the wooden surface. On completing the performance, as if to solicit my approval, she raised her eyebrows.

"Why not?" she asked.

"Why would I bring her back here?"

"To sleep with her…"

"I don't want to sleep with her."

"You slept with Mum…though, of course, she *was* your girlfriend."

"For the record, your mum and I never…" Talking to a girl about my relations with her mother seemed wrong, grotesquely wrong, like discussing the merits of the future with a dying man.

Kendal gave me the look that adolescents give adults when they want to make it known that they cannot be hoodwinked, or patronised, because they know the truth, they know the myriad follies of their elders and the absurd lengths to which they go to hide their dirty linen.

"Of course you didn't, Daniel."

We watched each other eat and drink. I simply put the cake in my mouth, chewed it and swallowed it. Kendal saw fit to turn the consumption of the unsavoury mess before her into an act of seduction. I simply washed down her gruesome creation with a few mouthfuls of tea. Kendal copied me, move for move, down to the blink of an eye, except that, when she was placing her empty mug on the table, she was fulfilling a quiet, bridled consummation.

"Can I come with you tonight?"

"No…"

"Are you worried that I'll cramp your style?"

"I'm worried about the next verbal savaging that I shall get from your mum."

"You can handle her."

"I can…but she has right on her side."

"We're doing nothing wrong."

"That's not how she sees it."

"She needs to get a life."

"The only reason why she's letting you stay here for a few days is that you two had such a cataclysmic row that she can't bear the sight of you."

"The feeling's mutual."

"She's questioned my motives for letting you stay here."

"Do you care?"

"I resent her accusations." My temper was just about under control.

"Why?"

"Why do you think?"

"I'm not a child."

"You're sixteen."

"I'm old enough."

"And young enough to ruin my reputation…"

Kendal glared at me. She glared at me some more. She looked down at the crumpled newspaper on the table. She snatched it up and scanned the front page. "'Dead man identified,'" she read. "'See page three for details.'" She opened the journal at the said page. "'Police today named the man found dead yesterday in Oxford,'" she went on. "'A spokesman for Thames Valley Police said the body had been identified as Philip Haygreen, forty, founder and proprietor of publisher Odyssey Books. The spokesman said: "The next of kin have been informed. Officers believe the circumstances to be suspicious." Mr Haygreen was found dead at his home in Canal Reach, in Oxford's Jericho district, by his neighbours yesterday. Neighbour Phyllis Mortimer raised the alarm after she peered through Mr Haygreen's kitchen window and saw him hanging from his staircase. Following a post-mortem examination, the police spokesman added that the likely time of death was during the early hours of Saturday morning. An inquest into the death will open in Oxford on Thursday.'"

The silence that ensued could not have been broken more emphatically.

"Canal Reach!" Kendal exclaimed. "That's my bloody street!"

"I know it is," I replied from behind trembling hands.

"I know that man!"

"Do you?" The words were muted by shaking palms.

"And that Phyllis Mortimer is a nosey cow!"

"Is she?" My voice was faltering now.

"What was she doing looking through his kitchen window?"

"I don't know."

"What's the matter with you, Daniel?"

My head had been in my hands since Kendal enunciated – in her usual cynical, mocking tone – the second sentence of the report on page three. There were no tears. I was not shocked. Shock had barely registered. I was stunned.

"Come out from behind your hands, you baby."

"Get me a beer out of the fridge, will you?"

"Get a grip, man."

"On second thoughts, make it a whisky…a large one."

"You didn't even know this man."

After a pause, during which the whisky never came, I told Kendal that I knew the man, I knew him all too well.

Four

I had told Kendal not to open the front door if and when the bell rang, to let me open it, so, of course, when the bell rang, she went to the front door and opened it. A rather startled-looking blonde woman, with striking curves, strode down the hallway and entered the communal part of the house. Before I rose from my armchair to greet my guest, Kendal regarded me peevishly, as if I had betrayed her in some way. Sabrina looked at me imploringly, silently, demanding an explanation.

"Hello, Sabrina…"

"If I'd known you had company," the newcomer replied, "I wouldn't have come."

"Kendal is my – "

"I'm Daniel's friend," Kendal interrupted, "who just happens to be his ex-girlfriend's daughter."

"Your mum was never…" Jousting with the girl on the nature of my friendship with her mother was tiresome, and I wished to signal an end to it, so I shot her with a look of impatience and sighed in exasperation.

"You two seem to be a bit confused about each other." Sabrina's tone was snide and a touch self-righteous. "Shall I leave you alone to work things out?"

"Please, sit down," I said irritably. "Kendal, would you mind pouring Sabrina a glass of wine, and keeping her company, while I get changed?"

"What am I, a waitress?"

"As I'm giving you refuge from the harsh realities of teenage life, you won't mind being my *hostess*, will you?"

My favourite album was playing. *Femme Fatale* had just given way to *Venus In Furs*. *Run Run Run* would follow. Sabrina tiptoed into my room, closing the door behind her. Seeing that I was half-dressed – thankfully, the half below my waist – she looked at me sheepishly. She pulled a funny face, as if I were a child and she the adult with all the answers. Her creeping became a dance, a little skip, nimble as a ballerina. Then the dancing stopped. It was a strange performance. It reminded me that I didn't know Sabrina that well.

"Let yourself in," I said.

"What are you listening to?"

"*The Velvet Underground & Nico…*"

"Oh…"

"Do you know the album?"

"No…"

"Then it's going to be a long evening," I joked.

Sabrina looked around the room whilst I pulled a black polo shirt over my head and made the necessary adjustments. I tucked the shirt into my black jeans. My guest roamed the room like a genie just released from a bottle, looking at this and that, and not much liking what she was seeing.

"Kendal has a lot to say for herself," she submitted.

"Tell me about it…"

"That girl has a lot of spirit."

"Too much for her own good sometimes…"

"She adores *you*."

"I adore *her*." The statement needed qualifying. "I look out for her."

"She sees you as a sort of…father figure."

"I reckon so."

"What's her story?"

"She never had a dad." The words nearly choked me, they were that sad. "Every girl needs her dad."

"What happened to her dad?"

"He ran out on Kendal and Rosie, her mum, when Kendal was a month old."

"That's tough."

"Kendal acts tough, but there's a lot of pain there."

"She's vulnerable."

"We're all vulnerable in this mad world."

"Why does she cling to *you*?"

"When I was friends with her mum, Kendal and I…bonded. Now I'm stuck with her."

"I think you two are rather sweet together."

"Don't tell *her* that, whatever you do."

Sabrina planted herself on the end of my bed. I sat beside her and slipped on my newly-purchased boots with the zip on the sides. I studied them lovingly, regretful that I would have to spoil them by walking North Oxford's pavements on my way to the pub.

"She said that you were upset about something."

"We're all upset about something."

"What's bugging you?"

"Today, I learned that my best friend was…murdered…in his home, two days ago."

"I heard about a hanging."

"That was my friend, Philip, whom we talked about last time…"

"If he was your best friend, how come you only found out about his death today?"

"We'd been estranged for years."

"How come?"

"We shared the same childhood sweetheart, one Sylvia Blackman, and remained rivals for her affections long into adulthood."

"I'm sorry about your friend."

"Let's not talk about Philip."

Sabrina wanted to talk about Philip. "Why do the police think your friend was murdered?" She sounded more than mildly curious, she was interested with a vengeance, so much so that her breathing had quickened markedly.

26

"I don't know. They're experienced. They have their reasons."

"There was no sign of a forced entry."

Sabrina's comment made my stomach churn and my heart miss a beat. My body tingled from head to foot as the blood twisted in my veins. It was all I could do not to shudder. "How do you know that?"

"Oh, well, I'm just guessing."

Sabrina was not looking at me now; instead, her eyes were dipped and fixed on the floor. My eyes were fixed firmly on her. She looked up and around the room, at the shelves by the window stacked with CDs, about nine-hundred of them, at the hundreds of DVDs filling the unit hugging the next wall, as she scanned the room clockwise, at the myriad books housed by adjoining shelves, until she came to the framed photograph of Roseanne, which had been taken when she was twenty years old. The photograph was all that I had of Roseanne. I had even less of Albert, my dad. Sabrina seemed disconcerted by what she had just seen, intimidated even. Whatever her thoughts at that moment were, she kept them to herself.

The silence between us was unpleasant – more so for Sabrina, I guessed – so we were both relieved when Kendal put her head round the door.

"Not interrupting you two, am I?" she asked.

Though Sabrina jumped to her feet, suggesting that we *had* been disturbed at a crucial moment, I stayed rooted to the bed, mindful that I had much thought to give to my nascent friendship with a woman about whom I knew disturbingly little.

"We're going out now," Sabrina told Kendal. "What will *you* do?"

"I'll stay here, I guess, but I won't be listening to this shit."

"This is Nico singing," I declared, defending my heroine's honour and her chilling espousal of *All Tomorrow's Parties*.

"She sounds constipated."

"I was going to ask you to come with us," I returned with mock gravity, "but I shan't bother now."

"Leave me here all on my own," Kendal replied. "See if I care."

The girl looked so like a lamb that had just lost its mother that I wanted to adopt her ten times over and never let her out of my sight. I knew that, ever the actress, she was playing with my emotions, pulling at my heartstrings, exploiting my affection for her with neither shame nor mercy, but I could not help but divine the part of her that she strove to hide, the part that felt acutely isolated from the rest of the human race.

"Sabrina, you don't mind if Kendal comes with us, do you?"

My friend looked doubtful as a turkey at the approach of Advent. "Why would I mind?" she replied facetiously.

"She'll keep you company while I talk with a client."

"You're meeting someone in the Dew Drop?" Kendal enquired.

"I am."

"Who?"

"Let's just say that, tonight, my illustrious career as a private detective takes a new and exciting turn."

Five

Rain was falling when the three of us stepped out into Grove Street, though not heavily enough to warrant taking an umbrella. Kendal liked to take my arm when we walked together. Sabrina liked to do the same, judging by her demeanour during our only previous meeting, so I wondered which of them would make the first move. In the event, each kept her distance, as if I had been afflicted by a terrible smell. I was about to link arms with Kendal, for no reason in particular, when I saw that my car had received a gift from the sky.

"Sabrina, do you have a tissue?"

Though perplexed by the question, Sabrina rummaged through her handbag and produced a rather careworn square of white material which looked enough like a tissue for the job in hand. Aided by the moistness of the glass surface, courtesy of an hour's rain, the tissue-substitute did the job nicely. I stood back and admired my windscreen.

Sabrina eyed the car disdainfully. "Please tell me this museum piece isn't yours," she said.

"It's this year's model…or it was in nineteen-seventy-three."

"I've seen more contemporary pieces in the Ashmolean."

"It's a Jensen Interceptor. It's a classic."

"Thank you, Kendal…"

"Going on about the same things all the time is one of your biggest faults, Daniel," the girl replied.

"I've never talked to you about this car."

"Oh, yes, you have."

"I can't think when."

"Forgetfulness is another one of your faults."

"Where did you get the car?" Sabrina asked.

"From a former colleague…"

"Really?"

"I covered for a superior officer, when he was accused of taking bribes from a crook, so, when he retired, he gave me this masterpiece of British engineering."

Sabrina was giving me the strangest look.

"I've probably broken some rule or other about taking inducements, but he wouldn't take no for an answer."

I was looking now at a spitting cobra that was about to spit.

"I suppose I did preserve his good name and reputation for posterity."

"You were a *copper*?"

"You needn't sound so disgusted."

"I'm…surprised."

Sabrina *looked* disgusted, there was no doubting that.

"I never knew."

"Why would you know? This is only our second meeting."

The look of disgust had given way to one of contempt, which I guessed was some improvement. I looked away from Sabrina. The light from the lamps of a passing car made the rain look heavier than it was.

"Can we not stand here all night?" Kendal sounded like a mother scalding a recalcitrant child. "I'm getting soaked."

Before we entered the Dew Drop, I asked Sabrina whether it was safe for the two of us to be seen together.

"Why wouldn't it be?"

"Oxford's a small place and Jimmy has a lot of friends."

"He has no friends in Summertown."

"When we came here ten days ago, we ran into one of Jimmy's friends."

Sabrina reflected for a moment. "Danny Webber…" she said, smiling. "He's sweet on me. He won't say a word."

"I don't share your confidence."

"Jimmy's a taxi-driver. He gets around. He could see us anytime. He doesn't need Danny Webber telling tales."

"Are you still Jimmy's girlfriend?" Kendal asked Sabrina impatiently.

"No…"

"Then it doesn't matter, does it?"

"I guess not."

"Jimmy has other ideas," I said.

"It's not like you and Daniel are an item, anyway, is it?"

"I guess not," Sabrina repeated.

"Daniel doesn't want to sleep with you," Kendal told Sabrina. "He told me." She looked at me. She looked at Sabrina. "So Jimmy has nothing to worry about, has he?"

I looked at Sabrina. She looked at me. We both looked at Kendal. We followed her into the pub.

"Good evening, Barry…"

"All right, Daniel?" As ever, the Black Country enunciation sounded like a song.

"There's only one Albion," I said.

"Aye, there is."

My companions were giving me searching looks.

"Barry's West Bromwich," I explained. "I'm Brighton and Hove."

"And I'm thirsty," Sabrina replied.

"So am I," Kendal added.

"Mine's a double-gin and tonic."

"So's mine."

"Kendal, I can't buy you alcohol."

"Then why'd you bring me into a pub?"

The evening was going to be longer than I thought.

"My usual, please, Barry, a double-gin and tonic, and…whatever you deem appropriate for young Kendal here."

"How old is she?"

"Not old enough…"

"You could have fooled me."

We three stood in silence as our host busied himself with the drinks. As I surveyed the scene around me, and beheld the usual gang of old heads and cap-bearing younger heads, an old man with thin grey hair and buck teeth staggered into the pub like a punch-drunk boxer with a same-day hangover. He raised a hand to greet me. I waited for the thud of impact as he hit the ground, but, somehow, he managed to stay on his feet.

"Hello, young Daniel!" he called.

"He knows your name, then," Sabrina muttered, "but not your age."

"Hello, Mandy!" I called back, mindful that my drink could not come soon enough.

"Got another lass, I see," Mandy returned. Like a canine stud trying to mount a non-consenting bitch, he climbed onto the stool to my left.

"Another lass?" enquired Sabrina in jest.

"He's shot away," I replied. "When he saw us in here last time, he was so drunk, and his vision so impaired, that he thought you were Jennifer Lopez."

Sabrina frowned. At last, I had rendered her speechless. Mere cleverness would not be enough to leave Kendal dumbstruck. For that, I would need a miracle.

Mandy nearly fell off his stool when he spied Kendal. "Stone the mothers!" he exclaimed. "You've got two lasses!"

"No, Mandy, you're seeing double again."

The old man squinted heavily. Like the famous bulldog chewing a wasp, like a dyspeptic hag, he screwed up his face. Some of the wrinkles produced thereby were so deep that they must have hurt. He peered through the fog of alcohol in a determined effort to discern exactly how many women I was standing with. He seemed to have settled on the figure two. Suppressing a belch, he swallowed hard. He could not take his eyes off the younger of my companions.

"By heck," he said, "if I were twenty years younger…"

Kendal was not unaware of the attention that was on her. "Make that sixty years…" she returned, a tad caustically.

Barry placed the drinks on the bar. He told me the cost. I was surprised to receive change from a ten-pound note.

"Looking forward to the new season, then, Baz?" Mandy asked.

"I am…but I hope it's not as dramatic as the last one. That last game, against Pompey, turned my hair grey."

"You were born looking sixty."

"One more word from you, Mandy, and you're out on your ear." Barry raised a glass of whisky. "Here's to a successful season for the Albion."

A pint of ale met the whisky with a clink. "I'll drink to that," I said.

We had retired to a dark corner of the Dew Drop, to a vantage point, where I could more clearly see than be seen. I could see straight ahead, through the area by the bar, to the lounge at the front of the house. Thus could I see the entrance to the lounge bar. I could look right and see the door to the toilets and the saloon bar. From the saloon bar came most of the noise: raucous laughing and shouting. The lounge bar was relatively sedate, occupied as it was largely by couples, talking the talk of lovers, and parties of people dressed for a night out at the theatre.

"Why do you keep looking at the door?"

"Because, Sabrina, my client is due any second now…"

"Have you met him before?"

"No…"

"Do you know what he looks like?"

"No…"

"So how will you recognise him?"

"He gave me a description over the phone."

"Does he know what you look like?"

"Yes, Kendal, he does."

"How come?"

"He's read my book. There's a photograph of me on the inside cover…a most unflattering one, I hasten to add."

"I started reading your book," the girl confessed, "but I kept getting sidetracked."

"By what?" Sabrina asked.

"By rows with Mum, mostly…"

"I still row with my mum, and I'm twenty-eight."

"That means that you are exactly halfway between me and Daniel."

"In what sense?"

"Our ages…"

Kendal was making mischief. I could tell easily enough. I hoped that she wasn't going to spend the entire evening provoking Sabrina. Though the elder was more than capable of looking after herself, of hitting back with a withering look or a barbed comment, she was being foolish if she underestimated for one second the younger's capacity to hold her own in repartee of the most venomous kind.

"In what other way could you *possibly* come between me and Daniel?"

Sabrina responded by regarding her interlocutor in the way that a pedestrian regards a stray dog that has just sprinkled urine over a lamppost. The look lingered. It was reciprocated with a vengeance. They were like two boxers at the weigh-in, heads locked together, and eyes narrowed to harness mutual loathing.

"Give it a rest, you two."

Sabrina turned her back on Kendal and moved closer to me, closer to a disconcerting degree. She crossed her blue-denim legs, the right leg over the left, a movement made to look all the more invasive by the sight of black leather forming an axis of malevolence under the table. Sabrina was the Venus in furs, with the shiny boots of leather, Kendal the whiplash girl-child in the dark. I was simply waiting for the man.

"So, tell me, when did you leave the police force?"

Though Sabrina's question was harmless enough on the surface, I couldn't help but sense that she was fishing for information; it seemed to me that, rather than permitting an identity to emerge from the natural course of human interaction, she was trying hard, piece by piece, to construct a biography, as if she were embarked on some mission of espionage.

"If I didn't know you better," I said, "I'd say you were spying on me."

"You don't know me at all."

"Quite…"

Elegant as ever, Sabrina sipped her gin, before replacing the glass on the table with the surgeon's precision and the assassin's calculated sense of mission.

"Well?"

"I left the Met four years ago, after fifteen years' service."

"He was a detective," Kendal declared proudly.

"Why did you leave?"

"Ostensibly, because I failed the police medical on mental-health grounds, but, in reality, because my methods were considered too unorthodox for an organisation wedded to procedure."

"Were you a…maverick?" In hesitating before releasing that last word – as it happened, in whispering the word perilously close to my right ear – Sabrina gave me the impression that she was not mocking me so much as taunting me.

"I relied too much on my intuition."

"Did your intuition get results?"

"I was always more concerned with the truth than with results."

"You must have seen some horrible things."

"I got off lightly." I was trying hard to hide my irritation at Sabrina's tone. "In any case, real crime is not like the crime of books and television. Most crimes are the product of stupidity or recklessness, not malice or calculation. I never had to do battle with a brilliant criminal mind."

"Did you work on any murders?"

"A few…"

"Were they...*gruesome* murders?"

The way that Sabrina emphasised the word – she pronounced it with relish, as if blood were dripping from her lips – made me jolt, almost shudder, and twist around so that our eyes met mere inches apart.

"I found someone hanging once."

The woman withdrew from my space. She leaned back into the cushioned wall-seat and put her right arm along the top of the wooden casement, as if she were trying stealthily to slip it around Kendal's shoulders, possibly to strangle her.

"What do you do for a living, Sabrina?"

Crafty as ever, Kendal posed the question to ease what had suddenly, almost unaccountably, become a liaison infused with tension. Sabrina failed to perceive the meaning of the question, but, then, she did not know Kendal like I did.

"Thank you for asking, young lady."

"I'm keen to learn about you," Kendal returned with more than a note of sarcasm.

"With a single question, you've shown more interest in me than Daniel has in all the time he's known me."

"This is only our second meeting," I protested, "and, during the first, you told me that you're a life coach."

"What's a life coach?"

"When Daniel abandons us to attend to his client, I'll tell you."

"That's him," I said. "He's here."

Six

The meeting with my client over, I returned to my two companions, but found only one of them there.

"Where's Sabrina?"

Kendal looked pleased with herself. She looked pleased with life in general. I envied her, for she was young, very young, the myriad possibilities of life were arrayed before her, and she, despite her tender years, had sense enough to pick the most promising opportunities and bring them to fruition. From her seat, she peered up at me through a mane of black hair. At that moment, I was struck by her resemblance to Roseanne. I wondered how I had not noticed it before.

"She left."

"Why?"

"She said she knew all she needed to know about you."

"What did she mean by that?"

"I think she was spying on you." Kendal sounded convinced. "I think you think that too."

I fell into the seat. I sighed. "But why would she spy on me...and for whom?"

"You're the detective."

My eyes lingered on Kendal. I had never studied her before, not least because I found her almost unspeakable beauty unnerving. In my mind, I rewound her life to when I first met her, through Rosie, two years before, just after *Crystal* was published. She was the same then as she was now, neither affected by the tunes of her peers, nor moved by the drumbeat of her generation. What I found most appealing about Kendal was her silence, her gift for withering one-liners notwithstanding, for she spoke as if she yearned for stillness of voice. This need for silence cut her out for solitude. She stood alone, away from the crowd. Few people got near her. The silence repelled them. Her likeness to Roseanne was no mere affinity of countenance.

"Why did I not see through her the first time?"

"How did she behave on your first date?" Kendal had a gift for looking bored whilst sounding interested.

"Thinking back – not that it *was* a date, mind you – she was rather intrusive with her questions."

"In what way?"

"For a start, she asked me why my book hadn't been published by Odyssey, the company that Philip founded."

"Why *didn't* your friend publish your book?"

"I haven't spoken to Philip for fifteen years."

"Oh, yes, because of that Sylvia girl…"

My nodding head affirmed the substance of Kendal's remark. "Anyway," I said, "that's not the point."

"No?"

"The point is: how did Sabrina know about my relationship with Philip?"

"Did you ask her?"

"I did."

"And?"

"Rather shiftily, defensively, she told me that she'd read somewhere that Philip and I had been friends since childhood. When I asked her where she'd read that, she said she couldn't remember."

Kendal now seemed enthralled by the story unfolding. She sat beside me, silent and still, thinking behind keen eyes. I liked the way she used words with many to spare, as if she were being forced to make her peace with a world that demanded words, eager, hungry words. Her movements, graceful as a swan's on a placid lake, stood out from the dross like works of art; they challenged a world which demands movement, plenty of it, and which must have deeds, the more of which the better to nourish the flesh. As Sabrina observed, Kendal had spirit; but, more than that, she had soul.

"Where did you meet her?"

"She approached me in here, a couple of weeks ago, when I was having a drink with Mandy at the bar. I saw her striding towards us, a full-bodied siren on a mission, so I nudged Mandy and told him that he'd pulled again. She took my hand and gave me a piece of paper with her phone number written on it. Then she walked out of the pub."

"So you called her?"

"Out of curiosity, yes, I did."

"Was she with anyone when she gave you her number?"

"I didn't see anyone with her."

"She's up to no good."

"So it would seem."

"What's her game?"

"I need to find out."

"You've got three mysteries on your hands."

"Have I?"

"Mystery number one is: who killed your friend?"

"The police will deal with that."

"Mystery number two is: why is Sabrina sniffing around you?"

"What's mystery number three?"

Kendal nodded at the item. "That is."

There it was, the brown envelope, on the table in front of me. It looked forlorn. It looked lost. It looked abandoned. As well as forgetting that it was there, I had forgotten what was in it. I reminded myself by recalling the meeting that I had just had with the strange – some might say, sinister – character at the other end of the lounge bar. The man was gone now. He had vanished into the wet August night, having promised not to see me again until my mission was accomplished. I picked up the envelope. I looked at Kendal. I stood up.

"Come on," I said. "Let's go."

As we left the Dew Drop, a little before ten o'clock, Mandy stopped us in our tracks. His attempt to suppress a belch almost succeeded.

"It's a glorious sight to behold, so it is," he spluttered.

"What is?" I asked, not caring to hear the answer.

"Young love…"

Looking around, I caught sight of several couples who might have done the epithet justice.

Taking the utmost care not to hurt me, Kendal elbowed me in the ribs. "He means us."

"You two look right together," the old man went on. "That other lass is a wrong 'un."

"You're not wrong there," Kendal said.

"Your love is a beautiful thing to behold."

"So you said, Mandy," I returned, the pain in my ribs subsiding as my discomfiture increased.

"It's enough to have every kangaroo in the western hemisphere jumping for joy."

With one last look at Mandy, I led Kendal away. In two hours, the man had degenerated into a minor shambles. His hair was streaked with nicotine-yellow. His eyes looked like they had just been pecked at by a murder of angry crows. A spent roll-up cigarette hung from his mouth, as if, having smoked the better part of it, he was resolved on eating the remnant. I wondered to which of North Oxford's genteel abodes he was bound to return. I knew that he lived nearby, but could think of no house in the neighbourhood that might have harboured such a creature.

Outside, Kendal was inquisitive as ever. "Why do you drink with that old soak?"

"If I see him, I give him the time of day," I replied. "He can be quite entertaining."

"*Clowns* can be quite entertaining."

"That suit of his has never seen the inside of a washing-machine."

"It looks like he slept in it."

"I've never seen him without it."

"Why do you call him Mandy?"

"His name is George Mandelson. He likes to be called Mandy."

We crossed the deserted Banbury Road without having to check our strides.

"That man you met looked scary."

"He was representing my client."

"Who's your client?"

"He's a very rich man who lives in Hampstead."

"Where's that?"

"North London…"

"What does he want you to do?"

"He wants me to find his daughter."

"Is that a photo of her in the envelope?"

"It is."

"Can I see it?"

As the rain had stopped, and the sky had cleared, I slipped the photograph out of the envelope and passed it to Kendal.

"Wow," she said. "You'll have no trouble finding her."

"No?"

"She's gorgeous."

"She's blonde," I argued. "Blondes are everywhere."

"She looks like Cameron Diaz."

"I wouldn't know."

Kendal gave me the photograph back. I put it in the envelope and waited for the next question.

"What's the girl's story?"

"Her name is Miranda Ward-Homer. She's twenty-one years old. She dropped out of Oxford University – Keble College – after her first year. She went back to London to live, though not with her parents, and worked as a model."

"What sort of model?"

With Kendal's innocence in mind, I hesitated before going on with the story. "A glamour model…"

"She's a stripper then…"

My concern for Kendal's innocence had been misplaced.

"She's done modelling of all sorts, including, I'm told, some at the less wholesome end of the market. The family suspect that she became involved in pornography."

"She's been busy."

"She's just another rich girl gone astray."

"Why have the family got you involved?"

"They have reason to believe that Miranda has returned to Oxford."

"What if she hasn't?"

"Then I'll go to London to look for her."

"Won't the family have someone on the case in London?"

"Mr Hardcastle assured me that I was the only person being paid to look for Miranda."

"Isn't it obvious that Miranda doesn't want to be found?"

"The family simply want to know that she is safe and well."

"Why did you become a private detective?"

"Because I'm here, and I have to do something."

"Will you start looking for Miranda tomorrow?"

"No, because, tomorrow, I have to go to my hometown, to see Mrs Haygreen…"

"Philip's wife?"

"Philip's *mother*…"

"Is she expecting you?"

"Yes, I called her this evening…before we came out."

"Can I come?"

"You'll be bored."

"I'll keep you company in the car."

"Okay, but I'm leaving early."

"I'll be ready."

All the time that Kendal was staying with me, she, as a minor, was my responsibility, so I could hardly have refused to take her to Lancing with me. The alternative would have been to send her back to Rosie, but that would have been like asking a Glasgow Rangers fan to wear his team's shirt in the home end at Celtic Park.

"You don't seem so upset now."

"Believe me, sweetheart, I *am* upset. I've known Philip all my life. We were born, two hours apart, in the same hospital, in neighbouring beds."

"Bloody hell, you're nearly twins!"

"We're very different. His family had pots of money. Mine didn't have so much as a pot to…put money in. When we left North Lancing, our primary school, he went to Lancing College, one of the most salubrious private schools in the land, whereas I went to Boundstone, a place that makes Wormwood Scrubs look like a convent. He played hockey and the flute. I played truant. He went to Oxford University. I went to Edinburgh. From boyhood, he had the love of Sylvia Blackman. I didn't."

Kendal linked arms with me. "That's life, darling."

"You are who you are, Kendal. You have to make the most of whatever hand life deals you. You have to be strong. You have to rise above the vicissitudes of life, most of which you can't control. Too many people react to adversity by allowing themselves to fall into an ever-spiralling cycle of self-abuse."

"Not everyone is as strong as you."

"You are."

"Am I?"

"You're one of the strongest people I know."

Kendal beamed with pride. I might have just told her that she put me in mind of Joan of Arc, or Boudicca, or some other woman the strength of whose will would change the course of history.

"Do you find my strength attractive?"

43

The question was not conducive to an immediate answer. In her delightfully snide way, the girl was laying down the gauntlet again, trying my patience, probing my integrity, testing propriety to the limit. We had reached my block of flats.

"You're a strong-willed person, Kendal," I said at last. "People of your age find that intimidating."

"Is that why I hang out with an old git like you?"

Another of Kendal's endearing qualities was that she always knew exactly how and when to break the tension.

Seven

Traffic on the Banbury Road seemed never to relent. It never ceased to murmur. It hummed beyond my bedroom window like an advancing swarm of bees, a monotone that would be speared by the regular squeaking of buses braking to a halt. It was against this auditory backdrop that Philip's death slapped me in the face with a brute hand, having spent the evening creeping towards me, casting a dilating shadow with its every ominous step.

I was sitting in my armchair by the window, listening to one of my Lou Reed albums, one of the compilations. *Pale Blue Eyes* was playing. The song reminded me of Kendal. Most things seemed to be reminding me of Kendal. She was very much on my mind.

It was getting late. I could hear Kendal moving about in the kitchen. I hoped that she was not baking another cake, for there is only so much punishment that a set of teeth can take. When I entered the kitchen, she was sitting at the table, peering down at a piping-hot cup of coffee.

"You shouldn't drink coffee at bed-time," I said.

"Who said I was going to bed?"

"You look sad."

"I'm sad for you, Daniel."

I sat down opposite her. We occupied what had become our usual places at my kitchen table. "Why are you sad for me?"

"Mum told me once what today, August the first, means to you."

"Did she now?"

"It's the day your dad died, isn't it?"

"It is."

"How old were you at the time?"

"Eight…"

"Mum said that he died in a car crash."

"He crashed his car into a tree. There were no other cars involved, so far as anyone knows, and the car was said to be in perfect working order, so nobody knows quite why he drove his car into a tree."

"He might have fallen asleep at the wheel."

"That's a possibility, but the only eye-witness – an old man walking his dog – said the car was doing eighty miles an hour before it crashed, as if the driver had deliberately accelerated into the tree."

"He killed himself?"

"He might have."

"Why?"

"God only knows."

"How long after your dad died did your mum leave?"

"A couple of months, just over…"

"October…"

"The seventeenth…"

"Why did she leave?"

"I've no idea."

"That must have been an awful time for you."

"Nineteen-seventy-three is a year that I care to forget."

"But you can't forget it."

"If only I could."

"I know how you feel."

"We're a right pair, aren't we?"

Kendal sipped from her cup of coffee and winced.

"You know when people say 'Drink it while it's hot'?" I submitted.

"Yeah…" Kendal replied, rolling her tongue in her mouth in an effort to douse her taste-buds.

"They probably mean that you should let it cool down slightly before you attempt to drink it."

"Thanks for the advice, Dad."

"My Auntie Hillary used to place before me a cup of scalding-hot tea, or coffee, or Horlicks – something, at any rate, that resembled volcanic lava – and say, 'Drink it while it's hot,' as if my mouth and stomach were made of asbestos."

Kendal laughed quietly. "She's the one who brought you up, right?"

I nodded. "She's my dad's sister. She had no children of her own, so she was delighted to become mine and Laura's guardian…with my Uncle Gordon, of course, though he was hardly ever home."

"Why was that?"

"He was a detective, CID, in Sussex. Then he joined the Sweeney."

"What's that?"

"It's Cockney Rhyming Slang for Scotland Yard's Flying Squad."

"I don't get it."

"Flying Squad equals Sweeney Todd equals the Sweeney."

"Right…" Kendal replied doubtfully.

"I wanted to join the Sweeney."

"Why didn't you?"

"I don't like guns."

"You coward…"

"That's what I am."

"Tell me about your dad."

"His name was Albert James Winter."

"Is that all you know about him?"

"I know him only insofar as he related to my mum, and I don't know much about her."

"I'm listening."

"Well…Let me see…Albert James Winter…Roseanne Mary Wordsworth…Okay, for a start, it was a miracle that they ever met, never mind married."

"Why's that?"

"Liddell Wordsworth and Miriam Baxter, my mum's parents, formed the most unlikely union. She was the daughter of a diplomat and he the son of a South Wales coalminer. They met towards the end of the Second World War, and married just after it. Emotions were running high at the end of the war. The war caused people to meet who would not otherwise have met. The class-system was shaken up a bit. My grandparents got jobs with the Inland Revenue and set up home in Worthing. That's how my parents came to live opposite each other."

"What about your dad's parents?"

"They were natives of Worthing, and had served in a civilian capacity during the war."

"I see."

"Anyway, as Albert and Roseanne grew up – I like to call them by their names – it became apparent that Albert was the only person in the world who could bring Roseanne out of her shell.

"The children met for the first time one hot Sunday afternoon. The Wordsworths were heading to the beach. Albert was playing football with friends, when the ball went astray. The four-year-old girl skipped towards her dad's car, retrieved the ball, and presented it to Albert. 'Here's your ball,' she said. Her parents looked on, astonished, for that was the first time that she had spoken without first having been spoken to. More incredibly, to her parents' eyes, she smiled.

"From that day, Albert and Roseanne grew ever closer. In Albert's company, Roseanne changed. She would talk, though softly, and she would smile, though shyly. At night, with his flashing torch, Albert used to send coded messages to Roseanne from his bedroom window. That's how he first told her that he loved her.

"Albert doted on Roseanne…and it was her fate constantly to need to seek his embrace as the world sought to crush her silence. She used to tell him about her sorrow that she could never be herself and about her hope that one day she could be. Roseanne sought Albert because he alone understood her. As the years went by, as the world refused to make its peace with Roseanne and her silence, she needed Albert more, and he found himself needing to be her guardian.

"As she grew up, Roseanne's vulnerability threatened to break her. The world was closing in. Life bore down upon her. Silence was not strength and stillness no bulwark."

"No what?"

"The world screamed at her to speak. Life demanded that she move. Albert was her only hope of survival; and she gave Albert's life purpose.

"Adolescence asked questions about their love. What kind of love for each other would they carry into adulthood? Would they become adults nourished or burdened by their childhood bond?"

"So what happened?"

"They knew that they would always have each other, but they couldn't be without each other, so they married. Albert was eighteen and Roseanne sixteen. Nine months later, they had me."

"How do you know all this?"

"I got most of it from Miriam, my maternal grandmother. The rest I got from Auntie Hillary."

"I'm going to help you find your dad."

"That's nice of you…but he's dead."

"I mean find him…in a real sense."

"And I'll help you find *your* dad."

"That's Mission Impossible."

"Nothing's impossible."

"Oh, yeah? So I can grow wings and fly to the moon, can I?"

"If anyone can, *you* can."

"Your mum's still alive."

"You think so?"

"I *know* so." She looked at me tenderly. "We're going to find *her* too."

Sleep and I were not the best of bedfellows. Sometimes, she and I got into bed together and spent the night wrapped in each other, lovers to the core. Such occasions were rare. For the most part, she ignored me, treating my advances with disdain, as if I were a leper with a need urgently to attend to his personal hygiene. Most nights, then, I cursed her for her stubbornness and her refusal to consider me a man worthy of her attention. If cursing failed then I would reduce myself to flattery. Eventually, she would submit to my blandishments and allow me a small portion of her beneficence, so that I felt more a part of the human race, taking from her gratefully what most people take for granted. That she found my entreaties contemptible was not in doubt. I hated being always at her mercy.

Sleep was eluding me, again, and I was in no mood to busy myself with damnation and flattery. I retrieved one of my favourite films and sat back in bed, filled with anticipation. Insomnia had its consolations. Then my bedroom door creaked open. I put the image on the screen on hold and watched as a satin-clad siren etched contours and curves in the dusk. She stood beside my bed, a woman in all but name. The words that I tried to speak were beaten back by a rampant heart. I wanted to tell her to turn back. My words, even had they come, would have fallen on deaf ears, for the girl was not for turning.

Eight

A sheet of August sunlight took advantage of a gap in my heavy black curtains to cut through the darkness, causing the room to be bathed in a cloud of charcoal, an effect that could not quite be touched, though I felt it on my skin as if it were a blanket smothering my strenuous efforts to work out where on earth I was.

When the forbidding blankets by the window were parted, the girl in my bed clutched at her eyes, moaning in complaint, before turning onto her right side, taking her naked breasts with her.

The kitchen was a sanctuary, full as it was with familiar things in familiar places. I looked around it, hoping that nothing was out of place. I beheld a gallery of order and restraint. It seemed to have survived Kendal's incursions.

I was eating from a bowl of cereal, a pot of tea before me, when the yawning Kendal, with the air of a model on a catwalk, conspired to enter the room. At that moment, as if it, too, had had its breath taken away, the fridge stopped its whirring and fell silent. It made not a sound as the girl, carefree and careless as a dowager duchess at a garden party, opened its door and took some milk. Before I could think what to say, she had brought a bowl and a mug to the table.

Still speechless, I sensed that a glare of indignation would betray my feelings eloquently, but, predictably, my silent admonishment was met with indifference. The girl's subsequent raising of her eyebrows was an attempt at provocation. Her eyebrows were the least of my worries, for her capacious breasts were spilling out of her nightdress and heading south, though, mercifully, there was every chance that they would be intercepted by the table.

"Is there tea in the pot?"

"What else would be in there, orange juice?"

"For a fifty-year-old man, Daniel, you can be very childish."

"For a sixteen-year-old girl, Kendal, your maths can be very poor."

As Kendal approached with unbecoming caution the bowl of cereal that she had just prepared, I poured tea into her mug.

"This is not ordinary tea," I said. "It's Assam."

"What are these things?"

"They're Kraves."

"I know that. But what are they made of?"

"Can't you read what's on the box?"

"I've just done my GCSEs, Daniel." The girl yawned, omitting to put a hand over her mouth. "I'm done with reading."

"You're done with manners, too, I see."

"What?"

The girl began chewing hungrily, as if she hadn't eaten for days, before washing down with tea the barely-chewed parcels of corn and chocolate, slurping noisily as she did so.

"I suppose I should be grateful that you've come to the breakfast table wearing something…even if it does barely cover your modesty."

Kendal absorbed the broadside with the equanimity that I had come to expect from her. I might have just told her that Elvis the King was alive and well and living on a traffic island in Dunstable.

"It was hot in your room," the girl replied. "You should open the windows."

"What were you doing in my room?"

"You said I could watch the film with you." Kendal was speaking with all the confidence of one who knew her power and how to use it. "You fell asleep after ten minutes. I watched the film to the end. Then *I* fell asleep."

"But you were awake enough to switch off the television?"

"How awake do you have to be to press a button on the remote?"

"Arguing with you is like discoursing with Socrates."

"Don't argue with me then."

"What would your mum have thought if she'd entered my room in the middle of last night?"

"She probably would have been congratulating herself on such a masterful breaking-and-entering."

"I was speaking hypothetically."

"Well, don't. It's stupid."

Largely in admiration, I shook my head. I finished drinking my second cup of tea of the morning. I watched my guest as she ate and drank, and wondered why so celestial a being bothered with mundane matters like food and drink.

"Would the lady of the house mind if I put on some music?"

Kendal was likewise facetious in reply. "Be my guest."

"Has the lady any musical preference?"

"Give Nico a rest. She's depressing."

"Oh, come on, Kendal. Nico is your kind of artist."

"So *you* say."

"I'll put on *Berlin*, by Lou Reed. Then we'll listen to it again in the car."

"As you wish…"

"That album is just right for today."

"Why? Are we going to Berlin?"

"The album tells the story of a down-at-heel woman trapped in a relationship with a violent, drug-addicted man. When her children are taken from her by the authorities, because of her perceived lifestyle, she commits suicide. It has been described as the most depressing album ever made."

"Oh, great, I need cheering up."

"While it's playing, I'll get ready to leave by nine-thirty. Will you be ready by then?"

"Yeah…if I haven't topped myself in the meantime."

Nine

"Are you all right?"

"Why do you ask?"

"We've been on the road for half an hour…and you haven't said a word."

"I've nothing to say."

"I see."

"Can you keep your eyes on the road, please?"

"Yes…but you're staring at the windscreen so hard that I'm scared you'll break it."

"I'm thinking."

"What are you thinking?"

"My thoughts are private."

"So are your breasts, but you exposed those."

"You have an answer for everything."

Kendal's middle name should have been Irony, though Perversity would have served equally well. "I was wondering what your plans were."

"What do you mean?"

"Well, you've just taken your GCSEs…"

"So?"

"So, what's your next step?"

"Oh, Daniel, you do disappoint me."

"How?"

"You sound like Mum. I thought you were above that kind of talk."

"Pardon me for taking an interest in your life."

"Mum thinks I'm staying on at school to do A levels."

"Aren't you?"

"Not likely…"

"Why's that?"

"I didn't turn up for half of my GCSE exams."

Kendal didn't need a lecture, and I wasn't about to give her one. "Perhaps you'll pass the exams that you *did* turn up for."

Kendal looked at me and smiled, almost lovingly.

"You don't think that school can teach you much, do you?" I suggested.

"You're starting to go back up in my estimation."

"That's good to hear."

"But you've a long way to go before I respect you again."

"I'll keep trying."

"You do that. You never know: one day, you might be cool."

"Thank God that's over."

"Lou Reed's *Berlin* isn't growing on you then?"

"It was bad enough the first time."

"Consider it part of your education."

"You're supposed to be looking after me, making me feel comfortable, not torturing me."

"Perhaps making you listen to it twice in a morning was a bit cruel."

"I liked the film last night."

"Then you must see more of Eric Rohmer's films."

"Have you got any?"

"I have them all."

"What's your favourite?"

"My favourite Rohmer film is always the last one that I watched."

"The guy in the film irritated me, though. I wanted to slap him."

"Gaspard was in the unenviable position of having three beautiful women to choose from."

"You would envy him, surely?"

"He's a decent, sensitive guy. He didn't want to hurt anyone's feelings."

"He ran away from all three of them."

"Yes, but he realised at the end that he loved Margot."

"But he fancied Solène."

"He was captivated by her vivacity."

"And Lena?"

"She was just his girlfriend: an unwanted legacy, as it turned out."

"Why do you like this man's films so much?"

"Because Rohmer's a Catholic, because he's French, because of the beauty of the people and their dialogue, and of the settings…Some art rouses the heart and the mind and the soul, all at once. When watching Rohmer's films, one's soul is caressed by grace."

"Is that why you fell asleep?"

"I was tired. I've seen *A Tale Of Summer* a hundred times…and I'll see it a hundred times more."

"How many films has Rohmer made?"

"Rohmer is not as prolific as, say, Fassbinder, but each one of his films is a masterpiece. Most of his films formed part of a cycle, such as the *Six Moral Tales* and the *Comedies And Proverbs*. *A Tale Of Summer* is one of the *Tales Of The Four Seasons*."

Kendal peered down at her lap, at the albums that I had selected for the journey. They were stacked five-high. To my surprise, she cradled them with no little reverence. The five plastic cases might have been a fragile religious icon, or relic, such was the care that my passenger was taking with them.

"What's next then?" she asked.

"You choose."

"*Exile On Main Street*…The Rolling Stones…"

"No, that's too long. We'll listen to that on the way home."

"*The Head On The Door*…The Cure…"

"Yes, put that on. It's quite short."

"Will I like it?"

"You'll love it."

My thoughts turned to Philip as I drove and Kendal immersed herself in The Cure.

Philip had lived a charmed life, he had been blessed with good fortune, but his many victories had not been achieved without effort on his part. He might have been shown the flute and the violin, by parents bent on vicarious fulfilment, and urged to play them, he might have been shaped by his Maker with a musical destiny in mind, but such endowments would not have found their fullest expression in one wedded to the principle of apathy, nor would they have made the least acquaintance with excellence had they been guided by one disposed to rest on his laurels.

My friend's sense of duty, harnessed to the faculty with which he was born, had seen his lean figure grace the most exalted playing fields of Sussex and his sharp mind adorn the hallowed portals of Oxford.

Once, before I had the first idea what he meant, he told me that the elect had a duty to set the standard for the damned, not because the doomed masses had the slightest chance of emulating the chosen few, but because the anointed were called upon to lead by moral example, to be dignified and beyond reproach in all that they did. The beautiful were beautiful, and the damned were damned, but, for the beautiful, theirs was the burden of leadership in this world of men. In all the time that I knew him, Philip was faithful to this charming ideal.

"What's this place?"

"It's the Sussex Potter, in North Lancing."

"Why have we parked here?"

"Because I'm hopeless at hill-starts, and Mill Road is on a hill."

"Where's Mill Road?"

"That's Mill Road," I replied, nodding at the steep slope straight ahead.

"Is that where the Haygreens live?"

"It's where *Mrs* Haygreen lives."

"Is Mr Haygreen dead?"

"Philip's parents are divorced."

"When did they get divorced?"

"They separated fifteen years ago. I'm not sure when they got divorced."

"Why did they separate? You said the Haygreens were the perfect nuclear family."

"Their separation had something to do with Philip's departure from the City."

"You've lost me."

"Philip was a stockbroker…a very successful one."

"So, he quit his job. Why would his mum and dad fall out over that?"

"I haven't seen either of them often since I joined the Met, and, whenever I did see them, I didn't ask questions, so I don't know the details."

"Perhaps grief will make her open up."

"It might."

"So why exactly did you and Philip fall out?"

"I've told you."

"You haven't told me the details."

"Just before he quit the City, he proposed to Sylvia. She said no. Two weeks later, I was walking on Worthing pier with Sylvia…and who did we run into?"

"Philip…"

"Of course, he jumped to the wrong conclusion…and hasn't spoken to me since."

"Nice work, Daniel…"

"What do you mean?"

"You broke up Philip and Sylvia, which made Philip give up on life and quit his job, which made his mum and dad fall out and then break up."

"What a wicked person I am."

"I was joking."

"I know…though your train of thought was worthy of a detective."

"Had Philip and Sylvia always been an item?"

"It's hard to say whether they were ever what you would call boy-friend-and-girlfriend. They were just always together. By that, I don't mean that they never left each other's side. I mean that their lives followed the same path. They lived in the same street. They went to the same school. They both left North Lancing at the same time to go to private schools of the same stature. Then they went to Oxford together. He went to Wadham. She went to Keble. The two colleges are in the same bloody street. So, it was considered inevitable that they would marry. I was as shocked as anyone when Sylvia rejected him."

"Why did she reject him?"

"She told him that she loved him, but not in the way that he wanted her to love him."

"I understand."

"Philip knew exactly how Sylvia loved him. He knew that their love was not of the passionate, sensual kind. They weren't exactly Burton and Taylor. But he didn't think that that was a bar to marriage. In fact, he considered it the type of love that makes for a healthy, lasting marriage…and he thought that she felt the same."

"Love is difficult to fathom."

"Sometimes, I have to remind myself how young you are."

"When you have to bring yourself up, you grow up pretty quickly."

"Your mum played *some* part in your upbringing."

"Yes…but I was often alone."

"She did her best in difficult circumstances."

"I've never had a dad…and that's given me this aching pain that seems to be all pain, all types of pain in one, which means that I can feel everyone's pain, whatever it is."

59

"How long have you had this pain?"

"All my life…"

"People feel *your* pain too."

"Most people *are* a pain."

I had to laugh.

"Mum told me who my dad is. So why is his name not on my birth certificate? Why is there no name where the father's name should be?"

"Perhaps the father didn't want to be named."

"Perhaps Mum isn't sure who my dad is. I've heard that she put herself about a bit. My dad could be anyone."

"Whoever your dad is, you are a credit to him, and he's a fool for letting you go."

"I used to want to find him, to track him down, but I don't anymore. He didn't want me, so I don't want him."

"We talked about this last night."

"I was tired."

"You might find each other one day."

"You might be the pope one day."

As we strolled up Mill Road, I told Kendal that North Lancing School was on our left, and Lancing Manor our right, but she was so immersed in her thoughts, in her world, that my words failed to register. It was nice to be home. It was even more agreeable to have space, for Oxford, beautiful though much of it was, could make one feel hemmed in, what with its narrow streets and eager tourists, many of whom insisted on coming in groups of fifty or more. Behind me, Tennyson's green Sussex faded into blue, with one grey glimpse of sea. The whispering plains of the sea called to me. Ahead, the gentle breezes of the Downs enticed me with their hypnotic suggestions. I looked up the hill, and saw the trees, great pagan gods, with the mighty beech lord over all, daring me to resist their animistic charms.

"Did Sylvia live in this street?"

"She did…and she still does."

"She still lives with her parents?"

"She does."

"Why?"

"It's a long story."

"Can you give me the highlights?"

"Sylvia had to leave Oxford halfway through her third and final year. She was an alcoholic and…well, she had a problem with drugs."

"Heroine?"

"Cocaine…"

"How does a girl with everything going for her get herself in that state?"

"The rich are as fragile as the rest of us."

"How is she now?"

"She beat her addictions soon after leaving Oxford, but she has been a virtual recluse for the last twenty years."

"How did she beat her addictions?"

"She beat them simply by going home. Oxford itself wasn't the problem. It was all that came with it."

"I don't understand."

"About six months after she left Oxford, Sylvia and I went for one of our walks along the pier. She had weaned herself off both the booze and the coke by then…but, still, at the ripe old age of twenty-one, she looked…ravaged…beautiful, but ravaged. I told her that she looked beaten. I told her that she looked like she had wanted, really wanted, something, but hadn't been able to get it, but the more she'd wanted it, and the harder she'd tried to get it, the more elusive it had been. So she'd given up wanting it and trying to get it."

"She must have been straight back on the drink and drugs after that little pep talk."

"For a long time – since the day she started university – Sylvia had craved normality, she had yearned for the familiar, for what she knew, even as she revelled in the great adventure that was life at Oxford. From

61

her first day at Keble, miles from home, she had been vulnerable to the adulation that came her way. Wherever she went, they followed her. They would offer to buy her a drink, then another, then another. To start with, she was too polite to refuse. Then she became too weak to refuse. Then it went beyond drink. It was all so heady, so addictive."

"Wasn't Philip with her?"

"He was…but he wasn't strong enough to cope with the circus that always surrounded Sylvia. The poor chap spent nearly three years fending off one admirer after another, male and female. I'm surprised that he didn't go the same way as Sylvia. He found the whole business very draining. To his credit, without Philip by her side, Sylvia wouldn't have lasted anywhere near as long as she did at Oxford."

"Why was Sylvia so popular?"

"Had Sylvia been merely captivating, she would have been popular. But she was more than captivating, she was compelling…and that brought with it the adulation that I'm talking about."

"I think I get you…though my head's starting to ache a bit."

"I'm sure you'll hear more about Sylvia in the next hour or so."

"She sounds like my kind of woman. When can I meet her?"

"If you ever meet her, the similarities between the two of you will freak you out."

"You shouldn't have said that."

"Why shouldn't I?"

"Because now I *have* to meet her…"

Ten

The house stood before me like a man trying not to cry at his son's funeral. I could have cried at the sight of it. The garden was its usual immaculate self: the lawn made a bowling green look like a cabbage patch and the flowers forming the border were arranged like soldiers on parade. It was one of those gardens that you wanted to make a mess of, to make it look more natural, or simply because you could not stand such pedestrian orderliness. I approached a rose. Its petals, frayed at the edges, withered in the drizzle, then shuddered when struck by a gust of wind. I held the flower in my hand and put it to my nose.

"Why are you sniffing that flower?" Kendal was admonishing me, not asking a question.

"I'm communing with nature."

"You look stupid."

"There's no poetry in your soul."

"Poets are full of shit."

"You're no fan of Shakespeare then?"

"He's the biggest bullshit merchant of them all."

"Didn't he write *The Bullshit Merchant Of Venice*?"

"I rest my case."

"Daniel…" Mrs Haygreen said, as she stood before me, looking all of her seventy-odd years and more. She opened the front door. "Come in." She looked at Kendal as if the girl were some kind of apparition.

We stepped inside.

"Excuse the mess." The only people who say that are those whose houses are insanely tidy and strangers to dust.

"Allow me to introduce Kendal."

"Hello, Kendal…"

"Kendal, Mrs Haygreen…"

"Hello, Mrs Haygreen…"

"Please call me Cynthia."

"Calling you Cynthia would be like calling the Queen Liz," I replied.

"You'll call me Cynthia, won't you, Kendal?"

"I will, Mrs Haygreen."

Our hostess narrowed her eyes and searched Kendal's features, as if narrowing her eyes somehow made Kendal's features easier to discern. "You look…familiar."

"We've never met," Kendal said.

"No, I don't suppose we have."

"I've never been down this way before."

"However, Kendal was a neighbour of Philip's," I said, "so you might have seen her in Oxford."

Bemused, Mrs Haygreen shook her head. "It really is a small world."

"I live in Canal Reach, down by the canal, in the house that was used in the first episode of *Inspector Morse*, so we get a lot of tourists coming to gawp at the house."

"The only people who gawp at this house are estate agents trying to persuade me to sell it."

"The old boy in the house opposite spies on Mum with his binoculars."

"That's too much information, Kendal," I said, trying not to laugh.

"Are you Daniel's girlfriend?"

"Kendal's my glamorous assistant."

"I see."

"Doctor Who's always had one, so why shouldn't I?"

"Daniel's a private detective now," my assistant added. "He needs help with his cases."

"Yes, Kendal carries my cases."

"Daniel said he was a private eye, but I thought that was just one of his jokes."

"I'll leave you my card."

"Are you on a case at the moment?"

"I am, but I haven't got into it yet."

Mrs Haygreen regarded me as if suddenly I had become a stranger. "Well, let's not stand in the hallway all afternoon," she said. "Come into the lounge."

We were led into the lounge by a woman with a purpose. Philip's mother had always had an air of purpose, always acting as if she had not a second to waste. She probably slept with an air of purpose, if she slept at all.

The Haygreens' house was large, though commonplace. It irritated me each time I set foot inside it, for it was insufferably middle-class, though not bourgeois like the grand dwellings of North Oxford. The room in which we stood was the house in miniature. It was the same then as it always had been. Each object was arranged as if placing it an inch to either side would have violated some cardinal law. The furniture consisted of a stolid mahogany, much of it embellished with embroidered flora. Rustic idylls were depicted within ornate frames which hung from solid walls. Photographs of Philip at various stages of life smiled at one from every corner. An aged collection of nineteenth-century novels – none of which seemed to have been opened, never mind read – adorned a single shelf, to the left of the mantelpiece. Since I last saw the room, twenty-four years before, only the fashion had changed, for the carpet and curtains were no longer mosaics of garish colours, and the push-button, wood-encased television set must have been replaced ten times over.

"I read your book."

"What did you think of it?"

"It was a nice story."

What Mrs Haygreen meant by that assessment was anyone's guess. I valued her opinion only because I had known her all my life. She was not the type of person who would have read the book had she not known the author, nor was her critical faculty developed enough for me to respect her judgement on the matter, but I was grateful that she had taken the time to indulge my first, and probably last, published novel.

"It saw the light of day only because I know the publisher."

"Nonsense, you're a clever *boy*, Daniel."

"Did Philip read it?"

Our hostess winced as if I had just touched a very raw nerve. "Yes," she said, lost in painful remembrance. "He…He…thought it rather…"

"Go on," I wanted to say. "Your opinion means little to me. You've never read a proper book in your life. But Philip might just have been able to contribute a meaningful assessment." My ugly, vainglorious thoughts dismayed me. I chided myself and resolved to examine my conscience as soon as time allowed.

"Please, both of you, sit down," we were urged. "I'll make us some tea." Mrs Haygreen shuffled out of the room with her head bowed. Seeing her go in so prostrate a fashion saddened me to the point of tears. My tears were stilled when I felt a sharp pain as my right arm was poked. I turned to Kendal.

"What are you laughing at?"

"'You're a clever boy,'" my friend returned, giggling like a schoolgirl. "I liked that."

When Mrs Haygreen returned with the tea, I could see that she had been crying. During the lady's absence, I had become fixated on one of the photographs above the fireplace. There he was, my old friend, resplendent in his academic gown, clutching his scroll for all the world to see, a silly hat on his head, a graduate of a peerless institution, destined for years of distinguished service in that overblown casino known as the City of London. Mrs Haygreen placed the tray on the coffee table and began to pour the tea.

"Do you still take milk and sugar?"

"I do…thanks."

"Kendal?"

"The same for me, thanks…"

We were given our drinks in turn. I tried to hide my irritation at receiving a full cup, together with a saucer, the former of which, as always, did not fit the latter in a way that made handling the combination easy. Kendal looked as if she had never seen a china tea set before, never mind had to negotiate one. I wondered why people could not simply serve tea in mugs.

When Mrs Haygreen was back in her chair, she expressed her regret that we had to meet in such desperate circumstances.

"We don't see you much these days," she added.

I wondered why Mrs Haygreen had not spoken in the first person, given that hers had become a solitary presence in the house.

"Philip and I lost touch," I replied.

"That was a great shame."

The last time that I had spent any length of time with Mrs Haygreen, she was only a little older than I was now. In days long past, she had worn the same florid dress that she wore today, though she had been neither so plump nor so grey and made up. I felt as oppressed by time as she looked.

"Philip's dead now." The mother's stark words were full of lamentation.

I glanced at Kendal. She was sitting with great dignity, almost regally, reclined, with a straight back, looking down gravely, respectfully, at her lap. She looked far from embarrassed. I had doubted the wisdom of bringing her to this house, but she was doing herself proud, as I should have known she would do.

"Doesn't it annoy you when people use words like 'fatalities' and the 'deceased', when they mean 'death' and the 'dead'?" Even as she purported to use the words without fear, Mrs Haygreen recoiled in horror on hearing them.

"The world's full of euphemisms."

"Did you know that Philip was in Oxford when you moved there?" Mrs Haygreen wiped a tear from each eye as she awaited my answer.

"I had an inkling that he was back in Oxford."

"In the weeks before he returned to Oxford, Philip behaved most strangely. He was stranger still on the day he came down from London to make the announcement about his future. He walked in here that day, looking like he'd just stepped out of a train crash, and announced that he had quit London and was on his way back to Oxford."

"Was that so drastic an act?" I enquired.

For a second, Mrs Haygreen looked affronted by the question. "Well, it was not so much what he said as the way he said it." The lady brought the cup to her lips and drank tea as if it were a dose of the hard stuff. "He sounded like he was on drugs."

Kendal's little cough would have sounded to our hostess like a little cough, but it reached my ears as a stifled gesture of mockery. I eyed Kendal reproachfully. She eyed me back with a girlish snarl.

"Oh, and the way he looked…" Mrs Haygreen sighed, a look of mild disgust on her face. "I've seen shepherds on the Downs look tidier."

"Perhaps he was just going through a bohemian phase."

"He said that he wanted to be an artist."

"An artist?"

"Oh, yes, an artist," Mrs Haygreen replied with a large dose of sarcasm. "He wasn't born to oil the wheels of capitalism," she added, mimicking what I presumed to be Philip's tone at the time of his announcement. "He was born to create in the midst of this desert."

"Philip must have been reading Albert Camus."

"Who?"

"Oh, just some French guy…"

"Anyway, off he went." As Mrs Haygreen sipped tea, an unsteady hand caused her cup to suffer a minor spillage, though the saucer did its job in catching the overflow. "As you know, Philip's father and I fell out over the matter," the lady continued. "I accused Ben of pushing the boy too hard…and he accused me of not pushing him hard enough. That was the end of twenty-six years of marriage."

"It seems perverse to me that you and Mr Haygreen should have fallen out over such a matter. It was not as if Philip were renouncing the material world. He wasn't about to join a commune. Oxford's hardly a wilderness."

"The change in Philip was too much for either of us to bear. We were shocked. It was as if Philip had changed beyond recognition, overnight, and Ben and I had changed with him."

The only conclusion that I could have drawn was that the word "artist", and the spectre of Bohemia that it invoked, had shaken a middle-class redoubt to its foundations. All the same, I couldn't help but wonder how and why a couple as solid as Benjamin and Cynthia Haygreen had not been able long ago to have effected some sort of reconciliation.

Mrs Haygreen sighed. "A month or so after Philip returned to Oxford, we learnt that he had set up Odyssey, his publishing house. Being a publisher must have been what he meant by being an artist. I asked him why he had given up on his music, when he was such a gifted musician, and he said that he got no satisfaction from regurgitating the music of others. I couldn't see the difference between playing someone else's music and printing someone else's words, but he insisted that there was a difference."

"Philip was exhausted after four years in the City."

"Yes, he was burnt out…but he made pots of money. Well, he must have: he died owning three houses."

"That's news to me."

"Two in Oxford and one in Portslade…" Mrs Haygreen shook her head. "Portslade…Of all the places…"

"There are worse places than Portslade…but it's an odd place for a second home."

"Do you know what people were saying about Philip's two second homes?"

"No…"

"That they were brothels. Can you believe that? Why do people gossip in such malicious terms? I mean, as if my Philip would have anything to do with a brothel."

As I made a mental note to find out if the malicious gossip had any basis in truth, silence fell upon the room. All that could be heard were the relentless ticking of the grandfather clock in the hallway and the clinking of china as I placed my cup and saucer on the coffee table. Mrs Haygreen was slumped in her armchair, head bowed towards her lap, looking like her life was over, mourning the loss of the two men in her life, wondering how and why life had gone so wrong.

"Of course, we both know what – or, rather, *who* – destroyed Philip, don't we?"

Knowing to whom the lady had alluded, I prepared myself for the venting of spleen.

"Sylvia Blackman…"

All I could do was listen.

"From the day Philip was born, she was there, teasing my boy. She never wanted him…but was happy to let him think that she did. She continued with her cruel hoax, her rotten confidence trick, for twenty-five years…until, finally, she broke my boy."

"I wouldn't judge Sylvia too harshly."

"When Sylvia came down from Oxford, Philip pandered to her. He came home every weekend to nurse her, as if she didn't have enough people waiting on her."

"Love is blind."

"I ask you, a drug-addict with her start in life? What's *her* excuse?"

"Sylvia simply can't cope with being Sylvia."

"Sylvia is a washed-up, middle-aged spinster, still living at home with her parents."

"Sylvia never meant to hurt Philip. She's just…careless."

"Please don't make excuses for her, Daniel."

"That's how I see her."

"Do you remember the business with that teacher, at her school, when Sylvia was fifteen?"

"I heard about it."

"Anyone who didn't know Sylvia was outraged by the breach of propriety…but anyone who knew Sylvia pitied the poor fellow."

"Trouble follows some people."

"Why do you look at me when you say that?" Kendal asked.

"I was just checking that you're still here, you've been so quiet."

"It's not my gig, that's why."

Mrs Haygreen peered at Kendal, puzzled as a camel in a snowstorm. She shook her head. Once the girl's strange words had been shaken out, the lady asked me if I remembered the time when Ryan Shawcross was run over by a car, down by Hill Barn Garage.

"I remember it all too well."

"Do you know what his last words were?"

"No…"

"'Tell Sylvia I love her.'"

"Was Sylvia told?"

"She didn't need to be told. She knew that every boy in Lancing was in love with her."

Death haunted the house with a presence more tangible than any ghost's. Everything was lifeless. The curtains hanging by the French windows on the far side of the room, the ornaments on the mantelpiece and the shelves, the tea-set and the pictures hanging on the walls: all displayed an emotion placed somewhere between dejection and despair. I had seen more life in Bognor Regis in November. Death, as the poet said, can be appeased by neither prayer nor gold, but the mother, looking as if appeasement of death had never crossed her mind, offered only a tear in supplication. The tear looked as if it had fought its way out of her eye. Exhausted by the struggle, it dropped into her lap and exploded like a miniscule bomb.

"We're going up to Oxford on Thursday, Ben and I," Mrs Haygreen announced. "It took the death of our son to bring us together, even if it is only for a day." She took a tissue from inside her sleeve and dabbed her eyes. "It'll be a busy day. We have to attend the inquest. We have to see a policeman. We have to speak with a reporter from the *Oxford Mail*, though we might give him a miss. We would like to visit Philip's house, but it's a crime scene. It's been cordoned off."

It's not just a crime scene, I thought, it's a murder scene.

"We'll have to talk to Philip's solicitor about…about his estate, about these other two houses…and whatever else he had to dispose of."

Benjamin and Cynthia Haygreen had been reunited by grief. If only for one day, they would come together to comfort each other in mourning. They would look back on their life together – as friends, as lovers, as husband and wife, and as parents – and celebrate what they had given to the world and to each other. They would hold each other and cry for the gift that was lost. They would weep for the jewel that was theirs and was taken from them. "In love, we gave our only son to the world," they would say. "In love, we shall preserve him."

"Of course, what we shall find in Oxford is that our son has left everything he owned to that Jezebel, Sylvia Blackman."

"Whatever Philip did in life, good or bad, he did for Sylvia," I said. "Because of Sylvia, Philip lived a good life. If Sylvia ever finds happiness, it will be because of what Philip did for her. Philip gave Sylvia life, because Sylvia gave Philip life."

"Life?" the lady returned. "She gave him death."

"Why do you say that?"

"My son was hanged in his own house."

"Can you blame Sylvia for that?"

"She might not have put the rope around his neck, but, you'll see, that girl, somehow, was the root cause of Philip's demise."

Eleven

"She's in there, is she?"

"I imagine so."

"Let's go and see her."

"Another time…"

"But I want to meet her."

"You *will* meet her."

"When?"

"Soon…"

"Not soon enough…"

"Sylvia doesn't want to be disturbed right now."

"How do you know that?"

"I can sense it."

"So, you're telepathic now, are you?"

"In a way, yes, I am."

"It's a nice house."

"I used to stand outside this house, when I was a boy, on my way home from school."

"Why?"

"I used to imagine what was going on behind that door and those walls."

"Couldn't you have just looked through the window?"

"In case you haven't noticed, there's a sturdy oak tree blocking sight of the lower windows."

"What are those other trees?"

"The one in the middle is a conifer…and the one on the right is a willow."

"There can't be much light in that house."

"Sylvia's never had much light in her life."

"I want to go on that swing."

"That house hasn't changed at all in more than thirty years. Even the swing was there, rocking and swaying under the oak tree."

"Have you ever been inside the house?"

"Never…"

"Why not?"

"I've never been invited in."

"That's weird."

"The house has mystique. I'd like to keep it that way. Sometimes, the way that you imagine something to be is how it should be…and should remain."

"Will Sylvia come to Philip's funeral?"

"You heard Mrs Haygreen…Sylvia hasn't been invited…"

"But?"

"But she'll be there."

"Then I can meet her…"

"Are *you* coming to the funeral then?"

"If you'll let me…"

"I doubt that I could stop you."

"Will Sylvia make a scene?"

"In her own discreet way, yes, she will."

"How do you mean?"

"I can picture the scene. The church is packed. The service is just about to start. The vicar is surveying the congregation. The organist's hands are poised. Sylvia is nowhere to be seen. Then, at the back of the church, a door creaks open. The measured footsteps resound ominously. La belle noiseuse, the beautiful troublemaker, has arrived. All eyes are upon her as she takes her place in the back row, but in the forefront of everyone's mind."

"It'll be just like *Eastenders*."

"Without the shouting…"

"Without the punching…"

"Without the pulling of hair…"

Kendal's laugh consoled me, for it was a little burst of youth, of innocent wonder, in a place where people were jaded and without hope. I wanted Kendal's innocence to last forever, but I knew that even she would fast become – was fast becoming, indeed – a cynic.

"Philip's mum and dad…" the girl resumed.

"What about them?"

"It doesn't make sense."

"What doesn't?"

"Philip quit his job in the City…but I still can't see how that caused his mum and dad to break up."

"You heard what the lady said."

"I just don't buy it."

"It's all about illusions, Kendal."

"So is magic."

"Middle-class people wrap themselves in illusions. They tell themselves, and each other, lies."

"You mean that they deceive themselves and each other?"

"Put it another way. The life of the Haygreens was a tapestry. When one stitch was taken out, the whole thing unravelled."

"It was a house of cards. When one card was removed, the whole thing collapsed."

"Yes, the whole edifice crumbled."

"Where are we going now?"

"We're going to the Sussex Potter for lunch."

"Good…because I'm starving."

"Lucy Hancock, a former classmate of mine at North Lancing, is the manageress there."

"You're so old-fashioned, Daniel."

"Am I?"

"Nobody says 'manageress' these days."

"What do they say?"

"'Manager'…"

"You would say 'actress', wouldn't you?"

"No…"

"What would you say?"

"'Actor'…"

"So, Kristin Scott Thomas is an *actor*, is she?"

"She acts. Therefore, she's an actor."

"I bow to your superior knowledge on the matter…and all other matters."

Kendal began her descent of the hill in a slow shuffle, her hood up as she made her way through the now-steady drizzle. I was about to make pursuit when I had my head turned by a curtain twitching in the upper part of the Blackmans' house. I looked up and saw a figure, a silhouette, standing at a window, the smaller of the upstairs windows. The figure was spectral, so much so that it seemed like it might pass through the window and float down to greet me. But this was one spectre that, even had it been able to move in so ethereal a fashion, would not have dared leave the sanctuary of the house. I had no reason to believe that the shadow looming over me welcomed the attention that I was according its home, but, all of a sudden, I was overcome with a sense of warmth, as if a balm had been planted at the core of my being and were radiating outwards. I smiled at the figure and hoped that it was smiling back at me. Then the figure was gone.

"Come on!"

Kendal was some fifty yards down the hill, looking up at me, her head resembling a boiled egg under the hood.

"I'm coming!"

What was heard as we passed the Haygreens' house alarmed me and disconcerted Kendal so much that she whipped the hood off her head and peered down the garden path as if she had just spied the Grim Reaper coming at her, his scythe brandished in anger and evil intent. That is how she should have reacted. That is how most people would have reacted. Kendal, however, still hooded, simply stared at the source of the noise, unabashed, though the parting of her lips suggested mild astonishment.

"Poor woman…" she said.

"That's real anguish for you."

"Losing any child is bad enough, but losing your only child…"

A response to Kendal's heartfelt words was on the tip of my tongue when my phone rang.

"Daniel?"

"How are you, Laura?"

"I'm still alive, you might be surprised to hear."

"I'm sorry that I don't visit you more often."

"The twins have forgotten what you look like."

"I can come and see you now." When no reply was forthcoming, I thought that I had been cut off. "I'm in Lancing."

"Why?"

"I've just been to see Philip's mum."

"I didn't know about Philip's death until today."

"Is that why you're calling me?"

"That's one of the reasons. The other reason is…well, I'll explain when you get here."

"I'll be there in ten minutes."

"Okay…"

"Are the twins there?"

"Of course they are. It's the school holiday."

"They might have gone out."

"You must be joking."

"Put the kettle on."

"It's on."

"And, before you ask, I had not planned to slip back to Oxford today without going to see you."

"Liar…"

The line went dead, abruptly, without ceremony, in a manner that only Laura could have fashioned.

"Change of plan…" I told Kendal.

"Yeah?"

"We're going to my sister's for lunch."

"Where does she live?"

"Down by the seafront…"

Twelve

"I'm not sure that we have time for this tour of Lancing, Kendal. My sister's expecting us, and she can't abide lateness."

"Just look around you and tell me what you remember."

"Why?"

"You told me that that last Friday in July in…What year was it?"

"Nineteen-seventy-three…and it was the second-to-last Friday in July…"

"Okay, well, you said that that Friday is the last memory you have of your mum."

"For some reason, I remember that night vividly, even though it was thirty-two years ago."

"That must mean something."

"Such as?"

"It means that the clues to what happened to your mum can be found in that evening."

"In my recollection of it, you mean?"

"Yes…"

"I don't see how."

"All you have to do is cast your mind back to that evening, take yourself back there, and tell me what you see."

"All I can see now are the school gates of Browning Road."

"That's a start."

"That's it. That's all that can be said about them: that they are there."

"Tell me about them."

"Well, I remember thinking that the school gates were powerless that afternoon, when school ended, to stop the waves of children from overwhelming them and pouring onto the streets. The gates looked chastened and contrite. I remember thinking that, six weeks from that day, the gates, in league with the teachers, would be the masters again. But to me, back then, six weeks were a lifetime – they stretched ahead, long and hot and full of sunshine – and the gates that would have caged us children melted away in the heat of an eternal summer."

"You're doing well. Keep going."

"What else do you want me to say?"

"Tell me what happened when you left the school."

"At the time, all I could think about was the fair."

"Which fair?"

"Every year, on the penultimate Friday of July – on the day that school closed for the summer – the fair came to Lancing. The whole village descended on the Beach Green. It was the highlight of the year. I was so excited. I couldn't wait to get down to the seafront, to immerse myself in the sights and sounds and smells of the fair: the gypsies who ran the fair, who wore clothes from another age; the children running amok; the flashing lights; the candyfloss and the toffee-apples; the rides and the games. By the time the school gates were flung open, I was crazed with desire. Captivity was over. The moment of blissful release had come."

"You're waffling a bit now, but keep going."

"At precisely half-past-three, Miss Hurd was labouring to be heard above the stampede for the door.

"'You're dismissed!' she cried at thirty-or-so eight-year-olds who were happily dismissing themselves. 'Have a wonderful summer!' she yelled. 'And don't forget that in September you will be joining Mr Hofton!' For her erstwhile charges, September was a month, a season, that would never come.

"Amid the anarchy, I sought Sylvia Blackman. Typically, she alone emerged from the scramble with her dignity intact. Somewhat apprehensively, for I knew that I was setting myself up once again to be cruelly rebuffed, I approached her. How magnificently haughty she was. Her glorious shock of black hair cascaded down her back like waters of ebony in free-fall. Her skin was smooth as velvet. Her bewitching eyes refused to acknowledge me. I looked for Philip, but could not see him. The coast was clear.

"Sylvia and I were the last to leave the classroom. I felt honoured at having escorted her from the embers of the school year. Neither of us spoke as we made our way to the point where we would part, yet there was a question that I was dying to ask her. I was scared of making a fool of myself. I was desperate not to insult Sylvia. So words failed me. I had waited so long for that moment, yet found myself hopelessly tongue-tied.

"Suddenly, Sylvia stopped walking. She waved at her mother. Then she turned round to face me, her eyes like chips of ice and her hair glistening and streaked with blue under the cloudless sky.

"It was a case of now-or-never, so I asked the question: 'Are you going to the fair tonight?'

"As I awaited the answer, I chided myself for having said 'going' rather than 'coming'. Roseanne had promised to take Laura and me to the fair that evening, and now I waited on Sylvia's promise to meet me there and to imbibe with me the balmy air that would be forever ours. The wait was agonising. She was punishing me, and I loved her all the more for her cruelty.

"'Maybe…' she said at last.

"She was like a sunflower, beaming, radiant, a queen among flowers. As she took her leave, I watched her, euphoric at the prospect of seeing her under the stars."

"This is the street where I grew up."

"Mountbatten Close…"

"Isn't it lovely?"

"Wasn't Mountbatten an aristocrat?"

"He was, indeed. Some joker at the council gave this street its name. Look around you. It's hardly aristocratic, is it?"

"So, what's the story here?"

"Who said there was a story?"

"I did."

"Yes, well, that evening – the evening of the fair – was sultry and full of possibilities for romance. I was at home with Roseanne. She alone gave me hope that my every dream would be fulfilled. She banished all my doubts. She gave me the breath of life. With her by my side, I was invincible. I was untouchable. Beauty, sheer beauty, was hers. People, even the worst sort, were drawn to her warmth. Such beauty as hers could never be defiled.

"At six o'clock, or thereabouts, as Laura danced and twirled around the room, a child in the heat of childish excitement, I sat on the sofa like a statue, except that I displayed greater economy of movement and offered still fewer words."

"What?"

"'I'm going on the Big Wheel,' my sister sang. 'I'm going on the bumper cars. I'm going in the Haunted House.'

"It had been hot indoors, but outside the air was no less oppressive. The sun hung in the sky, relishing its power, teasing us, mocking us, and showing no mercy. The air was thick with flying ants and the neighbourhood urchins were parading the street with their customary malice. The children were on the walls. They were on the grass. They were even on the cars. They were in the road, poking at potholes with sticks. They were prodding cracks in the pavement, upsetting the ants. They were prowling the street with menace, picking fights, cursing and swearing. When I looked down the street, I saw some boys playing with the Wembley Trophy football that Gerry Underwood had snatched from me a few days before. I reminded myself that Roseanne was with me. I was invulnerable. I put my chest out and passed through the hordes of bellicose children with my head held high. I even thought of trying to get my ball back, as we passed Underwood and his band of thieves, but I wasn't feeling *that* brave.

"Then Millie Lawson trotted up to us. Fascinated, her blue eyes narrowed, she looked up at Laura. Her blonde hair wriggled like rats' tails. With tomato sauce dripping from her chin, she gave the impression of having just removed her face from a basin of baked beans. Showing off, she jumped up and down on some of the flying ants that were crawling from every crack in every paving-stone in the street. The creatures scrunched and squelched under the demented girl's feet. Laura was held transfixed.

"'Come away,' urged Roseanne with a tug at the sleeve of Laura's summer frock.

"Clad in a long black dress, Roseanne stepped away, elegant as always, and Laura and I walked either side of her. As ever, she cut a melancholy figure. An anxious, intense gaze, the eyes half-shut, drew the whole face inwards to form a rather strained aspect which suggested an inner restlessness; as if she were yearning for something that she feared she would never have; as if she were aware of life's myriad possibilities but knew not how to realise them or how to connect them to the whole; as if only the fragments of a glorious vision had been seen.

"As we walked down Irene Avenue, I heard someone call: 'Hello, darling!' My eyes were drawn to the right, to the other side of the road, to the blonde, who, in a tight-fitting mini-skirt and high-heels, stepped gingerly over the ill-fitting slabs of pavement that threatened to bar her way. From her, I looked left, and saw two dust-covered workmen sitting atop scaffolding and drinking beer.

"'They didn't mean *you*,' I told Roseanne, hoping that I was right.

"'Ignore them,' she said.

"'They meant…' I stopped walking and turned around. The girl, the blonde, was gone. I wondered if she'd been there at all. Had I merely hoped that she was there? I turned to face the workmen.

"'What are you staring at, sunshine?' one of the men called to me. The other man offered a wave and a sly grin. It was my duty to face them down for Roseanne's sake. I chased after Roseanne…and have been chasing after her ever since.

"The sun was mellowing as the fair's commotion laid a benign hand on my expectant ears. A cool breeze kissed the back of my neck as I wallowed in the faintest stirring of the music. In the midst of the fair was chaos, a riot of noise, but, standing where we were on the other side of the Brighton Road, the multifarious sounds reached us as a lucid composition.

"The vision, too, was lucid from our final viewpoint at the lower end of South Street. We were standing over a maelstrom of dazzling colours.

The Big Wheel decorated the heavens. Wherever one looked, a colour glowed, only to expire and be replaced by another. Each flashing light knew its place. Las Vegas had come to Lancing."

"Look at the state of that grass."

"That's because the fair was here last week."

"Of course…"

"It will be back next year."

"Can we go?"

"I suppose so."

"The Mermaid Café looks rather bleak."

"It's always looked like that."

"Why are you laughing?"

"About fifteen years ago, there was a lawsuit involving the fair."

"Was there?"

"A man was on the chair-mobile – I think that's what you call it – flying through the air, when the chair became detached from the apparatus. Man and chair were sent into orbit. The man plunged head-first into the shooting gallery."

"Was anyone hurt?"

"No, but a few cuddly toys had their fur and feathers ruffled."

"Where's your sister's house?"

"Behind us…across the road…"

"Let's go then."

"The tide's in. I can hear the waves."

"Where is everyone?"

"This is Lancing on a busy day."

Thirteen

If it were possible to give Kendal a more searching look than Cynthia Haygreen had given her then my sister did just that.

"Come in," Laura said dubiously, her eyes glued on my companion.

Though Laura herself was no intellectual, she had married a teacher of Classics whose vocation had found an outlet at Lancing College. Thus was the house dominated by shelf after shelf filled with the sort of musty old books that would not have looked out of place lining the illustrious walls of Oxford University's Bodleian Library.

"You'll have to excuse the mess."

"Why does the hostess always say that, even when there is no mess?"

"Perhaps, by your lowly standards, Daniel, this isn't a mess."

"The place looks immaculate to me."

"I really must come and see your place sometime."

"There's a first time for everything."

"Aren't you going to introduce me to your...friend?"

"Laura, this is Kendal. Kendal, this is Laura."

"Hello..."

"Hello..."

"Do you often travel around the country with Daniel?"

"Somebody has to keep him out of trouble."

Judging by her look of inquiry, Laura wasn't sure what to make of Kendal. The feeling seemed to be entirely mutual. I resolved to make my annual visit to my sister's house as short as possible.

"Where's Malcolm?"

"He's out with a friend, taking photographs."

"Of what?"

"You tell me. Photography's his new hobby. He'll lose interest in that soon enough, like he loses interest in all his latest hobbies. He's constantly trying to fool himself that he's not totally obsessed with books. He reckons that he's going to spend the holiday cataloguing his books, all twenty-thousand of them. I told him that he'll need to take a two-year sabbatical for that."

"You two make an odd couple."

"At least I have someone, Daniel."

"Some of us were made for higher things than procreation."

"Is that what you tell yourself?"

"Where are the twins?"

"They went out after all. Some friends called round. I told them not to go on the beach, as the tide is right up, so they'll be on the beach."

"I'll see them next year then."

"They saw you coming, Daniel."

Kendal had a knack of disregarding propriety and, in so doing, establishing with a third party the nature of my relationship with her. It was her way of breaking the ice, of breaking down barriers, and, more often than not, of challenging people to make a judgement on the nature of our friendship. Thus was Laura made aware, upon a single utterance from Kendal, that the girl and I were bonded in a way that was on the very edge of propriety.

"Have you ever read *Lolita*, Kendal?" Laura had elected to take up the challenge.

"Who wrote it?"

"Vladimir Nabokov…"

"I don't speak Russian."

For a few unnerving moments, woman and girl were locked silently in mutual antagonism. As one excruciating moment ran into another, and another, I thought about going into the kitchen to make us all some tea, but was relieved to see that the woman had blinked first.

"Please," she said, "come through to the kitchen."

Laura's kitchen backed onto an expansive conservatory, which gave way to a colourful and decorative garden, my sister these days being quite the horticulturalist. I beheld a bird-table in the middle of the landscaped masterpiece; from it hung a bag of nuts, from which sparrows and robins were taking turns to feast. Nature was regulating itself seamlessly, without a human being in sight.

"These are nice."

Laura regarded Kendal, who was munching happily on a ham-and-cheese toasted sandwich. "You look hungry," she said.

"I *am* hungry."

"You must chew your food, or you'll get indigestion."

"Laura, don't talk to Kendal like she's a child."

"I presume that she *is* a child."

"Daniel told me that childhood is a state of mind."

I had never told Kendal any such thing, but I let her comment go for the sake of what remained of our three-way harmony.

"Did he?" Laura replied from her throne at the summit of the moral high ground. Nervously, as if she were expecting an assertive reply, from one or other of her guests, the hostess raised a hand and swept hair back behind her ears. "How's the private detection going?"

Before replying, I swallowed my mouthful of toasted sandwich. "It hasn't really taken off yet."

"Have you had any cases?"

"I've just received one."

"Shouldn't you be working on it?"

"To be honest, I don't really know where to start with it."

"What do you have to do?"

"I have to find a girl, a young woman, in Oxford."

"How hard can that be?"

"Too hard for me, I fear..."

Laura looked at me in disbelief. She shook her head. She stood up and went to a drawer, from which she took a letter. She placed the letter on the table in front of me. She sat down again and waited for me to speak. "Where do you start with that particular mystery?" she asked.

"What is it?"

"Take a look."

I pulled a postcard from the envelope. Kendal looked uninvolved, lonely, so I passed the card across the table. "What do you make of that, Sherlock?"

Kendal studied the card. She looked puzzled. She turned the card over and looked more puzzled still. "'Our Lady of Oxford,'" she read. She turned the card over again. "She looks like the Virgin Mary."

"She *is* the Virgin Mary," I said.

"Why is she called Our Lady of Oxford?" Laura asked.

"The Virgin's care and intercession is universal, even as she cares for each one of us individually," I replied. "That's why we can address Mary as Our Lady of Oxford."

"You a Catholic now, are you?"

"No…"

"There's a handwritten prayer on the back," Laura said. "The handwriting is the same as that on the envelope."

Kendal flipped the card back over. "'Merciful Father and God of all consolation,'" she resumed, "'you have shown yourself to be wonderful in the glorious Virgin Mary, Mother of Christ, and have given her to us as the Mother of Mercy. May all of us who venerate her with devotion always experience her powerful intercession and enjoy your immense mercy. Grant this through Christ our Lord. Amen.'"

"The word 'mother' appears twice in the prayer," Laura added. "Each time, it is underlined."

"The postmark is Oxford," I said. "I'm surprised that you haven't accused me of sending it."

"Why would you have sent it?"

"I live in Oxford."

"Yes, but you wouldn't have sent that."

"I might have, but not to you."

"So, who do you think sent it?"

"I've no idea."

"Do you know anyone in Oxford?" Kendal asked Laura.

"Apart from Daniel, nobody…"

Kendal had usurped my role as the detective. "Do you know any Catholics at all, who might have been passing through Oxford?"

For a few seconds, Laura was lost in thought as she searched her mind for an answer to the question. "I don't think I do," she said at last, surprised by what she had found.

Fourteen

"I'm sorry if my sister seemed a little hostile."

"It's me. I rub people up the wrong way."

"You do seem to provoke a reaction."

"As Mum would say, it was ever thus."

"Yes, she *does* always say that."

"It's her catchphrase."

"It will be her epitaph."

"Her what?"

"Oh, look, here come the twins."

"They haven't seen us."

"Let's keep it that way."

"You don't want to talk to them?"

"No…"

"Why not?"

"I don't want to disappoint them."

"Continue with your story, then, from when you arrived at the fair."

"Must I?"

"Yes…"

Knowing that the telling of the rest of the story would leave me feeling morose and all but spent, I sighed. "We had arrived," I began. "Amongst the glittering, ear-splitting throng, Laura and I rubbed shoulders with a host of familiar strangers, and Roseanne, friendless and painfully shy, acknowledged the odd passing acquaintance. She told us that we couldn't go on the Big Wheel, or on anything fast or dangerous, to which I protested that we had been reduced to virtual spectators."

"Did you talk like that when you were a boy?"

"I didn't use those exact words."

"That's reassuring."

"I was basking in the glory that was Roseanne…and somewhere amid the din and confusion was Sylvia. I felt her presence as surely as I walked on grass. Like an avatar, transfigured in the dusk, she would reveal herself to me. Such was our destiny."

"I think it's about to rain."

"Roseanne sent Laura and me onto the Flying Horses, which was a roundabout with shiny horses, slippery as wet soap. I spent five minutes holding onto the pole as if my life depended on it. It didn't help that the pole was equally slippery. The horses flew through the air as if they were being pursued by ravenous predators. I was terrified that Sylvia was watching my humiliation and reviewing the lofty esteem in which she held me. I rode the Flying Horses for Roseanne's sake. For her, I sacrificed my dignity. I would have given all that I had for Roseanne. I would have given myself. At any time since Roseanne left, I would have given my life for Roseanne's."

"I don't feel that way about *my* mum."

"Before going on the Flying Horses, I gave the fare, the money, to a man who looked all the more grotesque for standing beside the sublime figure that was Roseanne. His few remaining teeth were black, his dark hair was greasy and infested with scurvy, and a large wart sat regally on the end of his nose. I could not take my eyes off him. With nothing more severe than a wordless reproach, Roseanne rebuked me for staring."

"Perhaps he was a troll."

"He was less appealing than a troll."

"Perhaps he was a demon."

"Demons have a certain villainous charm. No, he was an amalgam of the subterranean and the nocturnal. He kept looking at me. He showed his teeth. He sniggered. Catarrh bubbled in the pit of his throat. A shiver went down my spine."

"He sounds demonic to me."

"I can see Roseanne now, gliding serenely over the churned grass.

When she was by my side, my breast almost ruptured with pride. Her brilliance illuminated me. It made someone of me. There was none so blessed as she."

"It *is* raining now."

"The Haunted House was an altogether more appealing prospect, but only because it gave me an opportunity to be heroic. Its frontage warned would-be visitors of the terrors within. Count Dracula and his host of women vampires dared me to step across the forbidding threshold, dangling shadows foreshadowed our likely fate, and ghosts reared their heads like ethereal predators. I went in pumped up with adrenalin and ready to show the supernatural poseurs that they held no fears for me. Laura was not so bold; she stood outside, looking guarded, until Rose-anne whispered a reassuring word in her ear; a few wary steps forward were enough to enable me to grab her by the arm and pull her into the abyss.

"Inside, there was nothing but distant screams and darkness. It was my job to protect my sister, so I reached for Laura's hand and held it, then screamed when a hooded, flesh-eaten figure, lit up by a flash of red, leapt out of a cupboard wielding a scythe; as I fell to the floor, I lost hold of Laura. Whichever way I turned, pitch-blackness devoured me. I looked for the entrance, which could not have been far away, but it too had been swallowed by the monster in the stomach of which now I languished. I was Jonah inside the whale. 'Lord, I repent!' I might have cried. 'If you will only come and save me, I will do as you command!'

"More flashing lights revealed a maze of corridors, and an army of ghoulish corpses drifting by. Count Dracula's laugh caused the walls to tremble. In desperation, I tried to retrace my steps onto familiar ground. As I groped around, people bounced off me. The ground became more and more unstable. I struggled to stay on my feet. The screaming became more intense, until it was consumed by a deafening cocktail of discordant sound. Yet more flashing lights uncovered more figures of doom; disjointed images assailed me until all my senses were scrambled. In a state of thorough disorientation, a nauseous dizziness overcame me. I called out for Laura. I had to save her. I staggered towards I knew not where.

"Then came the moment when I was convinced that I was going to die. Having fallen into a sort of ditch about two feet deep, I was picking myself up when a crushing weight landed upon me. Something heavy had fallen into the same trap that I had. For an agonising moment, the bulk smothered me. I was unable to breathe, never mind move. I lay there trying to assess how badly damaged I was. So that was life, I thought, and this is death. Albert had said that life was short.

"When the hulk lifted itself from me, my body was so racked with pain that I lacked the will to get up. I saw a snake-infested pit with me inside it. Serpents slithered over me and under me and around me, hissing and snarling as they went. In the hope that somehow they would pass me by, I tried not to move, but was made to writhe in pain as they sank their venom into me, and as they coiled themselves around me, squeezing tight. Surely, I thought, this is death.

"Finding myself back on my feet – in death, it seemed, anything was possible – I swayed from side to side, dizzy and disorientated. Corridors and alleys emerged again in the show of lights. The colours were brighter, quicker, and more brutal than before. I saw stairways, coiled like serpents. I saw balconies and balustrades. I saw towers. I saw ravens, crows, fiendish birds in black, and I heard their squawking. Everywhere, hooded figures danced and screeched. Though people ran and screamed around me, I was alone. The darkness was punctured by shards of light. I was lost, unable to step this way or that. I felt sick. Then I remembered Laura. What had become of her? I had to find her. I forgot myself. I was finished. But Laura, perhaps, might be saved.

"My efforts to find my sister foundered when a boy, glowing in purple, sprinted by.

"'Get me out of here!' I called to him.

"'Follow me!' he yelled back.

"I did not follow him so much as cling onto his shirt with all the strength left in me. All the way, though my eyes were closed, lights whipped me, they pierced me, they cut me into strips and left me bleeding. My ears were ravaged, raped by ravenous sound. My body was bumped and battered by people fleeing for their lives.

"Deliverance – if that is what it was – came when I spied a band of light at the end of a long tunnel. As the band became larger, my fear abated. Though my emergence back into the world was ignominious, I was determined to appear heroic. But assuming the appearance of a hero was no easy undertaking when I was wrecked, absolutely wrecked. I blundered down the steps and fell into the arms of Roseanne."

"The rain's getting heavier."

"Roseanne simply brushed my hair with her fingers and straightened my clothes."

"It's pouring out there."

"We wandered awhile, watching and listening, now and then nodding and waving at people we knew and some that we did not know. Strangely, the many flashing colours around us lit up the sky in its purest blue and the grass in its purest green; under the blue dome, and upon the lush green carpet, people bobbed and weaved, making patterns that moved and a concert of sounds subsumed within one greater sound. From above, the clamour would have been perceived as both a tapestry and a symphony: the chaos of life seen and heard as order.

"Lord over all was the Big Wheel. It looked down from its lofty height on the fair's many and various pieces, all of which were doing their best to please their master, so as to justify their respective places in the scheme of things. Laura and I looked up at the Lord in awe. It reached up to the sky and twirled like a giant firework. It was so much bigger and brighter than anything else at the fair. It was almost too big to see at once, and almost too bright for the naked eye. Beneath it, we felt small and naked. Roseanne regarded the Big Wheel knowingly, as if, though mighty, it were a friend. She gave a solemn smile. Then she led us away towards the dodgems.

"My eyes continued to seek out Sylvia: not a single nook or cranny was left unexplored as I trailed Roseanne around the fair. Sylvia was everywhere and nowhere. Here and there, I thought I heard her dulcet tones. My heart yearned for her, even as it yearned for Roseanne, who was right beside me. Why did Sylvia not appear? Then I realised that she would appear; that the evening, my evening, our evening, would have its consummation. I wanted it so much. I wanted the evening and its perfect ending. The evening was forming. Though its essence was there, its nature would not be cast until I saw that Sylvia had come, and come for me.

"Roseanne would not have allowed her children to take to the dodgems had the burly chap who controlled them not interceded on our behalf. 'Go on,' the handsome man said from the steps leading up to the platform. 'I'll look after them.'

"A blush signalled Roseanne's consent. She blushed again when the man winked at her. He led Laura and me to a car just inside the perimeter fence.

"As I drove around in the car, dodging and bumping, I could see the man, exuding Romany charm, leaning on the inside of the fence, talking to Roseanne; though she was listening to him, politely, she said nothing in return, preferring to remain silent and to smile, a picture of contentment and fulfilment. With her fingers, she brushed some hair behind her left ear, before doing the same behind her right. She was always doing that.

"Suddenly, a car thundered into the back of us, trapping us against the barrier. Laura jolted forward. Angry, I turned round to face the aggressor...and there, behind the wheel, was Sylvia. She had found me. She and her dad span the car away from ours and rejoined the fray. Laura and I were hot on their trail.

"'Your mummy's young, isn't she?' Sylvia asked softly as I escorted her down the steps. Gone was the shield of haughtiness. I had broken through.

"'She's twenty-five,' I replied. 'Isn't that quite old?'

"'Not really,' Sylvia returned. 'My mummy's thirty-eight.'

"Ahead of us, Roseanne and Mrs Blackman were chatting quietly, which, though pleasing, surprised me, as I hadn't realised that they knew each other. Behind us, Sylvia's dad humoured Laura. A bond between our families had been forged by magic.

"'Where's your daddy?' Sylvia asked.

"I told her that he was at work. She looked bemused. Her presence was intoxicating and, with the long holiday ahead, I wanted to spend more time with her. In a moment of uncharacteristic boldness, I asked her if she cared to join me at the beach at the weekend. She told me that, the following day, her family would join the Haygreens in Spain. I knew that Philip and his parents had gone to Spain, but had no idea that the Blackmans were joining them. Though crestfallen, jealous, I was determined not to let the cruel revelation spoil the evening.

"The Blackmans melted into the night, into the sunset, into the western sky, which bled with delight and with remorse. The balloon in the sky had burst. The ribbons of cloud around it had broken its surface, causing rivulets of blood to burst forth and trail away to the north and to the south. The sea, whispering near-silent melodies, blinked in silver and soaked up the warmth.

"Tired, but excited, I trailed Roseanne and Laura all the way home. We took a different route: up Orchard Avenue and along Manor Road. All that I saw around me was, and would remain, showered with the roses of that wondrous evening. Even the school gate, at the foot of Mill Road, seemed to have put our differences aside to share my jubilation. The familiar became so very strange. A fantasy had come true.

"The impressions of the evening drifted into my dreams. All the colours of the fair were there, together with the pure blue sky and the pure green grass. The red balloon and the silver-crested black sea were there. Even Laura, teasing me, was there. Sylvia, my princess, resplendent in her purple dress, was there. And, of course, my queen, my Holy Queen, the one who was always in my dreams, was there."

"That's a beautiful story. You can be quite poetic…for a policeman."

"I'm not a policeman."

"Let's not argue over details."

"Does the story have any meaning whatsoever?"

"Of course it does."

"What is the meaning?"

"Can you really not see it?"

"Not really…"

"Think about it."

"I *am* thinking about it."

"Think about what you've told me today – the story of that day, that special day for you – and think about what your sister has just told us."

"Do you know what?"

"What?"

"I'm starting to work it out."

"I knew you would."

"I couldn't have done it without your help."

"I have my uses."

"You're priceless."

"On the way home, please would you show me the spot where your dad died?"

"Do I have to?"

"It's the final piece of the jigsaw."

Fifteen

"*The Argus* is quite an interesting read."

"More interesting than the *Oxford Mail*?"

"I never read the *Oxford Mail*. Mum does."

"What does the paper say about the Albion?"

"Er…it says that…Mark McGhee is warning the fans that another season of struggle lies ahead."

"Tell us something we don't know."

"It says that McGhee hopes to have a new defender in place before Saturday's Championship opener at Derby."

"We'll need more than one more."

"How are Oxford doing these days?"

"It's funny you should ask that, because, last week, I went up to the Kassam Stadium to watch Oxford play Albion in a pre-season friendly."

"Who won?"

"Oxford won four-one."

"So Brighton are even worse than Oxford?"

"No, because Oxford are two divisions below Brighton…"

"But Oxford won."

"That was one game…and it was a friendly. It meant nothing."

"I'm looking at the Personal Services page now."

"Respectable papers like *The Argus* should not be advertising brothels."

"There's a two-for-one offer at Suzie's."

"God help us."

"Do you mind if we make this the last album of the journey?"

"No…I don't really get this type of music, to be honest."

"I had a friend, a Stones fanatic, who turned to God and turned his back on the Stones."

"Why?"

"Their music isn't exactly godly."

"Is it Satanic?"

"It is diabolical…to some people's ears."

"But you like it."

"I grew up with it. It's part of my world."

"The Stones are still going, so they're part of my world too."

"Yes, I suppose they are. But the Stones were a long way into their careers when you were born."

"Do you believe in God?"

"Does God believe in me?"

"That's a daft question."

"To every question that matters, Kendal, there is no answer."

Her soul glorifies the world, it radiates grace, infusing all that is, seen and unseen, with blessings and thanksgivings. Her soul takes the heart of man, the rotten heart of man, and makes of it something worthy to stand before God. Her soul gilds the tarnished fabric of life, it lights up the darkest recess, it opens a window to heaven. She is the very conscience of man; moving deftly among his dismal schemes, she conveys that still small voice that would speak to man; though man does not hear it, he responds. Without her, the abyss would be deeper, wider and darker. Without her, man would have one less angel to guard him, and one less gracious advocate whose eyes of mercy might be turned. Without her, man would be still firmer in the grip of Evil. Without her, man's exile would endure; it would stretch ahead, long and bitter, beyond even this vale of tears, towards that horizon that is never seen. There is no trumpet for her virtue, for her silence, her foremost virtue, is an all-too-eloquent harbinger of right temper and fortitude and the rewards intrinsic to both. Her silence exalts the world with neither herald nor acclamation. Her silence is her soul. In her silence God rests. Her silence is the breath of God, and some there are that hear it. Her silence is the face of God, the immanent face of God, and some there are that see it. When she is gone, she will take her petition to the altar in heaven. There she will abide, witness to God's mercy. Then she will come again. Though she never went away…

"What are you thinking about?"

"I have this rather fanciful notion about Roseanne."

"Tell me about it."

"I can't."

"Why not?"

"It's too fanciful, too wistful, too…nebulous…"

"Why did you become a policeman?"

"Because I'm here, and I have to do something."

"You've already used that line."

"I know, but it applies equally to the question that you've just asked."

"Why exactly did you leave the police force?"

"The official reason, as I think I've told you, is that I wasn't fit, mentally, to continue serving."

"They thought you were nuts?"

"In a sense, yes…"

"In what sense?"

"In Soviet-era Russia, anyone who opposed the regime was labelled insane, because it was considered inconceivable that anyone could take issue with communism, paradise-on-earth that it was, unless they had a screw loose."

"How does that apply to your job at the Met?"

"They disapproved of my methods and found my views on crime-and-punishment unacceptable."

"What was wrong with your methods?"

"What would you say is more important, truth or results?"

"The truth…"

"Is the right answer…"

"If you could not find the truth, would you settle for a result?"

"No…"

"Why?"

"Because someone's freedom is at stake…"

"Right again…"

"I'm always right."

"To value truth over results is an attitude that affects one's methods. In one case that I investigated, a woman was routinely beaten up by her husband. They lived in a high-rise block of council flats, in Lambeth, with their two-year-old son. Their electricity and gas had been cut off because they hadn't paid the bills. One night, a fire destroyed the flat and in the wreckage were found the man, with his head bashed in, and the boy, dead, in his bed."

"What about the woman?"

"She got out alive. A neighbour called the Fire Brigade. The woman was accused of murdering both her husband and her son. She maintained that her husband had started hitting her, that she had hit him with a vase to defend herself, fearing for her life, that, as he fell, he had knocked a candle onto the sofa – they had no power, remember – which had caught fire. The fire had spread rapidly and set the entire flat alight."

"What did your colleagues think?"

"Whatever they thought privately – one can never tell with detectives – they were more than happy to charge her with the murder of her husband and son. I happen to think that, had there not been a child involved, the attitude of the police would have been different. When it emerged that the child was not the woman's, but the product of one of her husband's many infidelities – the mother of the child had gone missing and, out of pity, the wife in this case had agreed to take him in, or had been coerced into doing so – the police set upon the woman like a pack of bloodhounds pursuing a fox. 'Get her for murder!' the police cried. The poor woman didn't stand a chance. I believed her version of events. I was in a minority of one. Actually, others might have believed her, but such was the febrile pack-mentality in this case, as is often the case in such investigations, that nobody dared say so. I was taken off the case for failing to pursue it with sufficient vigour. The Crown Prosecution Service pursued the woman with yet more vigour than the police had. 'We have a case!' they declared. There were no witnesses. They had nothing more than supposition and a desperate need, like the police, to get a result. A crime had been committed – or so they claimed – and a crime needs a victim and a criminal. Counsel for the Defence did its job, but the woman went down for the murder of her husband and the boy. Apparently, she killed her husband in cold blood, seizing her chance to rid herself of the man who beat her, and she set fire to the flat so as to kill the boy, out of revenge for her husband's infidelity, and to make the deaths look like the accidents which she claimed they were.

"The upshot is that three lives are now ruined, instead of two, and that a woman will spend the rest of her life in prison for a crime that she did not commit, or, indeed, for a crime that nobody committed, because there was no crime. This is how the law works. I tell you, there are thousands of people languishing in prison for crimes that they did not commit. All too often, the pursuit of justice is nothing more than a conspiracy against the individual in the name of results and the satisfaction of the public's need for vengeance.

"I found it all quite sickening."

Sixteen

"Well, here we are again, at your kitchen table."

"I'm reading *The Argus* and you're reading the *Oxford Mail*. We're like a married couple."

"Does Maureen give you the *Mail* every day?"

"Yes, it's a strange ritual of hers."

"Is she single?"

"As single as they come..."

"You could do worse."

"Behave yourself."

I went to the kitchen sink and started peeling potatoes.

"What's for dinner?"

"I thought I'd make shepherd's pie. Last time I made shepherd's pie, it came out of the oven upside down."

Kendal laughed. "Perhaps you put it *in* the oven upside down."

"It went into the oven with the potato on top and the mince underneath."

"So how on earth did it come out of the oven with the mince on top and the potato underneath?"

"I am to cookery what Ronnie Corbett is to sumo wrestling." I stole that line from the mouth of Arthur Daley, in series eight of *Minder*, but Kendal had no need to know that.

"Who's Ronnie Corbett?"

"Never mind..."

As Kendal immersed herself in stories of the latest muggings and burglaries to have come upon Oxford, I continued with the delicate preparation of my culinary flagship, the only dish that I could make without consulting a recipe.

"Is there anything about Philip in the *Mail*?"

"Not that I can see…"

"What are the main stories?"

"Oh, the usual," Kendal sighed. "A mugging on the Cowley Road, a spate of burglaries in Divinity Road, and – oh, how funny, listen to this – an old lady in an invalid car crashed into an off-license by The Plain. She took out the whole of the front window and ploughed into the food display, scattering crisps and peanuts everywhere."

"I once pushed an old lady in an invalid car from the shops in Summertown to the bottom of Islip Road."

"Yeah?"

"Are you listening?"

"I've no choice."

"Her battery was flat. She stopped me and asked me to push her home. I asked her where she lived. She said that she lived on the other side of the road, by the lights, a two-minute walk away. When we got there – to the place where, supposedly, she lived – she told me that, actually, she lived further along the Banbury Road. Each time we arrived at the place where she'd said she lived, she told me that she lived further along the road. This went on until I'd pushed her halfway to Kidlington."

"Really?"

"To add insult to injury, when, finally, we reached her house, she asked me how much money I wanted."

"I don't know, the old people of today…"

"Had she told me the truth at the outset, I would still have pushed her home."

"She didn't know that, though, did she?"

"No, to her, I was just another feckless youth." In the expectation of a withering retort, I laughed quietly to myself.

"How long ago did this happen?"

"I remember, it was my birthday, so it was seven months ago."

"Did you have to carry her white stick as well?"

"If I had a white stick right now, I know what I'd do with it."

"Daniel, keep your fantasies to yourself, if you don't mind."

"You're a piece of work, you are."

"Hey, what do you make of this?"

"What's that?"

"Do you remember when I said that Suzie's, that knocking shop in Brighton, had a two-for-one offer?"

"I put it down to their having to compete with Hove's Hive Of Honeys."

"Well, I'm looking at the Adult Services section in the *Oxford Mail*… and there's an advert for a Suzie's."

"That's interesting."

"Isn't it just?"

Leaning over Kendal, having abandoned the potatoes for a moment, I studied the advertisement. "That's a Summertown number."

"Are you planning a visit?"

"Mrs Haygreen spoke about a brothel in Portslade, which has a Brighton dialling code, and a brothel in Oxford."

"But she was talking about what the gossips are saying."

"Gossip is usually based on truth."

"Do you seriously think that your choirboy friend owned a couple of brothels?"

"I was a detective in the Met for fifteen years. I've seen it all. The word 'impossible' is no longer in my vocabulary."

"It's not likely, though, is it?"

Leaning against the worktop, my arms folded, I pondered the unlikely and the impossible together.

"And, even if you're right about this, it has nothing to do with your case. You have to focus on that, Daniel."

"Will you do me a favour?"

"Last time *Mum* said that to me, I had to go and look for one of her bra pads out in the street."

"Would you call those two numbers?"

"What two numbers?"

"The two Suzie's…"

"What do you want me to say?"

"Can you pretend to be a girl interested in working at each establishment?"

"Okay…"

"Say that you would like to visit them, to meet them, to talk with them about working at their…places."

"So you want their addresses?"

"That's the idea."

"Why?"

"All will be revealed."

"Can't you call them yourself?"

"I have something to do."

"What?"

"I'll tell you later."

"Where are you going?"

"To my room…"

One of the benefits of being meticulously tidy is that nothing is ever lost: things might get mislaid, but they never get lost. Everything has a place. Everything is in order. This order serves as a means to an end. It serves also as an end in itself.

The cards were in the box containing the bits and pieces relating to my early childhood. I took out some photographs of me, and of Laura, and of me and Laura together. I removed some photographs of Albert taken when he was a boy. The only photograph of Roseanne in my possession was taken when she was pregnant with me. She was sitting in a deckchair, on a bright summer's day, squinting in the sunlight, looking neither content nor fulfilled, though a tentative smile suggested both contentment and fulfilment ahead.

There were eight cards: one for each birthday. Looking at them made me feel old, though they had been preserved well enough. Only the first one was showing signs of age, for it was frayed around the edges and dappled with spots of yellow. That card was given to me in the name of Albert and Roseanne. The other seven cards were likewise signed, but they bore an additional signature, that of Laura. What all the cards had in common was the handwriting of Roseanne.

The words "birthday", "Daddy" and "Mummy" were crucial: they were singled out for my particular attention, for the letter that they had in common. That letter was looped in an idiosyncratic fashion, its tail crossing itself and ending in a semi-circle. It was more than idiosyncratic. It was unique. Before that day, I had never dwelt on Roseanne's unique formation of that letter; now, it exercised me to the point of obsession.

With great anticipation, I took up the comparative document and focussed on the word "Mary". I had to be sure. There it was: the letter was formed in exactly the same fashion. My heart was pounding as if I had just broken the world record for the one-hundred-metre race. Suspicion had given way to conviction.

Kendal entered the room with her customary regard for the occupant's privacy.

"Before you ask," I said, "I'm listening to *Strange Days*, an album by The Doors."

"How fitting…"

"Indeed…"

"I've just had a call from Mum," she announced.

"She wants you back?"

"She wants to see me tomorrow morning, at home."

"You'd better go then."

"I will go, but I'm coming back."

"You're always welcome here. You know that. I'm sorry that I was a bit unwelcoming to start with, but you put me in an awkward situation."

"I'm sorry."

"At least you're wearing some proper clothes now."

"Mum wants to see you too."

"When?"

"Tomorrow…"

"Where?"

"At our house…"

"Then I'll go with you."

"She wants to see us separately."

"Who does she think she is, the Queen?"

"She said she'll be in touch with you."

"That's all I need."

"I phoned those numbers," the girl declared.

"Did you get the details?"

"I did."

"You're a proper little schemer."

"It was *your* idea!"

"I was joking. You did well."

"What are you doing?" Kendal lowered herself onto the bed and peered down at my little collection of souvenirs.

"I have here some cards."

"You sound like Paul Daniels."

"Some birthday cards of mine from when I was a boy…"

"I can get them carbon-dated for you."

"And what else do I have?"

"The card that your sister received, the one with the Virgin Mary's picture on it…"

"Look at them and tell me what strikes you."

Kendal studied the cards, opening each one of them, in turn, and closing it. Then she examined the postcard that Laura had been sent. She checked two or three of the cards a second time.

"What do you notice?"

"It's the letter 'y'."

"What about it?"

"In the birthday cards, and on the postcard, it's written in the same way."

Seventeen

Courtesy of my guest's meticulous preparation, breakfast was ready when I stumbled into the kitchen just before nine o'clock. It was more than ready. It was an elaborate display, an exhibition, a pageant of my best crockery and cutlery, mugs and glasses, all laid out according to a blueprint designed for a king and his consort.

"You're a disgrace, Daniel."

Kendal was leaning with her back against the worktop, by the fridge, her arms folded, in the supercilious manner that I was given to standing. She was mocking me. She could be most amusing.

"Why am I a disgrace?" I protested as I took my seat at the table.

"You come to the breakfast table at this hour."

"It's only nine o'clock."

"The early bird catches the worm, Daniel."

"I've had my fill of getting up early…and of not going to bed at all."

"There's a girl out there who needs finding."

"And, this week, I'm going to find her."

Kendal sat down. She was in one of her playful moods. She liked to reverse the roles, to act as if she were the elder. When she behaved in this way, I saw intimations of her mother, but I told her so at my gravest peril.

"You sound confident."

"How hard can it be to find a strikingly beautiful blonde in Oxford?"

"If it was *that* easy, wouldn't your clients look for her themselves?"

"I guess they don't want to frighten her away."

"There's no chance of *you* scaring her off…not when you're not getting anywhere near her."

"Trust me."

Kendal shook her head by way of dismissal, though her manner was affectionate and replete with nonchalance. "Eat your breakfast, Daniel."

"What time are you due home?"

"Five minutes ago…"

It was disconcerting to find myself back in the Oratory, this time sitting at the back watching and listening as an arcane incantation issued from the mouths of thirty-three devout souls (I counted them) and diffused like incense from multiple burners. The people were scattered around the church, one to a pew, kneeling behind a black-haired priest, who knelt in the front row, on the right, all of them facing the Sanctuary. I had walked in just as Mass was ending and the devotion about to begin; some people had left the church between the two events and others entered. They were praying the Rosary – the Holy Rosary of the Blessed Virgin Mary, that is – and, as it was Wednesday, they were praying the Glorious Mysteries, starting with the Resurrection and ending with the Coronation of the Blessed Virgin Mary. Some of what I was observing, I knew about; the rest I gleaned from the Catholic Truth Society prayer book that I took from the shelves at the back of the church and sat studying as the devotion unfolded; though most of it made sense, in both theory and practice, I wondered why the Hail Mary needed to be recited ten times after the announcement of each of the five mysteries. It all seemed so secretive, as if the prayerful huddle were members of an esoteric cult, as opposed to a Church with more than a billion adherents, and were chanting with a fervent persistence in the hope of propitiating some adamantine guardian of some cosmic rune or unleashing some overwhelming creative power.

It was hard not to feel like an intruder. Even though the devotees had their backs to me, I felt as if each and every one of them were watching me; and that is not to mention my sense of being watched from above. Daunted as I was, then, I waited until halfway through the saying of the Hail Holy Queen, the culmination of the devotion, before I paid for the prayer book, by putting two pounds in a metal box, and taking my hurried leave of the church.

Perplexed by my brief encounter with the praying of the Holy Rosary of the Blessed Virgin Mary, I found that I had walked down Saint Giles' and into Cornmarket Street. I interrogated myself as to where I should go from there. Though I liked wandering aimlessly around the city, I had not that luxury today, for I had a job to do and I had to think hard about how to do it. I was about to take a firm hold on the situation when my phone rang. The doghouse beckoned.

"Rosie…"

"I'd like you to come to the house."

"What's for lunch?"

"You'll be lucky."

"I'm busy."

"Since when?"

"I'm working."

"Oh, yes," came the cynical sneer from my handset. "Kendal tells me that you are playing at being Sherlock Holmes."

"Not exactly," I replied. "Holmes was an exponent of deductive analysis. I'm more…intuitive."

"She says that you have got precisely nowhere with your first case."

"Well, these are early days."

"So you won't mind taking a bit of time out to come and see me."

"When you put it like that, how can I refuse?"

"Will you be here at midday?"

"It's nearly midday now."

"See you at midday."

"Charming, as ever…" I told my handset after the connection was severed with a matron's severity.

A drink was imperative. Facing the wrath of Rosie Waterhouse without at least one large whisky in me was unthinkable. I looked up Cornmarket Street, the commercial hub of Oxford, and beheld a sea of heads. Children on their school holidays had been added to the army of European language students that invades the city every year. I was looking at the parting of the Red Sea, except that the parting was conspicuous by its absence.

The Grapes suggested itself as a suitable venue for my libation. I had read somewhere, probably in Maureen's *Oxford Mail*, that it was on the verge of closure. The least that I could do, then, was buy a couple of large ones to help keep it afloat.

The man behind the bar had looked surprised to see a customer. "Why not start early?" he said as I savoured my first large one of the session.

I looked at my watch. The time was twenty-past-eleven. "I don't normally start this early," I replied.

"A bit of Dutch courage, like, is it?"

"You could say that."

"A woman?"

"Yes, but not in a good way…"

"Trouble?"

"Trouble and strife…"

"Your wife?"

I laughed at that. "Not likely…"

"Just stand your ground," my counsellor went on. "Disagree with her, but appear to agree with her. That's the trick."

"Any man who can do that deserves the Nobel Peace Prize."

"A couple of those inside you…and she won't stand a chance."

"You read my mind." I placed the empty glass on the bar. "I'll have another double, please."

"Coming right up…"

"You remind me of someone."

The barman had his back to me as he fed more whisky into my glass. "I'm often mistaken for Tom Cruise."

"It's not him that you remind me of."

The man placed the replenished glass before me. "Then it must be Robert Redford."

"No, it's Dave."

"Dave?"

"The owner of the Winchester Club, in *Minder*, played by Glynn Edwards…"

"Oh, right, that old geezer…"

"You even sound like him."

"If I'm Dave, I hope you're not going to be Arthur Daley and tell me to put these drinks on the slate."

The ten-pound note that I had taken from my wallet was pushed along the bar. "For my drinks…and get one for yourself."

"Much obliged to you, sir…"

"Call me Daniel."

"And you must call me Dave."

"Really?"

"David Haywood…at your service…"

Eighteen

The walk to Canal Reach was not a pleasant one, not least because morning had slipped headlong into afternoon when I left The Grapes. Dave had kept me amused with stories of some of his regulars down the years. He told me that three elderly gentlemen had been coming to the pub at midday for years to play dominoes together, and had not missed a day since nineteen-eighty-seven. He said that they were "old codgers" back then, so he dreaded to think how ancient they were now. Sure enough, as I finished my fourth double-whisky of the session, the geriatric trio staggered to their places in the far corner of the pub as if they were dropping into their local day centre for coffee. They even ordered a drink each. Dave was adamant that those three pints of beer would last all afternoon.

"How nice of you to come, Daniel…"

"You know I like this part of town."

"Close the door behind you."

I did as I was ordered, before following Rosie into the kitchen. As I passed through the living-room, I couldn't help but notice the pile of bills, final reminders all of them, languishing on the coffee-table. Rosie's situation had not changed for the better. I decided to be nice to her, whatever the provocation, not to antagonise her with sly comments.

"As you can see, I *have* made lunch."

"You shouldn't have troubled yourself."

"You've been feeding my beloved daughter," was the ever-so-sly retort. "The least I can do is feed you in return." Rosie lowered a bowl of pasta-salad onto the table. She urged me to take a seat.

I took a seat and peered into the bowl. I was looking for something recognisable. I spied olives and chopped peppers. Tomatoes were evident, as was cucumber. I was dismayed to see butter beans, but was mindful that I knew Rosie well enough to express my hope that she would not be offended if I spurned them.

Rosie joined me at the table. "I know why you're late."

"Can you smell the whisky fumes?"

"I reckon the entire street can smell them."

"I needed inspiration."

"You're turning into a degenerate. That's what happens when a man has too much time on his hands."

"When a woman has too much time on her hands, she gets grumpy and argumentative."

"I'm on leave."

"So relax and enjoy it."

The food looked less impressive on the plate than in the bowl. Rosie directed my attention to the bread, which was piled in the basket beside the bowl. By the look of it, the bread would have been useful for any carpenter who had run out of sandpaper. Luckily, I was not hungry.

"Are you not having any bread?"

"I'm not into DIY."

My hostess looked offended. She thought for a moment. Then she eased her way into the interrogation. "I guess you're wondering why I've asked you here."

"The thought had crossed my mind."

"I shouldn't have had to summon my own daughter to her own home, but she came, she listened, we talked…and then she went…back to yours."

"I've tried to persuade her to return home."

"Have you?"

"Do you think I like having her at my flat all the time?"

"I think you do, yes."

"All right, I admit, she's good company. I like having her around the place…though not for the reasons that you're suggesting."

Arguing whilst eating was not easy, though Rosie was managing it easily enough.

"What's going on between you and Kendal?"

"Why don't you ask Kendal?"

"I did ask her...this morning."

"And?"

"And she said that nothing was going on between you."

"There's your answer."

"But she's bound to say that, isn't she?"

"Kendal's no liar."

"I'm appealing to you, Daniel, as the mature adult in this...irregular relationship...to give me a straight, honest answer."

"If something *were* going on between Kendal and me, she would gladly tell you, because she would revel in the drama that would ensue."

"You're as accomplished an actor as she is."

"Just say what you have to say, Rosie."

"I've said it."

"You think I'm screwing Kendal?"

"One last fling with young flesh before you hit middle-age..."

Rosie's carefully crafted dish was fast becoming unpalatable. "You'll recall that my 'inadequacy as a man', as you so charmingly put it, was the reason why we broke up...not that we were ever..."

"Kendal's a nubile teenager. I'm a spongy forty-six-year-old. I can see how a girl like Kendal would rouse even your flagging libido."

"I'm very close to walking out of here, Rosie."

"At least finish your lunch."

"I've hardly *started* it."

Orange juice was poured into a glass and passed across the table; the juice had so many bits in it that I feared I would have to eat it rather than drink it. Several mysteries had come upon me in recent days, and I was struggling enough chewing on *them*.

"Would you like a beer?"

"I've had enough booze for one day, thanks."

"I'll make you some coffee later."

"I won't be here later."

"It was ever thus."

Rosie's hair was much shorter than I had seen it before. It was manicured, with each strand arranged with military precision. It reminded me of the Edinburgh Military Tattoo, but without the pomp and circumstance. I had known her hair only as being shoulder-length and wild, more than a little greasy, sweaty even. That's how I preferred it. The new hairstyle made her look older than she was; and her frumpy new clothes did little to accentuate any lingering youthfulness.

"Kendal told me about your friend."

What was I to say in reply to this new conversational broadside, when there was every chance that it had been launched with an attribution of blame? I was being made culpable for every other crime and misdemeanour, it seemed.

"I can't begin to tell you what Philip meant to me, even if Philip and I had long been estranged, and even if my feelings for him were bound up with my feelings for someone else."

"Isn't it incredible that he lived in this very street, and that neither you nor I knew it?"

"You were hardly likely to have known, were you, when you'd never heard of him?"

"You know what I mean." Rosie saw that I was picking at the pasta-salad, arranging bits of food into what appeared to be the shape of a crucifix. "You're struggling with that, aren't you?"

"I'm not hungry."

"Have some bread. It has to be eaten today."

"It looks like it should have been eaten yesterday."

Rosie sighed in frustration at our inability to find a common wavelength upon which to communicate. "What do you think happened to your friend?"

"I've an inkling, but it's a fanciful one, like most of my inklings… though most of them turn out not to be too wide of the mark."

"What is this *fanciful* inkling of yours?"

"Cherchez la femme…" I replied. "Cherchez les femmes…"

"What are you talking about?"

"Bring me a case and I will say, 'Look for the woman.'"

"What?"

"Woman…women…the Eternal Woman…"

"You're drunk."

"They are all connected. I don't know how, but they are, and I shall find out."

"That's reassuring to know."

"But I won't do so sitting here."

"Thanks very much…"

"I have to go."

Rosie followed me to the door.

"I will try to persuade Kendal to come home," I told Rosie, who stood now in the doorway, looking out onto the street.

"She might just listen to *you*."

"Things will improve between the two of you."

Rosie nodded hopefully. "You probably think I'm an ogre, don't you?"

"I wouldn't want to disabuse you of your prejudices, Rosie," I replied. "You would be lost without them."

The woman pondered my words for a moment, before slamming the door in my face. I was standing six feet away from the door, but I felt closer, for the force of the closure reached me like a smack in the face with a coffin lid.

Nursing the effects of the assault, I trudged the few yards up the street to Philip's house. It was cordoned off by tape, courtesy of Thames Valley Police. A police officer was standing outside, looking bored. A different officer had been guarding the house when I passed it on my way to Rosie's house. He had looked no less desperate to be somewhere else. The house looked desolate. I tried to get close enough to be able to see inside. As his colleague had done, the guard observed me reproachfully, his eyes threatening me with arrest should I dare take another step closer. The curtains were closed, anyway, so the house was guarding its secrets from prying eyes and twitching noses.

Seeing the Bookbinder's Arms, I thought about imbibing a pint of Tribute, in tribute to Philip, but thought better of it. I looked down the street known as Canal Reach. A melancholy summer haze shrouded it, making all its edges appear fuzzy. Waves of heat rose from the ground. At the very moment that the bells in the splendid Italianate tower of the Church of Saint Barnabas proclaimed the half-hour, a narrow-boat, on the canal, drifted into view, and out again, heading towards the city centre. I managed to catch the name emblazoned on its side. That single word, "Tribute", was much more than poignant.

My heart sank at the thought of the dead of Jericho.

Having eaten virtually nothing since breakfast, and all too conscious of the whisky swilling around anarchically in my stomach, the Jericho Café, my favourite place to eat in all Oxford, enticed me. Its Gallic ambience was always embellished with a sultry jazz soundtrack, the food was never less than exquisite, and the fans, whirring busily on the ceiling, were bound to keep one cool on the hottest of summer afternoons. I had taken one step in the direction of the café when my phone rang.

"Kendal?"

"How's it going?"

"How's what going?"

"The case…"

"Your mother's been on my case, if that's what you mean."

"I didn't even bother talking to her this morning."

"You showed up. Rosie told me."

"I showed up. I sat down. I listened. I let Mum say her piece. Then I left."

"She didn't try to stop you?"

"How could she stop me?"

"She has the law on her side…as I keep telling you."

"I don't care."

"Is there something you're not telling me?"

"Why should there be?"

"It's just that…well…the two of you seem incapable of resolving your dispute, and I can't believe that what you fell out over was so serious."

"We just don't get on."

"I hope that's all it is, because I really don't need another mystery."

"You have a lot of loose threads hanging, Daniel."

"I'll tie them, don't worry."

"When?"

"Soon enough…"

"I'm not seeing much progress."

"Right…Suzie's…you got the address for me yesterday, didn't you?"

"You know I did. It's in Middle Way, just round the corner from your flat."

"I'm going there tonight."

"Why?"

"I shall pretend that I'm a client."

"You mean that you'll pretend to pretend."

"Then, tomorrow, I shall visit the other Suzie's."

"The one in Portslade?"

"Yes, the other Suzie's the address of which you got for me."

"Because you think that your friend Philip had something to do with both Suzie's?"

"I *know* he did. It seems incredible that the Philip that I knew could have had anything to do with brothels, but he *was* involved, I'm sure."

"Shall I go with you tomorrow?"

"No…"

"Why not?"

"I want you to attend the inquest."

Nineteen

From the other side of the road, I saw Dex propping up the bar in Jude the Obscure. He was a hardy drinker. He was trying to engage in conversation the only other person in the pub, the barman, but was being studiously ignored, a state of affairs to which he was thoroughly accustomed. I was one of the few people who gave him the time of day, because he amused me, though I would spend the next hour with him only because there was a chance that he would be useful.

"I thought I'd find you in here," I announced, wishing to seem that I had sought him out.

Dex looked up at me with bloodshot eyes. "I'd take my hat off to the power of your sixth sense," came the slurred reply, "but I don't possess a hat." He took a swig from his pint of lager.

I regarded his ginger head. "No hat would dare attach itself to hair that greasy," I said.

Dex patted his head. "I'll have you know," he said, "I washed these locks of mine only three weeks ago."

"That recently?"

"It was a special occasion."

"What did you wash it in, chip fat?"

"Some green stuff I found in the bathroom when I moved into the flat…"

"It's called shampoo."

A man in his twenties, wearing regulation sweatshirt and jeans, came to the bar on the other side. "Can I get you anything he asked?" He was friendly as a Greek in a Turkish bath.

"A whisky, please…"

"Make that two," Dex put in.

"Haven't you had enough?" I asked.

"Something has to chase down the beer." As if his throat were sore, he swallowed hard. He belched.

"Did your mum never tell you not to belch in public?"

"My mum was too busy screwing Tom, Dick and Harry to tell me anything."

Or, as Lou Reed put it, I thought, with Harry, Mark and John…

"That'll be three pounds, please."

I gave the barman the money. I pushed one of the drinks along the bar towards Dex. "I heard that your money came through."

Dex nodded. "All fifty-thousand glorious pounds of it," he said. "Thank God for Auntie Pam."

"When I hadn't seen you selling the *Big Issue* for a few weeks, I thought: either he's dead, or his money's come through."

"If the money hadn't come through, I probably *would* be dead."

"What will you do with the money?"

"I'll spend it."

"Where are you living?"

"Glandford and I have forsaken the delights of a tent in Port Meadow for the relative opulence of Kidlington."

"Where is Glandford? I thought you two were joined at the hip."

"He's gone to get some gear."

I shook my head. "Isn't it time you gave up that stuff?"

"I have to do something with my time."

"You could get a job."

When Dex raised his eyebrows at me, a thousand freckles on his forehead moved with them. He allowed his eyes to fall towards the whisky that he had taken up. He laughed quietly to himself. There was melancholy in his laughter.

"What will you do when the money runs out?"

"I'll worry about that when it happens," Dex replied. "I'll probably be dead by then."

"How do you figure that?"

"My dear friend, five years on the streets take their toll."

"Don't take this the wrong way," I said, "but you looked smarter when you were on the streets."

"Yeah, well, I made an effort back then, didn't I? After all, nobody wants to buy the *Big Issue* from a tramp."

Laughter was upon me when Dex belched. I recoiled from the smell.

"Got a smoke?" The question was posed in the wake of the belch, and smelt as bad. "I've run out."

"I don't smoke."

"Do you have any vices, Saint Daniel?"

"I drink too much tea."

"You've been knocking back the whisky. I can see it in your eyes."

The conversation had taken a turn for the downright perverse. It was time to be serious. "In all your years selling the *Issue*, did you ever see this young lady?" I showed him the photograph of Miranda.

In his clouded vision, Dex struggled to make sense of the image. "No," he replied, "but I wish I had." He strained his eyes. He leaned forward slightly. He took a second look. "I don't know, though," he said. Lucidity passed almost before it arrived. He shook his head. "She looks like any other blonde."

"Saying that all blondes look alike is like saying that all carrot-tops look alike."

Thinking God only knew what, Dex regarded me for a moment. "Why do you ask, anyway?" he enquired.

"I'm looking for her."

"Are you stalking her?"

"In a way, yes…"

"Has she got lost?"

"It would be more accurate to say that she's gone underground."

Dex nodded at the floor on the other side of the bar. "Try looking in the cellar then." As his laugh tailed off, he belched again.

My body was repulsed by the prospect of more whisky, but I drained my glass regardless.

"If she's gone AWOL in Oxford," Dex resumed, "the Great Dane's gaff might be the place to start looking."

"You mean The Aquarium, on the Cowley Road?"

"That's the place."

"Why does that man's name keep cropping up?"

"Because he's everywhere…"

"He's even inside my head."

"He's lowlife…but he's not *that* low."

"How come you know so much about the man?"

"You don't spend five years on the streets without hearing a thing or two."

"What have you heard about this character?"

"That he's a gangster…"

"Everyone knows *that*."

"That he kidnaps girls…"

"Come off it."

"Have you not been to that place of his?"

"Have you?"

"I know people who have."

"What have you heard?"

"That it's a fuck club…"

"Most people assume that it's not a monastery."

"I've heard that he puts these girls, the ones that he kidnaps, to work."

"You're saying that he takes girls off the streets, against their will, and forces them to sell their bodies?"

"I'm saying that he picks them up, gains their trust, and then *persuades* them to sell their bodies." Dex gulped at his lager. "He has an eye for the vulnerable girl, for girls that he can take under his wing…and for girls that are legal, but only just."

"You *Big Issue* vendors are a great untapped resource."

"We make great snouts."

"A couple of my snouts were *Big Issue* vendors."

"You were a *cop*?"

"Of a sort…"

"Well, knock me down with a feather."

"You look like you're about to *fall* down."

"Perhaps you can help me."

"How do you mean?"

"You could help me find a purpose in life."

"People keep saying that to me."

"I am a sheep that has gone astray."

"You want to lean on *me*, someone who will have to leave his car in town overnight, because he's drunk too much whisky to drive it home?"

Dex gulped down more beer and, thank the Lord, suppressed another belch. "Your vices illuminate your virtues," he intoned miserably. "My vices swamp my virtues."

"Nobody's perfect."

"Not even you?"

"Not even me…"

"From where I'm standing, you look like a saint."

"Every saint has a past, Dex, and every sinner has a future."

With a hand unsteady as a tremulous granny's, Dex raised his pint glass. "I'll drink to that," he announced.

"You would drink to anything."

The glass was raised again. "Here's to drinking to anything."

"I have to go."

"But it's your round!" Dex protested. Doubtless, he genuinely thought that it was my turn to buy the drinks, so addled was his mind. The shame was that behind the fog of drink and drugs was a brain to match the best of them. People like Dex swell the streets and remind one that most of us are casualties of life, in one form or another.

"In case you've told me anything that proves to be useful, I thank you."

I returned the photograph of Miranda to my jacket pocket. I placed the empty glass on the bar.

"You look terrible."

"But, Dex, I'll be sober in the morning."

"It *is* morning."

I wasn't sure whether to nod knowingly, at the perverse inevitability of the situation, or shake my head in despair. Torn between the two acts, I accomplished neither.

"I would give you a lift home," Dex slurred, "but, as you can see, I'm somewhat indisposed."

"Are you telling me that you have a car now?"

"I left it somewhere." Dex shook his head. "I can't remember where."

"We're a right pair, aren't we?"

"I doubt that it would get you home, anyway," Dex continued. "It's running on vapour."

Holding my breath, wincing, I took a step back. "The vapour from your breath, I shouldn't wonder..." I returned.

Though Dex strained every sinew to suppress a belch, he failed.

"Do yourself a favour," I said, "and get some food inside you." I regarded my interlocutor's coat. It was too big even for him. "You need to grow into that thing."

Dex raised his glass of whisky. "This, my friend, is all the food I need." He drained the whisky. He put the glass on the bar. "Another one in there, please..." he told the underemployed barman.

Though the barman suspected that his patron had drunk more than enough liquor for one day, he was not about to argue with a man twice his size.

"Do you ever take that coat off?" I asked.

"What coat?"

127

"The one you're wearing…in the middle of summer."

Dex regarded the decomposing grey-green blanket that all but engulfed him. He looked surprised to see it. "Oh, that coat," he said. "It's been part of me for so long, I'd forgotten it was there."

Jericho is an offbeat place. Legend has it that the name derives from the flimsiness of the houses built to accommodate the workers putting together the new home of the Oxford University Press, that splendidly haughty edifice in Walton Street: when trains shot by, on the other side of the canal, the houses would shake and the walls threaten to come tumbling down. When Thomas Hardy set his novel *Jude the Obscure* in Jericho, the district was a thoroughgoing slum. Intimations of the old Jericho abound, not least the shabby public houses that adorn every street corner, their thresholds so rarely crossed by customers that you wonder how they can so stoutly defy the laws of finance and economy. But defy them they do, and defy them they will continue to do, for years to come, not receiving so much as a lick of paint, whilst the nearby oyster bars and sandwich bars, all chrome and glass, undergo one incarnation after another. Some say that Jericho is being spoilt, for it has been discovered by the rich. What is worse, so people say, is that it has been discovered by folk who aspire to be rich and are well on the way to being so. Soon, so the lamentation goes, the only walls around Jericho will be those keeping out the poor and the not-so-rich.

Cornmarket Street was heaving, a seething mass of human flesh, much of it naked. I had just stepped out of Boots, having bought some earplugs: Kendal's regular trips to the kitchen during the night were so disturbing my sleep that I needed some form of insulation, no matter how flimsy. A young man stood outside the shop trying to sell the *Big Issue*. He was competing with an African evangelist, who paced up and down, back and forth, wearing a white gown and a fez-like hat, exhorting the infidels to see the light, to repent and be saved.

"Open your hearts to the Lord!" he bellowed. "Let the Saviour, Lord Jesus Christ, into your lives!"

"Shut up, will yer, mate!" cried the magazine-seller. "I'm trying to sell the *Big Issue* 'ere!"

At which point, the Scotsman outside the Virgin Megastore, stamping his feet as he played his beloved bagpipes, began a rendition of *Scotland The Brave* that drowned out even the manic street preacher.

Around these three staples of the Oxford scene, the world went about its business, indifferent.

"Hey, man! Can I trouble you?"

My first thought was that I had been intercepted by a clipboard-wielding charity worker.

"If you must…"

"You listen to hip-hop?"

"Not if I can help it…"

"What you listen to, man?"

"Fleetwood Mac, Supertramp, The Carpenters, Eagles…" I joked.

"That's good, man." My new friend looked somewhat baffled by my admission. "That's what you's about. But you need to move with the flow, man."

"I tend to find myself swimming *against* the tide."

"You wanna let yourself go and see what happens?"

"How much will it cost me?"

"Three pounds…or two for five…"

"One will do, thanks…"

The man brandished one of the CDs that he was holding.

I studied it. "'Big Bad Brian,'" I read. "Is that you?"

"I'm the man."

"You don't look like a Brian."

Confusion was written slowly across the man's face.

"I'll add it to my collection," I said.

"This is what's happening, man. The streets are what I know. I take my sounds from the streets of Britain, man. I don't ape no gangster-rap shit from America, neither."

A third man, this one more round than tall and wearing a bandana, came between me and Big Bad Brian. He, too, was clutching a small pile of discs.

"Three pounds for the latest sounds from Jay Zed…" he announced.

"Are you two a double-act?" I asked.

"We're just a couple o' black dudes tryin' to make good, man," Jay Zed replied. "What's good for one is good for the other, and what's bad is bad."

"That's how it is, man," Big Bad Brian said.

I gave one of the men six pounds, and told them to sort out between them the division of the spoils.

"You're a true brother, man," Big Bad Brian proclaimed.

"You're one of us," echoed Jay Zed.

"We're thinking of taking up the bagpipes, man," Big Bad Brian declared.

"Yeah, man," Jay Zed added, "for every one that slags the noisy fucker, there's another two that chucks coins at 'im."

"Probably, to shut him up…" I suggested.

Big Bad Brian held up the pound-coin that I had given him. "I'm gonna knock him out with one of these beauties, man."

"Don't waste your money," I said.

"Be lucky, man!" Big Bad Brian called as I walked away.

"Dig the music, my friend!"

But the call of Jay Zed was all but lost in the hustle and bustle of a fading Cornmarket Street.

Twenty

When I got home, Kendal was waiting for me. She had made some coffee, having worked out how to use the percolator that I had owned for years – it had been a birthday present from my sister – but never taken out of the box. Gratefully did I accept her offer to dish up some of the previous day's leftover shepherd's pie, and I watched with pleasure as she heated some baked beans and planted them lovingly on the plate beside the mince and the potato. The food filled an enormous hole in my stomach and soaked up much of the whisky. We agreed that we would not talk about Rosie until further notice.

"I've been playing some of your music."

"Let me guess…Blondie…"

Kendal nodded.

"Pink?"

She nodded again. "Go on."

"Mott the Hoople?"

"Who?" Kendal took a most ladylike sip of her coffee. "No, the Stones…I played *Their Satanic Majesties Request.* There's a great song on that album, called *She's A Rainbow.*"

"That's one of my favourite Stones songs."

"I played the song three times."

"You're hooked."

"Do you prefer the Beatles or the Stones?"

"It's a false comparison. The Beatles disbanded just as the Stones were getting into their stride; and the Stones are still making albums and playing to live audiences."

"They are growing old disgracefully."

"Some would say so."

"Any progress on the case?"

Cryptically, I tapped my forehead twice.

"What does that mean?"

"It means that it's all happening up here."

"What is?"

"The case..."

Kendal was sitting next to me on the sofa. Her frown betrayed a touch of scepticism. Then she smiled her gorgeous smile and brushed some hair behind her ear with her fingers. I was put in mind of Roseanne at the fair.

"I guess that I have to trust you."

"What does that mean?"

"It means that...I have to trust that you know what you're doing."

"It's all smoke and mirrors, isn't it?"

"The case?"

"This whole private-detective thing..."

"It's not a science then?"

"Not for me..."

"You need to clear the smoke so that you can see the mirrors."

"That's what I'm doing."

"And what do you see in the mirrors?"

"I see several people."

"Who?"

"I see Philip and Sylvia, I see Dane Goldman and Sabrina, and, of course, I see Miranda."

Kendal's expression was difficult to read. She was the little girl lost, trying to be a woman, but lacking either the hard-nosed fortitude or the cold-eyed cynicism even to affect such maturity. Precocious as she was, I could see in her face both the past and the future, the girl and the woman, and the tension between what she was and what she was becoming. Her present fate was to sit uneasily on the cusp dividing girlhood from womanhood, a plight rendered all the more burdensome by the body's having long ago won the race to maturity, leaving the mind floundering in its wake. I wanted to tell her that her pain would soon be over, that very soon she would have crossed the bridge over troubled waters, the conduit between the girl and the woman.

"What's wrong?" I asked.

"It's probably nothing."

"So tell me."

"Well, it's happened before…and it's happened again."

I expected Kendal's revelation to have something to do with being caught short at the onset of menstruation, or some such womanly predicament, but the reality was much less prosaic.

"I've been followed."

"By whom?"

"I don't know."

"Did you get a look at him?"

"I left the flat this morning. A silver Mercedes, with black windows, followed me all the way to Mum's house."

"It was waiting for you outside?"

"Yes…"

"And it just crawled along Woodstock Road, then down Polstead Road and into Jericho?"

"Pretty much, yeah…"

"How did it maintain walking speed along Woodstock Road?"

"I don't know, Daniel. All I know is that it was there when I left the flat, it was there every time I looked up, and it was there when I got to Mum's house."

"Was it there when you left your mum's house?"

"No…"

"You said that you've been followed before."

Looking challenged, but nowhere near beaten, Kendal nodded.

"By the same car?"

Kendal nodded once more. "I left school one afternoon, about Easter time, and noticed the silver Mercedes parked in a lay-by on the Marston Ferry Road. It was an odd place to park, but I thought nothing more of it…until I got home and saw the same car parked on the corner of the street, by the Bookbinder's Arms."

"It had followed you all the way home?"

"Somehow, yes…"

"Let's work this out. Four months ago, a car follows you home after school. This morning, the same car follows you from here to your mum's house. So whoever's driving the car knew this morning both where you were staying and where you live. But if he knew where you live then why follow you?"

"Perhaps he thought I was going somewhere else, and wanted to find out where."

"But why?"

"I don't know."

"It makes no sense."

"I think that someone just wants to freak me out."

"I think you're right."

"I have a person in mind."

"Who?"

"I think you know who."

"Dane Goldman?"

Kendal nodded calmly, but firmly, her affirmation.

"You know him?" I could not believe that she did.

"Who doesn't?"

"And Dane Goldman, the one they call the Great Dane, is connected in some way, I'm sure, with Sabrina."

"Your friend, Sabrina?"

It was my turn to nod. "And the connections don't end there."

"No?"

"All should be clearer after my visit to Suzie's this evening."

"You've really got it sewn up, haven't you?"

"I could be completely wrong."

"I doubt that."

"Let's crack this together."

"I'm enjoying being involved."

"I've tried to get you involved, but on *my* terms. Now, it seems, a third party has forced you to become involved on *his* terms."

"I'm not scared."

"I know you're not."

"What else is a girl with no prospects supposed to do, but get involved in a private detective's mystery…or mysteries?"

"You have to be careful, Kendal."

"*You* have to make another date with Sabrina."

"Do I?"

"You need to find out what she's up to."

"Sabrina's purpose will emerge in good time."

"So you *won't* make another date with her?"

"No…"

"You're the boss."

"You could have fooled me."

Kendal bewitched me for a moment with her smile. She reached over to the coffee-table and took up the postcard of Our Lady of Oxford. She regarded it reverently. Our Lady looked reverently back.

"What are we going to do with Our Lady of Oxford?" the girl asked.

"That's a case with which I've made some *definite* progress," I replied.

"How?"

"You know how."

"I know that you think that you've matched the handwriting."

"The two sets of writing *have* to be the work of the same hand."

"It's possible."

"It's more than *probable*."

"But it's not definite."

"The evidence is compelling."

"I'm just trying to protect your feelings, Daniel. I don't want you to get your hopes up, only to be disappointed."

"I *won't* be disappointed."

"How can you be sure?"

"How many convents do you think there are in the Oxford area?"

"A few…not many…"

"So it wouldn't be difficult for me to do a little research and draw up a short list, would it?"

"I guess not."

"So that's what I did."

"Nice work…"

"Then I phoned each convent…and, when speaking to someone at the third establishment on the list, established that it harbours one Rose-anne Mary Wordsworth."

"Your mum?"

The word sounded wrong, false, like an imposter. It had no place in my life. It was a word that others used. I could not remember my ever having used the word. It was an idea, a nice idea, but nothing more. There, in the realm of ideas, it would stay, never to be rescued, never to see the light of day. Mindful, then, of the word's lack of substance, as it applied to me, I simply nodded.

"Bloody hell, Daniel, that's awesome! Why aren't you excited?"

"I *am* excited. But I have to keep my excitement in check. I've a job to do."

"But your mum…you haven't seen her since you were eight years old…and she's here…nearby…"

"And she'll still be here, nearby, when my job is done. She's not going anywhere, is she?"

"Wow, Daniel, there's so much going on at the moment."

"Rather too much, I would say…"

"It's all good fun, though, isn't it?"

"*You've* made it fun."

"Which convent is your mum in?"

Again, I balked at the word. "The Carmelite of Our Lady…"

"Where's that?"

"It's in Upper Midmarsh, just north of Yarnton."

"That's just up the road."

"It would be crass to call my discovery a miracle, but I can think of no other word for it."

"It *is* a miracle, Daniel."

"Though how Roseanne knew Laura's address remains to be discovered."

"She might know yours."

"That would be *more* than a miracle."

"So what's the next step in the master plan?"

"I'm going to listen to some music – I'm in the mood for Jim Morrison and The Doors – then I'm going down the road to Suzie's."

"You're going to pretend to be a client?"

"Up to a point…"

"I was thinking…if you have to, you know, in the line of duty…"

"Discretion is the watchword, Kendal."

"If they think that you're a journalist, or a policeman, they will throw you out on your ear before you can say Fanny Hill."

"It's just as well that I'm neither a journalist nor a policeman, then, isn't it?"

Twenty-One

Perpendicular to Grove Street, and linking South Parade and Squitchey Lane, is Middle Way. A long road, it is lined on either side by sturdy, regular houses of roughly the same shape and size, though the odd ivy-clad cottage dares to stand out from the crowd. The street could hardly be more suburban. It is the type of street where a member of a bridge club would live. Number Twenty Eight A Middle Way dares to be different from the other dwellings in the street by virtue of its standing sideways on to the road, rather than facing it, and being somewhat larger. Its bearing affords it discretion, not least because the pathway to its door is beyond the reach of the dismal light cast by the nearest street-lamp. I walked down that path to the door, on either side of which was a room that was barely lit, the one on the left by white light, some of which seeped from small gaps in the blind, and the other by a blue light standing in the window behind pastel-blue curtains. I rang the bell.

Giggling came from the room on the left.

"I bet he's for you," a voice said.

"He'll be for you," another voice replied.

"He might be for both of you," a third voice put in.

"I bet he's a fat minger," the first voice said.

"Then he'll be for you," the second voice retorted.

"Of course he'll be a minger," the third voice returned. "He's a man, isn't he?"

Ever so slowly, and only partially, the door was opened.

"Hello," I said.

"Oh," said the third voice. "Hello…" On her guard, she peered into the dark.

"You look surprised," I said.

The woman opened the door to let me in. "All that black of yours was a bit of a shock," she said, her accent suggesting that she was not without education. "I thought you were a priest."

"Have you ever had a priest in here?"

"Not to my knowledge…"

"You must be Suzie?" I was hopeful that she was.

"I might be," the woman replied, smiling at me pleasantly.

She was pretty, but plain, under hair that was brown and curly. The odd freckle decorated her face. I couldn't work out whether the absence of make-up enhanced or detracted from her appearance. In a loose-fitting, pale-blue, roll-neck sweater, and tight, stone-washed jeans, she was dressed for a night in front of the television.

"Follow me," she said, before turning on her heels and making for the blue room.

From behind, I was able to appreciate an alluring shape and to wonder if she, too, were on the game.

"I'll send in the girls."

As I waited, I inspected the room. A Monet, one of his *Water Lilies*, hung at the back. I wondered if Picasso's *Demoiselles d'Avignon* would not have been more appropriate. Below the picture, on a chrome-and-glass coffee-table, stood a wooden sculpture of a couple performing oral sex, the woman on top. On another wall was a large, designer-style mirror. Having looked at it for a moment, I looked away, for I was not flattered by the image that struggled to reach me through the gloom. On the other side of the room was a wooden table, upon which were displayed magazines of the soft-pornographic type, together with print-outs of descriptions of girls seen as posted by punters on the internet. I perused the various laminated sheets and took in some of the phrases deployed. Tara, apparently, had legs that went on forever; Carey possessed a backside for which one might die; Chelsea's breasts were ample enough to gorge on; and Angeline never failed to give one a satisfying climax. I was about to give Lucia's profile some attention when a shadow darkened the room. Standing before me was a girl whose legs went on forever.

"I'm Tara." Though she adjusted her white cotton dress, it was so tight that it remained firmly where it was. She was painfully shy. "Would you like to go upstairs?" she squeaked. Embarrassed, like a schoolgirl caught with her pants down, she brushed some of her dyed-blonde hair behind an endearingly petit right ear.

"Could I meet the other girl?" I enquired, exercising the customer's prerogative.

"Sure..." All legs and arms and hair and heels, the girl left the room and closed the door behind her.

A moment later, another girl, more curvaceous than Tara, came into the room. She wore a loose-fitting, see-through red dress, the hem of which threatened to encroach on her thighs. Like Tara, she wore heels that were needlessly tall. "Hi," she purred.

"Hello..." I had been unnerved and intimidated by hardened criminals, but never so much as I was by this damsel, smooth, hardboiled and loaded with sin as she was.

The girl approached me. She put a hand on each of my shoulders. Then she planted a lingering kiss on my left cheek. "I'm Carey," she said in a hushed tone. "Carey Seymour..."

I knew that Carey Seymour was no more this girl's name than Tara was the other girl's, not least because working girls never reveal their first names, never mind their second.

"Believe me," she whispered in my ear, "when you've seen a bit of Carey Seymour, you'll care to see more of her, much more." She stepped away from me. She regarded me with widened eyes. Then she left the room as Tara had done, though with maturity and greater self-possession, as if she were in complete control, an old hand to her colleague's novice. As she went, I noticed that her backside was not covered entirely by her dress, and that what passed for her underwear was as much in as under.

Within seconds, Suzie was back in the room. Like Tara and Carey, she was tense behind the relaxed façade. The girls seemed both to offer everything and desperate to give nothing. "Take what you see," they seemed to say, "not what you don't." "Take my body, but not my soul." Suzie, moreover, seemed distracted, vacant, her mind both elsewhere and nowhere.

"Which girl would you like to see?"

I made a rapid calculation. Tara was younger, more innocent, which made her more likely to yield to discreet enquiries; but it meant also that she would know less and therefore have less to tell. Carey was a woman of the world and, as such, would be more alert to the slyness implicit in a line of discreet enquiry, but she would have more to tell and might not shrink entirely from telling it. The choice facing me was between listening to the songs of innocence and the songs of experience. I chose the latter.

"I'll fetch her for you."

During the interlude, I noticed the television by the window. It was on, with the sound down, and showing was a nature documentary – the usual: wildebeest being stalked and eaten at the water's edge by crocodiles – which made a change from what I had been used to seeing on screens in bordellos that I raided as a policeman.

"Follow me."

I followed Carey out of the room and up the stairs, until we came to one of three bedrooms. It was not a small room. The room was a study in scarlet, a riot of scarlet, with curtains, carpet, duvet, pillows and wallpaper all matching Carey's dress. A dressing-table stood against the wall, beside which, by the window, a white synthetic wardrobe, with gold-coloured slats, took up more space than seemed necessary. To the right of the doorway, as one entered the room, was the large wardrobe's smaller sibling. On either side of the bed was a little table, on top of which were arrayed a lamp, a bag of cotton wool, a box of tissues and a packet of wet-wipes. A chain of lights – they, too, were scarlet in colour – was draped across the headboard. The room was brightened only by these lights.

"Are you getting ready for Christmas?" I asked, nodding at the fairy lights.

The girl might have heard the wisecrack before, for she looked at me as if I were a schoolboy unable to recite the two-times-table.

"I'm all yours."

"How much do I owe you?"

"That depends on what you want."

"Well, the usual…"

"Eighty pounds should cover it."

The girl took the screwed-up notes. She told me that she would take the money downstairs and come straight back.

While she was away, I allowed my eyes to adjust to what little light there was in the room. I took the horsewhip from atop the dressing-table, swished it once at an imaginary tennis ball, backhand style, then replaced it. I looked in the mirror and asked the barely-visible reflection what on earth he was doing there. I went to the window. Behind the curtains, white blinds were fitted tightly to the glass. I lifted one of the slats. I peered into the gloom outside. I looked north, towards Squitchey Lane. A young couple skipped past, heading south, holding hands and talking aimlessly in the fashion of lovers. Their chatter and their footsteps faded into silence. A car went by at walking pace, its driver, I guessed, looking for the brothel that he had just called on his mobile. I came away from the window. My view as I had followed Carey up the room, three stairs below her, returned to me. I tried not to dwell on the image that my mind had conjured.

The girl returned to the room with slow, but eager, footsteps. She closed the door behind her. She walked towards me, all breasts and thighs. She kissed me on the cheek. Then, with a disarming sleight of hand, she removed my jacket. She took the garment to the door and hung it on the peg. With a curvaceous languor, she came back to me. She kissed me on the mouth.

"Take me," she whispered.

"There's no hurry," I replied.

"Why did you choose me?" Carey was kissing my neck.

"I preferred you."

"Most men choose Tara."

"Why?"

"Because she's blonde and skinny…"

"She's very young."

"She's old enough."

"Only just, I would say."

"Would you like oil or powder?"

"Can we just…talk…for a moment?"

Carey stood back from me as if I had just metamorphosed into my old friend Dex. "Oh, you're one of those, are you?"

"One of what?"

"A talker," Carey replied, not entirely without appreciation. "You'd be surprised how many of those we get in here."

"It's all the same to you, though, isn't it?" I returned. "You get paid, whatever happens."

"I get paid…without getting laid."

"Quite…"

"I had a bloke this morning who spent half an hour telling me how his mum used to make him kneel at her feet, naked, while she spooned him baby food…when he was a teenager."

"Did he ask you to do the same?"

"No, he just wanted to be horsewhipped."

"Did you hit him hard?"

"I smacked his bare bottom so hard, and so often, that he left this place looking like he'd been sitting on hot coal for an hour."

"You could get done for assault and battery…or worse."

"Are you a copper?"

"No…"

"You sounded like one just then."

"I assure you that I'm not a copper."

"What are you, then, a journalist?"

"What makes you think that?"

"I don't think anything. I just asked you a question."

"I'm not a journalist."

"Well, you're something, or you wouldn't be here just wanting to talk."

Seeing that Carey had sat on the bed, I turned around and took the couple of steps to the window. I looked behind the curtains again. I parted two slats of the blind and looked down the street. The car that I had seen before was cruising down Middle Way in the opposite direction.

"There goes another one, looking for answers."

"We're all looking for answers."

That Carey replied at all, never mind so sympathetically, surprised me. I scented an opening. "What questions are you asking?" I came away from the window, but remained a couple of yards from Carey.

"The same questions as everyone else…"

"I notice that you're wearing a crucifix."

"I'm a Catholic. What of it?"

My gladness was tinged with sadness, profound sadness.

"You're wondering why a girl like me is wearing a crucifix in a place like this, aren't you?"

"Yes, but not in a judgemental way…"

"Christ came to save sinners, not the righteous." She spoke with the fervour of an evangelist and the intensity of one desperate to repent.

"He did."

"Where there's sin, there's Christ, and there's sin here, that's for sure." In looking around the room, she was looking inside herself, and what she saw in the room did not please her. "When this is all over, I shall return to the fold, to the Church, and make a grand confession."

"Why do you do this?"

"I have no choice."

Carey waited for me to reply, as I waited for her to continue.

"My ex-husband was a drinker. But that wasn't the worst of his vices. He was a gambler too. It wasn't just the occasional flutter on the horses, either. If he wasn't in a betting shop, he was gambling online. I borrowed thirty-thousand pounds to pay off his debts. Then he left me. I worked as a travel agent, on low pay, so I was able to borrow only five-thousand pounds from a bank. My dad lent me ten-thousand and I got a few thousand from the sale of the jewellery that Mum left me in her will."

"Where did you get the rest of the money?"

"From a loan shark…"

"Whom you now owe considerably more than you borrowed?"

Carey nodded mournfully. "I told him that I owned my house, and that I was planning to sell it to make some money, but I lied."

"He didn't check?"

"Do they ever?"

I leaned against the flimsy-looking wardrobe and hoped that it would take my weight; though it rattled in protest, it stood firm.

"I figure that I have another six months on my back. Then I'll be free."

"Was there really no other way?"

"I saw none. My body is my only asset. I've nothing else to sell. I hope that God will forgive me."

"God *will* forgive you."

"He will punish me too. God is merciful. He is also just."

"It seems harsh to punish you when you had no choice."

"In God's eyes, there is always a choice."

Carey seemed pleased that she had told her story to someone at last. I had the impression that nobody among her friends and family knew about her work, that it was a well-kept secret, and that none of them would ever know. It was a secret that she shared with God only. I didn't count, of course, because I was a stranger, and one that had paid to hear her story. I felt as if I had just paid a snout for information.

"You're the first person I've told that."

"I'm not sure whether I've violated you or counselled you."

"You certainly did not violate me."

"I guess that you needed to tell someone."

"It just came out."

While Carey's tongue was loose, I would gamble on its remaining so.

"Has the loan shark threatened you?"

"Not exactly," Carey replied, "but he likes to remind me that he's not going away until he's paid."

"A friend of mine has got himself involved with a rather unsavoury character."

"Is that your problem?"

"He's a close friend. His problems are my problems."

"Then he's lucky to have a friend like you."

"He's spokesman for an organisation that's opposing the building of a leisure centre on the site of a disused farm. The man who wants to build the leisure centre is a local gangster."

"Who?"

"Dane Goldman…"

"I might have known."

"Do you know him?"

"I know *of* him. Who doesn't? He owns that dodgy nightclub, The Aquarium."

"I guess that you're bound to know of him…being in this…line of work."

"One of our girls, Dana, used to work for him."

I wanted to show Carey the photograph of the blonde, and to ask her if it were Dana. Was it possible that Dana was Miranda Ward-Homer? My heart was racing with expectation as I asked Carey if she had met Dana.

"No," Carey replied. "She's only been with us for a month or so."

"But you've spoken to her?"

"On the telephone…" Carey said. "A few weeks ago, she called Suzie on the landline, but she was out. We got talking, you know, like girls do."

"She uses quite an upmarket moniker. I imagine that she's quite refined."

"She's posh, if that's what you mean."

"What did Dana say about Dane Goldman?"

"She said that he was a despicable slime-ball and an evil tyrant."

"Do you know why Dana stopped working for Dane Goldman?"

"I don't know exactly what, if anything, happened between Dana and

146

Dane Goldman, but I do know that she had been seeing the owner of this place for some time – romantically, I mean – and had agreed to work for him here."

"How *very* romantic…"

"We live in a sordid world."

"Do you know Dana's real name?"

"Why do you ask?"

"I'm just curious."

Carey shook her head. "We're bound by the rule not to let other girls working at Suzie's know our names."

"That's a pretty silly rule."

"It's supposed to keep things professional."

"It's a rule that you could quite easily break."

"In this game, we learn to do what we're told."

Carey regarded me with suspicion. My questioning had gathered so much momentum that I had lost sight of caution and discretion. I reflected that caution and discretion would have gleaned much less information than Carey had given me and might yet give me. Then surprise hit me: the girl, the woman, had been quite happy to answer my questions. Now her sudden suspicion mirrored my sudden surprise. It occurred to me that Carey not only wanted to talk, she needed to. I felt bold enough to ask one last question.

"Do you know much about the owner of this place?"

"I met him once. I had to fulfil the one condition stipulated before any girl can work for him. He's just as sleazy as Dane Goldman. His name is Philip."

Though the substance of the revelation was not in itself a shock, I would not have been more stunned had the Archbishop of Canterbury just entered the room on a donkey. My suspicions had been nagging, merely nagging, but they had been my *worst* suspicions – in fact, they were very nearly unthinkable – so to have them confirmed hit me like a heavyweight punch in the face. So it was that, reeling, I took a step back, then another, until only the window prevented my toppling out of the room and onto the pavement outside.

"I know what you are," Carey announced.

Her tone might have been vindictive, cruel and sadistic, but it was nothing of the kind; instead, it was soothing, reassuring, and served to bring me out of my troubled state.

"You're a private detective."

"Is it that obvious?"

"It wasn't…until you started asking questions."

"Forgive me."

"What's to forgive?"

"I'm here under false pretences."

"Like I said, we get all kinds in here."

"Do you feel compromised?"

"I might have told you more than I should have told you…but there's no harm done."

"I'm looking for the girl."

"Dana?"

"I think so."

"A lot of girls in this game are living secret lives, or hiding, or both, so I'm not surprised that a private detective has come looking."

"A lot of girls in your game are hiding from themselves."

Carey nodded sadly.

"Thanks for your time, Carey."

"Thanks for being such a gentleman…albeit an inquisitive one."

As Carey stood up and adjusted her dress, my attention was drawn to the picture hanging above the headboard.

"Do you know the painting?"

"It's a Picasso, isn't it?" Carey replied.

I nodded. "*The Harem*…" I said. "I knew there would be a Picasso in this house somewhere."

As we descended the stairs, I looked down at Carey's head, and saw that her black hair was streaked with scarlet. I had not noticed the embellishment before. When the front door was open, though only by about thirty degrees, I asked Carey what time she finished work for the night.

"Ten…" came the reply.

"Not much longer then…" I said.

Carey waited for me to step outside. She closed the door. I was saddened by the lack of ceremony. I stepped into the night, my footsteps sending cracking sounds into the quiet streets. I had taken a giant stride in my quest to find Miranda Ward-Homer. Before the day was out, I would take another giant stride yet.

Twenty-Two

In the Dew Drop, passing the time, I enjoyed a pint of bitter. I needed a drink to help me think, and, more than helpful though she could be, I did not want my thoughts to be crowded out by Kendal's relentless adolescent curiosity.

"Evening, young Daniel," Mandy said, having entered my refuge, the lounge bar, and disturbed my perusal of the pub's copy of the *Oxford Mail*.

"Good evening, Mandy."

"What's the news?" he asked.

"The good news is that there is no bad news," I replied, "and the bad news is that there is no good news."

"As bad as that, is it?"

"And as good…"

"What do you think of that footballer then?"

"Which footballer?"

"That Dwayne Clooney…"

"I think you mean Wayne Rooney."

"That's the one."

"What about him?"

"I'm all for a bet, but he's gambled away six-hundred-thousand smackers."

"Listen," I said, "if a footballer had a bet on whether he would give up gambling, he would bet on his not giving it up, then give it up. That's how stupid he is."

Mandy screwed up his face in painful thought. "You not with your girl tonight?" he asked.

"In one-third of a three-word sentence, no."

"I know true love when I see it."

"So you keep telling me."

"It's enough to make every kangaroo in the western hemisphere wish to make a gigantic leap of faith."

"All love has ever done for me is turn me into a kangaroo of the western hemisphere so nauseous that he wants to skip lunch."

The old man pondered my words for a moment, before, as if his team had just scored the winning goal in the last minute of the European Cup final, cheering uproariously. He then burst into laughter.

"I love it!" he roared. With disarming suddenness, he calmed down. "I would have thought of that, you know."

"Feel free to use it," I urged. There was no prospect of my suing the old man for plagiarism, after all. "Just don't use it on me."

Barry crossed the floor from the lounge bar. "What's all the noise about?" he asked, every inch the landlord.

"Mandy was just revealing his inner kangaroo."

Barry looked at the old man and shook his head. "Mandy, behave," he said. The landlord turned to me. "Can you believe that there is a Northampton Town fan in the other bar, giving me grief about last week?"

"Yes, I saw that the Cobblers beat the Baggies."

"It was a pre-season bloody friendly!"

"Yes, but six-nil…"

"Remind me, how many goals did Oxford put in the Brighton net last week?"

"It was just a pre-season friendly."

Barry smiled at that.

"I noticed that the two Northampton players who scored hat-tricks were called Harper and Lee."

"So?" Barry had no idea that a punch line was coming.

"I bet the noise at Sixfields would have killed a mocking bird."

Barry looked at me as if I had just exposed my person. "Noise?" he said. "There were two men and his dog there...and I was the other man."

Barry's wife Lesley appeared out of nowhere. "You were the other man, were you?" she trilled, almost unconcerned. "Is there something I should know, darling?" She bustled into the lounge bar.

"You've been spending too much time with him," the landlord told me, with a nod at Mandy.

Much to my relief, Mandy wandered off to annoy someone else, leaving me to work my way through the local rag a second time, searching for a piece on Philip's death. Part of me was not unhappy to find not so much as a word on the matter. I was starting to wonder whether I had imagined the demise of my closest friend, and to speculate whether my apparent reluctance to grieve could be attributed to the fact that, in the real world, beyond my delusions and fantasies, he was very much alive.

In the time that it takes one to read Christ's Sermon on the Mount, my life, in what seemed like chronological order, passed before my eyes, a montage of episodes, to each of which I had been able only to react, neither to control nor to influence. My reactions had been instinctive, unthinking; no thought had been given to the cosmic importance of each minor detail of life, or to the universal inherent in the smallest drama. Still less thought had been given to the presence of God in all things visible and invisible. Now, again, able only to respond, and from a distance of many years, I viewed each episode, and the series thereof, through a new prism, so that all that I had seen and heard, as both man and policeman, was seen and heard through the eyes and ears of God. The effect left me heartbroken. Humanity was squalid, yet I, even I, was human, all too human. For a moment, I was God, and I wondered whether humanity deserved redemption when he did not condescend so much as to petition My favour. Then I was Man again, and I yearned, with all my heart and soul, to take it upon myself to rush to God's altar in heaven, to petition, on behalf of mankind, to beg for mercy, to plead for one more chance at redemption, for we are inveterate sinners and – this, perhaps, the most compelling argument in our defence – we know not what we do. I put away such thoughts of God and of being God.

The Dew Drop was packed with the usual reprobates from the neighbourhood, together with a host of strangers.

I recognised Frank Sawyer, a security officer at the Bodleian Library.

Not long after coming to Oxford, through the devious acquisition of a reader's ticket, I had insinuated myself into the musty world of dusty book covers and yellow pages. On the inside of the stout walls of the Radcliffe Camera or Duke Humphrey or the New Bodleian, feeling like I had penetrated the university's inner sanctum, expecting to be inspired by my surroundings, I masqueraded as a scholar and nurtured the delusion that I could write. In times past, Frank had searched my bag as I left the Old Bodleian; nowadays, as he limped around the suburb – he lived in Aldrich Road, on the council estate – he would acknowledge me with a grunt and a nod of his grey-thatched head. Though he was always alone, he never looked unhappy. I wanted to buy him a drink, to chat with him, and to learn about him and his life. But I was not staying long.

Also present was Tom, known as Speedy. From the lounge bar, I saw him sitting in the saloon bar, holding forth on some obscure topic. When last I had strayed into the saloon bar, Speedy chastised me for having diluted my drink with soda and ice, whisky, apparently, being too precious and aristocratic a distillation to suffer contamination by such plebeian embellishment. He had gone on to say how the finer properties of whisky were destroyed, not merely compromised, by the addition of soda and water. He had accused me, then, of vandalism. The man had asserted that, his being a biochemist, I should defer to his expertise, to which assertion I had replied that, though I could not argue with his science, my being a layman on such matters, I was within my rights to question the value-judgement on the sanctity of the purity of his favourite libation.

In the alcove, over by the window, were gathered the latest inmates of the women's refuge. There was no mistaking them, for they looked as furtive and as liberated as any of their predecessors. They were hunched in the far corner, hiding from the predatory male, not daring to stray more than a stone's throw from their refuge. Indeed, as was always the case with these broken girls, they seemed reluctant so much as to visit the bar to replenish their glasses.

"What do you reckon, girls from the women's refuge?"

"Without a doubt, Gabriel, without a doubt…"

"Can I get you a drink?"

"I've had enough for one day, thanks."

"Barry, my usual, please…and whatever this man's having…" Gabriel called, ignoring my half-hearted protest. "I once went out with one of the girls from the refuge."

"Aren't we supposed to treat refugees with compassion?"

"Her name was Shannon. She was Irish…a redhead. She was from Hackney, in East London. She'd run away from her alcoholic boyfriend, who was given to knocking her into the middle of next week. It was the same old story. Anyway, Shannon attached three conditions to our liaison: that we should meet only here, in the Dew Drop; that we should never stray more than fifty yards from her fellow refugees, Polly and Barbara; and that I should never visit the refuge, it being imperative that I should never learn of its whereabouts."

"It's that place over the road, disguised as a nursing home."

"Is it?"

"It is."

"How do you know?"

"I'm a detective."

Barry delivered the drinks. Gabriel gave the landlord the cash. He told him to have a drink himself and to keep the change.

"She went back to him, of course, like they all do."

"It was ever thus."

"The three of them – Polly, Babs and Shannon – all seemed so normal when I met them, just three lasses having fun, until I got to know them…and realised how fucked up they were."

"Tell me," I began, as I took the photo of Miranda from my jacket pocket, "does she look fucked up to you?"

Gabriel looked as if he had just seen the Dalai Lama enter the lounge bar on a camel. "Bloody hell!" he exclaimed

"I know. She's indecently attractive."

"And I've seen a lot of her lately. In fact, I've seen all of her."

"I hope you're not saying what I think you're saying."

"She's one of Suzie's girls."

"Bloody hell," I sighed.

"Do you know her?"

"She's the girl that I'm being paid to find."

"You've got a result then. I've just dropped her into your lap."

"I so wish it hadn't happened this way."

"I'm your lucky break."

"Now I owe you."

"After all the grief I've given you down the years, *I* owed *you*. Now we're quits."

"The girl's real name is Miranda. But you know her as Dana, don't you?"

"I do."

"Do you know which days she works at Suzie's?"

"Well, I saw her last Friday…and I'm seeing her this Friday."

Two days ago, Gabriel had made a vow of chastity, or something like one, but, in my excitement, in my consternation, I had forgotten that.

"Don't judge me too harshly," he pleaded. "I thought I'd have one more half-hour of unbridled pleasure before embracing the life of virtue."

"What?" I said, my mind a million miles away.

"Lord, make me a paragon of virtue…but not yet."

"When I hear Gabriel Tolpuddle paraphrasing Saint Augustine of Hippo, I know that I'm having a weird day."

Black clouds swirled menacingly in the night sky as I ambled down South Parade on my way to an uncertain destination: only when I was within sight of the house in Middle Way would I know whether I should lurk outside, hidden somewhere, or turn right into Grove Street, without delay, and head home.

The Royal British Legion building offered credible cover, so I stood by its entrance, my hands in my jacket pockets, looking up at the sky. It had turned blacker, the clouds having congealed and coalesced into several abysmal factions, which, even now, were shifting, gathering, collecting themselves, united in a single purpose. I stood there and hoped that they would allow *my* purpose for the evening to be fulfilled before they shed their burden and dumped it upon me.

I looked at my watch and saw that the time was just after ten. Then I had my head turned by an old boy in a blazer leaving the club. He looked as if he had seen action in at least one of the global conflicts of the twentieth century.

"Are you waiting for someone?"

"Er…" Caught unawares, and feeling unaccountably guilty, I uttered the first old-fashioned name that came into my head. "Yes, I'm waiting for…Cyril." I might have known that there *was* a Cyril drinking in the social club of the North Oxford branch of the Royal British Legion.

"You'd better go in if you want to see him, because he won't be out for at least another hour. He's always the last out."

"Don't I have to be a member?"

"You do, but…" The man was kind, avuncular and reassuringly decent, and he smiled at me in like manner. "You must be the nephew that he talks about."

"That's me," I replied, wishing that I had never begun the charade.

"He's a good lad, your uncle. He was too young for Hitler's war, but he saw action in Korea. But you know that, of course."

"He was a fine soldier," I agreed.

"He speaks highly of you too."

"He flatters me, I'm sure."

"My name is Donald Carfax," the man announced. "A good Oxford name is that."

As I did not know what my name was supposed to be, I kept my mouth shut.

"It's been nice chatting with you, Marcus."

"It's been a pleasure talking with you, too, Donald."

The man began to shuffle away, before hesitating and regarding me with curious eyes, wondering, evidently, why I was so rooted to the spot.

"I've a phone call to make," I told Donald. "Then I'll go in."

Donald nodded. Gingerly, as if every slab of concrete overlaid a mine, he stepped away into the night.

"Marcus, indeed…" I said.

"What's that smell?" Maureen asked as I walked towards her. She was reaching into her letterbox.

"Chips…"

"Oh, Daniel, not again…"

"I'm afraid so."

"Why don't you come round to mine one night? I'll make you a nice shepherd's pie."

"That's a most tempting offer, Maureen."

"I bet your mother makes a lovely shepherd's pie, doesn't she?"

"I don't remember."

The lady fished out a copy of the *Oxford Mail*. "I won't be able to let you have the paper today, I'm afraid. I've only just got back."

"Don't worry. I read it in the Dew Drop."

"Oh, that den of iniquity…"

"Have you been somewhere nice?"

"Only to Gee's…"

"Only to the most expensive restaurant in Oxford then…"

"Eric can afford it." The lady blushed.

"Eric?" New developments were afoot in my neighbour's life, it seemed, and I wished playfully to elicit the details.

"Just someone who likes to treat me now and again…"

"Why don't you invite *him* round for shepherd's pie?"

"These things take time, Daniel. You youngsters could learn a thing or two from us senior citizens about the art of courtship."

"There's someone in my flat, Maureen, who thinks that I'm a certified ancient monument."

"Oh, yes, the girl…"

"She's my…" I began. "I'll tell you about her someday."

Maureen looked curious and circumspect, in equal measure, as if my alluding to Kendal had given the lady license to question me about the girl, but had, at the same time, aroused her sense of propriety. She smiled at me. I smiled at her.

"I ought to check *my* mail," I said. I went to my letterbox. "I haven't checked it for days."

"You've left it unlocked again, I see."

I withdrew a clutch of envelopes. "What do you know?" I sighed. "Nothing but bills…"

"That one's not a bill," Maureen said, pointing at the white envelope which bore my name but no stamp. "I found it in the lobby, on the mat, last Friday. I tried to put it through the slot in your letterbox, but the box was stuffed full, so, suspecting that it was unlocked, as usual, I lifted up the lid and pushed it in. You really ought to be more careful, Daniel. There are thieves about."

"You're talking to a former policeman, Maureen."

"I meant to mention the letter to you sooner, but forgot. I'm old and senile…but you have no excuse."

We walked up the stairs, chatting idly, as neighbours do. Three times, I had to stop and wait while Maureen caught her breath. When we reached the landing, Maureen told me that I had left my chips behind.

"I'd had enough."

"What did you do with them?"

"I left them in the letterbox."

Bless her, she was watching *The Green Ray*, or had been, when I found her asleep in front of the television. The film was about to finish, the last scene was showing, the one in which the heroine Delphine and her new love – her true love, so the viewer is led to believe – sit and watch the sunset, waiting for the moment when horizon and sun conspire to emit the green ray, la rayon vert, a phenomenon which Delphine has built up in her mind to be some kind of consummation.

I turned off the television. I removed the disc. Then I switched off the DVD player. Kendal was sleeping like an angel. I would not wake her, but I would place a tender kiss on her forehead and bid her goodnight.

She had a tough day ahead of her tomorrow. She looked so vulnerable, lying there under the duvet, her right thumb almost in her mouth, so quiet that I wondered whether she had stopped breathing. It was a shame that she had missed the film's ending, but I looked forward to discussing it with her and to watching it with her soon. I was touched by her interest in the films of Eric Rohmer, as, indeed, I was touched by her very existence.

My ablutions beckoned and the letter, that strange missive from out of the blue, screamed to be opened. I would not open it before I got to bed, nor would I sleep easily once I had read it.

The content of the letter was disturbing enough, but my sleep was made yet lighter and more troubled by the constant irruption of the words that had passed between me and Carey Seymour following my hour in the Dew Drop and my stake-out by the Royal British Legion.

"I'm not stalking you."

"I did wonder."

"What are you doing on Friday?"

"Are you asking me out?"

"I need your help."

"That's usually why men come to me."

"You could help me save a girl's life."

"Don't give me melodrama after the day I've had."

"Believe me…"

"I'm working on Friday."

"Here?"

"In Banbury…"

"I'll pay you."

"How much?"

"How much would you earn?"

"Five-hundred…"

"Consider yourself paid."

"Where shall we meet?"

"At the Randolph Hotel…"

"What time?"

"Ten o'clock…"

"Morning or evening?"

"Morning…"

"It will be morning, love, if we don't get a move on!" the driver had yelled from inside the taxi.

"Go on then," the woman had said. "I like an adventure…and I like a mystery even more."

At thirteen minutes past one, I lay awake, looking at the ceiling, praying that sleep would soon take me, so that the old day could end, and the new day begin, with at least the bare minimum of nocturnal repose between them, dividing them, bridging them, making two days out of the one long day which threatened to stretch further ahead of me than I could see.

As soon as I replayed in my mind the image of Kendal asleep, an image that was so blessed that it was tantamount to a prayer, the ceiling became less irksome, less of a fiend, and sleep took a firmer hold on me.

Had I been able to pray, I would have spoken of sin and suffering and passion and victory and death. Were these commonplace truths – were they truths at all – or were they lies that we told ourselves to make life bearable? I wondered whether the silence of one could atone for the sins of the tongue of all, whether one's going without food and alcohol earned forgiveness for all the gluttonous and the drunken, whether being cruel to one's flesh somehow redeemed the many that pamper their flesh. I wondered how many sinners Roseanne's virtue had saved. I wondered how many proud souls now walked as little children in Roseanne's footsteps with humble and contrite hearts.

"Roseanne," I said on the brink of sleep, "you save souls, and might yet save mine, but why did you forsake me?"

Twenty-Three

Getting up at six o'clock had not been easy, notwithstanding my eagerness to join up the dots of the picture-puzzle that absorbed me. As I washed and shaved, I wondered if I really needed to drive down to Portslade, to the other brothel in Philip's life, only to find out what I knew already to be the case. The urge to see the whole picture, however, was one that I found impossible to resist. That is why I had been a less-than-adequate policeman: to me, the wood and the trees were both very much in the frame.

Rousing Kendal from sleep had been like trying to inject life into a sack of coal. During the night, she had crawled into her bed from the sofa, and I found her sleeping crossways, entangled in the duvet, her pillows on the floor. When she opened her eyes, her mind had been alert enough to ask me why the inquest was being held so soon after Philip's death, to which question I replied that the time between death and the ensuing inquest would vary, depending on the circumstances of the death and the availability of a coroner.

Kendal Waterhouse was the kind of sixteen-year-old girl who would take an inquest, with all its trappings of the law, in her stride. The formal nature of an inquest might well baffle her, but it would not intimidate her in the slightest. Today was one of the many days when she would give me cause to celebrate her uniqueness.

In my time as a detective, I had seen many worse council estates than Mountbatten Close, though few of them, if any, had such aristocratic connotations: it was hard to dissent from any claim that councillors with a singularly wicked sense of humour were behind its appellation.

Some of the estates that I had frequented made Mountbatten Close look like Beverly Hills.

I had been to places where wrecked cars littered the roads like tanks in the aftermath of battle; where emaciated stray dogs wandered the streets with menace, lifting their hind legs to sprinkle urine on anything that could not move, and crouching down to defecate on any surface unlucky enough to be in their paths; and where underfed toddlers trotted around with evil intent, their shabby clothes recording the most recent meal intended for their foul mouths. I had been called to places where spent tin cans, discarded toys and mangled bipeds, where damp and disarranged cardboard boxes, where mouldy shoes and miscellaneous leguminous escapees from ill-secured dustbins, all of these and more, were scattered liberally across the landscape like broken chattels in the wake of the apocalypse.

These were just what my eyes had seen. None of my God-given senses was spared the assault to which, in the discharge of my duty, I had been subjected by some of the capital's more squalid environs. The music of such places was tumultuous: the boom and clatter of cars fit only for the scrapheap; the sinister war cries of young hoodlums, budding malfeasants all; the perpetual rowing; and the barking and the howling. Though there were times when nothing more threatening was heard than the ominous beat and cries to arms of rap. Even the silence served as an ugly portent.

It was the smells for which such places had reserved particular odium. Urine, excrement, stale leather, rotting cardboard, decomposing provender, and food being prepared for constitutions that could have known nothing better: all sent forth rank odours into an atmosphere already corroded by rust. In winter, as they flowed into rivers of congealed stench, in air that was crisp and brittle, somehow, I was able to make out any one of these festering aromas from another. In summer, when the air simmered, the smells blended with ease to form a sea of pollution which made me wonder if living beside a sewage farm might not have been altogether a more seductive prospect.

These sights, sounds and smells, various, but united in their foulness, together had produced an elixir that, if consumed, would have reduced the hardiest of constitutions to a shuddering wreck. The sights, sounds and smells of Mountbatten Close, distilled, would have fashioned nothing more disagreeable than a rancid potion.

The people of Mountbatten Close had been decent, though somewhat eccentric, and, at times, both alarming and ridiculous.

When Albert and Roseanne brought Laura and me to Mountbatten Close, to number three, as the twentieth century's seventh decade petered out, we found ourselves living next door to the Sandersons, who made for the noisiest possible of neighbours. I cannot say what alarmed me more, Pete and Terry's near-incessant rowing, or their middle-of-the-night lovemaking, the latter of which phenomena took place inches behind my bed, on the other side of the wall, and produced orgasms, from man and woman alike, which might best be described by recourse to a Richter Scale measurement. The squabbling of Nicola, Darren and Kim engendered the notion that the Battle of Waterloo was being permanently re-enacted next door. However, it was their need to have their television on at full-blast that caused maximum irritation, for it always put Albert in one of his incendiary moods and induced consternation in the cage of Bobby, our budgerigar. The noise would have been sufferable, the bird's sensitivities notwithstanding, had the Sandersons ever been watching the same channel as us, for our clapped-out television set was often in dire need of amplification.

Let it not be said, however, that the Sandersons were not likeable enough as individuals; and whether they found the Winter family to be model neighbours is a moot point. Terry, the mother, would smile at me, without speaking, which I took to be a gesture of fellowship, and, on the rare occasions when words passed between Pete and me, he was never less than pleasant. On warm summer evenings, he would sit in his front garden, smoking a pipe, and tell me of his many adventures in the Eighth Armoured Division, most of which featured a narrow escape from the jaws of death. One sultry evening, he thrilled me with tales of his time as goalkeeper of Tottenham Hotspur. Enthralled, I went home and pored over my football annuals, but was dismayed to find no evidence to support Pete's claim, and I consulted Albert and both of my grandfathers, but none had the faintest recollection of a Pete Sanderson ever having kept goal for Spurs or any other club. I had often wondered what was in that pipe of his.

Mrs Patricia Jackson, whose clan was harboured by number fifteen, was a formidable woman. Thanks to my being sent to her house by Roseanne, once a month, with payment for the catalogue club, I saw much more of this lady, Mountbatten Close's answer to Raquel Welch, than I had ever wished to see. Clutching Albert's hard-earned money, I would knock on the door and wait, jumpy as a cat on a hot tin roof. Mrs Jackson would come to the door, cigarette in hand, wearing a low-cut blouse, miniskirt and boots, her high-cupped breasts making a mockery of the law of gravity and her thighs solid as a pair of mahogany sideboards. The woman would then bend down to take the crumpled notes and reveal the black roots of her dyed-blonde hair and the spectacle of a thousand freckles dancing haphazardly across her chest. She would always end our trysts by running a hand through my hair, and clawing my skull with her red-varnished nails, before planting a kiss on my cheek and whispering, "You be good now, won't you?" The ordeal was like submitting to the benign authority of a Sister of Mercy whilst being pecked at by a committee of vultures.

Peter, the second-eldest of the Jackson Five, as the children of the clan were known collectively, was a monster of a boy. He used his long, hulking frame to put the fear of God into his fellow schoolboys. He would strut around the playground, prodding, cuffing and cursing, stealing marbles, and, on autumn days, rapping heads with conkers-on-a-string. Whenever I was unfortunate enough to encounter him, which was depressingly often, I would be subjected to verbal abuse if I was lucky and bodily provocation if I was not. He would express his profound civility with cries of "Hey, Winter, your mother's a whore!" and "Your sister's a slag!". Albert would be branded a "whore-fucker". He would accuse me of habitually wrapping my mouth around male sexual organs and of having unchaste relations with various well-hung beasts. Peter Jackson was utterly beyond redemption. His older brother Cameron, who at least hinted that he was a fellow member of the human race, did little to restrain him; and his father, spending most of his time as a guest of Her Majesty, was unable to.

The Pilgrims, of whom there were eight, lived at number twenty. Telling a Pilgrim from a Jackson was many times harder than trying to distinguish between one chimpanzee and his twin brother. The head of the family was known as Tubby, which was generously to understate his proportions: he was always messing about with clapped-out cars, and would have to jack these wasted machines into the stratosphere before he could ease himself under them. There was even more of Mrs Pilgrim, who went by the name of Big Lil. For every pound carried by the copiously tattooed Tubby, his wife carried two pounds; where the man's fat was spread over his frame in generally consistent layers, the woman's was stacked up like so many spare tyres; and, where Tubby's belly was so large that it ought to have required planning permission, Lil's backside was so immense that a man standing on one of her buttocks would have needed a compass to find his way off it. Affection between the couple was unthinkable, sexual congress apparently impossible, yet six offspring managed to issue from their substantial loins.

The constant sparring, scuffling and scrapping, which was endemic in Mountbatten Close, would have, all too often, a Sanderson or a Jackson or a Pilgrim – and, not infrequently, all three – in their midst. But the Underwoods and the Felshams, the Halletts and the Lawsons – less populous tribes all, but no less belligerent – were never far from the fray. The violence was random and had no meaning. It was not invariably confined to the children, either.

By accident, or by design – I cannot remember which – I befriended the oldest child of the Morgan clan, which lived at number one. Willy Morgan was the shortest and the thinnest of all the seven Morgan children, and they were all short and thin. But he carried the menace of a villain. The Morgans eschewed the society of fellow residents of the Close, they went about their business quietly and without fuss, shrouding themselves in a mystique that garnered respect and fear in equal measure. Nobody knew what Mr Morgan did for a living. Nobody dared ask him. Outside the Morgans' house was parked an enormous truck that was weighed down by a precariously balanced cargo of broken furniture, rusty cookers, rolls of wire fencing, worn-out tyres and sundry other bits of junk. Nobody knew to whom this gruesome creation belonged. The consensus was that it was not unrelated to the Morgans, though nobody dared ask them. Willy's friendship, then, aided my survival in the rough-and-tumble that was life in Mountbatten Close. I had needed to be seen with him only once for word to get round that I was not to be messed with.

This or that posse of unwashed ruffians was cause enough for trepidation, but I had also to endure a feud with a whippet, a rancid creature that prowled the street with a nose for my blood only, it seemed. Other people ignored it, and it ignored them, but, when it saw me, it would growl and foam at the mouth, threatening me with a hideous end.

How Roseanne Mary Wordsworth ever came to a place such as this, God only knows.

Sitting in the Jensen, looking around, I saw that little had changed in the street since the seventies. There were a few varnished oak doors on display, signalling owner-occupation, and the odd satellite dish, and the Ford Anglia had been replaced by the Renault Clio, but the smells were the same, and such children as were in evidence – taking a break from the rigours of their twenty-first-century gadgets, no doubt – were clones of their predecessors. I even saw a pair of what I guessed to be eight-year-olds, a boy and a girl, poking a pothole with sticks. I wondered why poking potholes was particular to children of Mountbatten Close. I had never seen it done anywhere else. In my dotage, I would return to Mountbatten Close and behold children poking holes in the road with sticks.

Our house, which had not been our house for twenty years, stood as a memorial to Roseanne. For a little over four years, it had been her home, an abode humble enough for humility such as hers. Here, she had been a mother and a wife. Then, one foggy October evening, she went out and never came back.

That was the night that England said goodbye to Alf Ramsey.

That night, I kept a lonely vigil by the television, watching England trying in vain to beat Poland, a victory that would have seen them qualify for the following summer's World Cup finals, in West Germany. The redoubtable Poles, thanks to the heroics of their goalkeeper, got the draw they needed to take England's place. Jan Tomaszewski would have stopped a cruise missile that night. As I watched my white-shirted heroes lay siege on the Polish goal, Melody slept. How my fourteen-year-old babysitter managed to sleep through the onslaught is beyond my comprehension. She lay there, the girl from round the corner, sprawled out on the sofa, her *Look-in* magazine, open at the centre-page spread of David Cassidy, resting on her burgeoning chest and rising and falling with the rhythm of her breathing. Never mind the Polish goalkeeper's stopping a cruise missile, Melody would have slept through a nuclear holocaust that night.

At about ten o'clock that night, Frank and Lucinda Johns, whose daughter Jenny had spent the evening playing upstairs with Laura, came to the house. The crestfallen Frank slumped into an armchair and stared at the wall ahead, a man in shock, a man who had just discovered that we really were living in the strangest of times.

Frank was a slip of a man who looked like Norman Wisdom and sounded like Larry Grayson. His black hair was brushed back with Brylcreem, and he always wore a pin-striped, three-piece suit, even when mowing the lawn. Thick, gold-coloured jewellery adorned his tiny frame, so that one wondered if he were not weighed down by it all. A necklace could be seen just inside his collar; and a large identity bracelet, together with a signet ring that would have stopped a Sherman tank in its tracks, completed the walking bonanza of bling that was Frank Johns. With him around, it was like having a chain-gang stalking the neighbourhood.

The man was apoplectic. "Did I hear that right, up at the school," he began, "that England drew one-all?"

"Yes," I replied.

"Is it true, Melody?"

If Frank needed corroboration from a second person then Melody was the last person he should have asked.

Melody stood up. "Yeah," she said, "one-all, it was." She stretched her body into a star shape, yawned, then left the room.

Frank was indignant. "She doesn't seem to give a damn," he said.

"She slept all through the game," I put in, "and *I* didn't tell her the score."

"Why should she give a damn?" Lucinda said. "She's a teenage girl, for heaven's sake!"

Lucinda's height was real. The rest of her was a fake. Her accent was so contrived that she had to contort cheeks, lips and tongue, in unison, so as to pronounce each syllable with the desired refinement. Then she wore a black fur coat that even a boy of eight could tell was no more real than the Tooth Fairy. Her face struggled to breathe under layers of cosmetic decoration, and was crowned by a fountain of burgundy hair, the artificiality of which was highlighted by regiments of black roots. Frightening, indeed, could Lucinda Johns be to look at, though she had a heart of gold.

The Johns were the most unlikely couple, and the Winters and the Johns had been a yet more unlikely foursome.

"England are out of the World Cup," Frank lamented. "Do the young of today care about nothing?"

"Get a grip of yourself, man."

"England had lots of shots," I said. "It was that goalkeeper...He stopped everything."

"That goalkeeper..." the disbelieving Frank returned. "He's nothing but a bloody clown."

"That's what Mr Clough said."

Frank took a packet of cigarettes from his coat pocket. He took a cigarette from the packet. He put the cigarette in his mouth. He took a lighter from another pocket. He lit the cigarette and dragged hard. For some fifteen seconds, he appeared to hold his breath. Then, like a missile, smoke shot from his mouth and formed a cloud over Bobby's cage.

"We went to war for the Poles," he resumed. "And how do those bastards repay us? They knock us out of the bloody World Cup."

He sent another volley of smoke into the haze. Having made barely a sound all evening, Bobby, in protest at the gathering pollution, began to tweet manically.

"Now look what you've done," Lucinda moaned. "You've set the budgie off."

"Do you know what makes this disaster ten times worse?"

Nobody answered.

"The bloody Jocks qualified." Frank shook his head in despair. "My God, we'll never hear the end of this."

I thought he was going to cry.

"Frank," Lucinda said, "do you really think that you should be fretting about a football match at a time like this?"

Frank sighed. He nodded. "Yes, I'm sorry," he replied. "But, as I said earlier, there'll be a perfectly rational explanation."

"Oh, yes, of course, people often disappear into thin air for no reason whatsoever."

"She probably just needed some air…and went for a walk," Frank insisted. "Any second now, she'll come walking through that door."

How wrong he had been.

Twenty-Four

The woman who peered at me from behind the door was in the latter part of middle-age. Looking wary, a tad frightened even, she looked left and right before she opened the door to let me in. I stepped inside and the woman closed the door. In keeping with the surroundings, she looked tired and beaten. Her eyes were bloodshot and glazed, her greasy hair was a tangled mess, and her skin was so dry that it was starting to flake. She had been pretty once. She stared at me as if she were waiting for me to speak. She blinked. In the blink of an eye, she was lost, adrift in a morass of fallen women and lustful men; she yearned for lost years; she longed for a time when hope was her friend and regret a stranger, when the fall was always taken by someone else. She was locked in a cycle of degradation and seemed to lack the will to free herself from it.

"Follow me," she said, her voice educated and refined. She led me to a large room. "Please," she urged, "take a seat."

I looked around the room. All four walls displayed patches of baldness, as if someone had begun to strip them of paper, but given up. The paper needed scraping off, for it looked as if it had been hanging for thirty years or more. Whatever colour it had been, it had decayed to an unsightly greyish green, though parts showed signs of yellow. On the far side of the room, near the join with the ceiling, a strip of paper had begun a sorry descent to the floor. The ceiling was stained with smoke and spotted with age. The windows were so covered in dust and grime that the garden beyond could not be seen through smears and smudges. Threadbare to the point of oblivion, the brown carpet was marred by black puddles, as if an oil-like substance were seeping through the floor. The sofa, its patterned flowers having long since wilted and withered, was fit only for the rubbish tip. It cried at me not to go anywhere near it. I was bound to heed the advice.

"I'll stand," I replied.

"As you wish…" the lady returned. "We have three girls for you to-day."

"Okay…"

"I'll send them through."

I watched the lady leave by one of the room's two doors – we had entered by the other door – then turned around to see a sturdy oak table. I wondered how I had missed it before. As well as being large enough to seat an extended family for dinner, upon it were stacked, in numerous columns, knickers, bras and towels. A heady smell of detergent tempered the rancid air.

A girl lumbered into the room so like a Panzer tank that I expected to see rubble crashing down in her wake. Thickset, with big arms and legs, she looked out of place in a skimpy, see-through nightdress, a nightdress that was an exceedingly feminine pink. She held out her right hand. "I'm Justine," she said. She looked and sounded bored.

Her hand, limp as a leaf of lettuce in a thunderstorm, was not easy to shake, but I made the effort. I let the hand go. Observing her hair, I marvelled at how she had persuaded it to stick out sideways and to stand up on top. I noticed the tattoo on each arm: on the left, the word "Adam", and, on the right, in the same Gothic letters, "Eve". She stood in black leather boots, high-heeled and knee-high, attached to which were so many straps and buckles that it must have taken her a week to put them on. They were less like footwear and more like a pair of prosthetic lower limbs.

"I'm pleased to meet you," I said.

Justine turned on her considerable heels and rumbled out of the room.

I went to the door. I pulled it ajar and peered through the gap. I saw the girl cross the short part of the L-shaped hallway and enter a kitchenette. I wondered why four people would cram themselves into such a small space when they had a room the size of a small Alpine nation in which to sit. "I wouldn't bother with him," I heard Justine say. "He's a time-waster." Seeing another girl coming my way, I closed the door and returned to the middle of the room. I watched in horror as a malnourished stick-insect approached me.

"Hello," the girl whined. "I'm Flora."

Unlike Justine, Flora was neither colourful as Siouxsie Sioux nor wild as a banshee. As if to apologise for a wrong that she had done me, she smiled like a child and blinked long and softly. She was wrapped in an ash-grey all-over-body dress, which had long sleeves and pinched her ankles. There being no flesh to speak of, the dress clung to bones. Her pale skin sagged because there was no flesh to stretch it. On her feet were two-inch-high shoes, each of which was fastened by a single strap across the top.

"Flora's a pretty name."

"Do you think *I'm* pretty?"

The honest answer – that she was pretty once and could be again – was unspeakable. "You're beautiful," I said.

"What's your name?" Not only did Flora smile like a small child, she spoke like one.

"Daniel…"

"That's a nice name."

The sight of this emaciated girl trying to be seductive, with fluttering eyelashes and a childlike whine, was truly saddening. I cursed Philip and what he had become.

"My parents deserve all the credit for it."

Her attempt at laughter was so laden with nerves that only a girlish squeal emerged. "Maybe I'll see you later," she said. "I need the money for food."

Her last comment might have been a joke; it might have been a state-ment of fact; whatever it was, it made me want to rid the world, in the click of a finger, of all people except the two of us, so that I might care for her, free of demands on my time, free, more to the point, of those who had left this poor girl so ravaged. I was desperate to be with her. For thirty minutes, or thereabouts, I could be the best friend she ever had.

"Can we go upstairs?"

Flora was taken aback. "Oh," she said. "But you haven't met Belinda." Her words came out in a pathetic drawl.

"I don't need to."

"She's very nice."

"I'm sure she is."

"Do you like me?"

I nodded. I nearly cried. "I like you."

To my astonishment, Flora curtsied. "I'll just go tell the girls."

All skin and bone, she returned to the kitchenette. I heard her announce that she had been picked. She sounded excited. I heard clapping and words of approval and encouragement. "Go get him, girl," someone said, probably Belinda, as the voice was neither Justine's nor the maid's. A minute later, Flora was back in the sitting-room.

"Would you like to follow me?" she asked, before leaving by the door on the other side of the room.

As I followed Flora, I noticed a door on the left of the hallway. "What's through here?" I asked.

Flora carried on walking until she reached the first stair. "I don't know," she replied.

"How long have you worked here?"

"Six months…"

"And you don't know what's through here?"

"My ex-husband told me never to ask questions about matters that don't concern me."

"He's not here, though, is he?"

Flora resumed her ascent, somewhat quickly, for, when I reached the top of the stairs, I was unsure whether she had gone left or right. Giggling came from one of the rooms on the left.

"There you are," I said as I entered the room.

Flora was sitting on the end of a bed, her legs crossed and her right index finger on her lips. "Here I am," she said.

I walked to the end of the bed. I looked down at the girl. She looked unsure what to do. She looked lost. "What do you do for a living, Flora?" Under the circumstances, the question sounded absurd, but I had my reasons for asking it.

"This is what I do."

"You have no other job?"

"I work on reception sometimes."

"Here?"

Flora nodded.

"What's your boss like?"

"Suzie's nice. She lives in London, but works here and in the Oxford branch."

"You make it sound like a bank."

Flora giggled.

"Is the boss here today?"

"She'll be back soon. She's gone to the shops."

Knowing that Suzie could return at any moment, I resolved to keep my visit as brief as possible. I had known that there was every chance that she and I would meet today, but, at the same time, had denied that our meeting was a possibility.

"Suzie gets around," I said. "Oxford one day, and Brighton the next…"

"She's a busy lady."

"Do you live in Brighton?"

Flora nodded. "On the Whitehawk estate…"

"I've heard some tales about *that* place."

"I've lived there all my life," Flora said with a smile. "I have friends there."

I smiled back at her. "I'm glad that you have friends."

"Everyone has friends."

After a pause for thought, I asked Flora how many of her friends, were she to die today, would have forgotten about her by the weekend.

"*This* weekend?" she asked, puzzled.

Amused by her question, I nodded.

"None!" she exclaimed, delighted by the realisation.

"Then you're blessed."

Like a flat-out patient in the dentist's chair, Flora looked up at me. She smiled. She giggled again. "You're not going to kill me, are you?"

174

Alarmed by the question, I shook my head. I took my wallet from my jacket pocket and withdrew sixty pounds. I handed the money to Flora. "Take this," I said, "before you get into trouble."

Flora counted the money. "It's my lucky day," she said, her voice a mouse-like squeak. The squeak became yet another giggle. She stood up and fixed her gaze on me. Languidly, she blinked. "I'll be right back," she said.

While Flora was gone, I stood by the window. Though, like the place in Oxford's Middle Way, the house was perpendicular to the main road, I was able to get a good view of the industrial paraphernalia of the eastern end of Shoreham Harbour. Here was raw industry: giant warehouses, immense cranes, gigantic crates, great trucks caked in mud, rusty pipes that seemed to come from nowhere and to go nowhere, huge containers loaded with coal, and drums filled with oil. This end of the harbour, unlike the other, was not adorned with yachts and little fishing boats. I was looking at nothing so picturesque.

On my journey south, the sun had shined. Now, in a gust of wind, rain lashed the window with a vengeance. Against the dark background of the port, the swirling rain could be seen. A teenage girl, a small boy in tow, hurried a pushchair across the road as she made for the shops of Portslade. A car turned right into Middle Way and parked behind the Jensen. A large man struggled out of the car and ran his eyes over my pride and joy. He walked towards the house. The doorbell rang.

The door behind me creaked open. Though the house looked solid enough from the outside, it gave every impression, from the inside, of being ready to collapse at the drop of a hat.

"One of our regulars has just arrived," Flora whined. "He always sees Belinda." Maintaining the seductive pose, though with no great aplomb, she stumbled towards me. "But, then, they *all* see Belinda."

"So how do the other girls make their money?"

Wide of eyes and broad of smile, Flora was upon me. "Not even Belinda can see every man at once." She pressed herself against me. She put her arms on my shoulders and held onto the back of my neck. "What would you like to do with me?"

Feeling her bony wrists digging into my neck, I told Flora that I was happy to talk with her for a while.

"Talk?"

"Yes…"

"Don't you want me?"

I sighed. Gently, so as not to hurt her, I pushed the girl away from me. "Tell me, Flora…" I began.

"What?" She was hurt.

"Why does this house look like it hasn't seen a lick of paint for thirty-two years?"

"Probably, because it hasn't…"

"I've never seen a place like it." I was lying. I had seen many worse places.

"There's no point in painting it now."

"Why's that?"

"The place is changing hands."

"It's been sold?"

Flora shook her head. "The owner died," she replied, "and left the house to a friend."

As policemen are apt to say of loose-tongued interviewees, Flora was singing like a canary, which was a bonus for me, as I had yet to begin asking questions in earnest. I had come to the house prepared to breach the walls of fear and suspicion by gaining the residents' trust with easy-going, laidback charm, or, at least, the pretence of it, by blending that charm with questions dressed up to sound innocuous, and by seeming indifferent to the answers. Such had been my plan at Oxford Suzie's. There, I had been challenged by the self-possession of Carey and thrown off course by the realisation that she was a Catholic. Flora was no such challenge. She was too easy. I felt as if I were using her, exploiting her, taking advantage of her good and credulous nature.

"Was he a nice man?" I asked.

"The owner?"

"Yes…"

Flora smiled a smile of sweet innocence. Whatever her age, she looked older. But, at that moment, she was a girl of eight, her face hinting at a fullness that might yet return, and her eyes suggesting a past – and, God willing, a future – of happier times.

"He was like the Godfather in the films," she resumed in her girlish voice, though with the attempt at seduction put aside, "though he looked more like a choirboy."

"Did you meet him?"

"I met him when I first came here, before I started working…I had to…He made me…"

I knew all too well what she was trying to say.

"And he came here once or twice…you know, to check on things."

Flora's naivety notwithstanding, my next question had to be put with rare finesse. "What was his name, Don Corleone?"

"His name was Philip."

The need to seem indifferent to this last reply offered a new challenge. Turning my back to Flora, I went to the window. Again, fine rain was swirling, rather than falling. Cars went by, heading for either Brighton or Shoreham. Seagulls screeched overhead. When droppings from one of them, propelled by another gust of wind, splattered against the window, creating an egg-like effect, I turned back to face the girl.

"Why do you do this, Flora?"

Flora pondered the question in grave silence. She sniffed. Words were not needed. Though she smiled, there was sadness in her eyes. The smile, I guessed, came from the hope that her life would take a turn for the better, the sadness from the expectation that it would not. I felt helpless. I could no more help her than she could help herself. Like the woman who had let me in, she was caught in a spiral of self-perversion. I knew the situation as if it were a stalker whom I could not shake off. From time to time, however, an opportunity to break the spiral presents itself. For Flora, perhaps, such an opportunity was imminent.

"Some girls do this for money, some do it for power, some do it for pleasure…and some do it for someone else."

"Walk away from him, Flora."

Flora came to the window. "When I started doing this, I was doing it for money…for drugs…heroine," she said in a mournful tone. "But I wanted to change. I was battling with myself. Then I met someone who promised to make me clean. Then he made me clean. Then he sent me here. Now I'm battling with him. Battling with myself was much easier."

"You *must* walk away."

Flora was not looking through the window. She was looking at it. She might as well have been looking at the wall. She sniffed again.

"You *can* change," I said.

"Can I?"

"Yes…but you have to want to change."

"I do want to change."

"Rely on yourself to do the right thing."

"I can't rely on anyone. Even my parents let me down."

"You can rely on yourself."

"Can I?" The girl took three steps towards me, so that only inches of the worn-out carpet lay between us.

"Flora, listen to me. When I first spoke to you, you sounded like a little girl. You were talking like the person you were when last you were happy. Out of habit, you retreat to another time, another place, another person almost. You want that little girl back, don't you, as part of you, a person from whom the woman grew, not as a crutch for the woman to lean on?"

With tears running down her cheeks, Flora nodded.

"Only the woman can get the girl back, Flora."

Flora nodded again.

"The girl's not strong enough to reclaim the woman," I added. "The woman must reclaim the girl."

Flora signalled her agreement as tears continued to flow.

I took a tissue from my jacket's side pocket. It was somewhat bedraggled, though clean. I handed it to Flora. She wiped tears from her eyes and mascara from her cheeks.

"I'm sorry," I said. "I did not mean to upset you."

Flora smiled. "You haven't upset me."

"I didn't mean to come in here and…" I was not sure why I was there.

"I'll make today my last day."

"Leave with me now."

Flora shook her head. "I'll see the day out," she said. "Nobody's going to pick me, anyway."

"I picked you."

Flora beguiled me with another of her girlish smiles. I thought that she and Kendal would get on well. That the two of them would ever meet was a pleasing fantasy.

"I would pick you every time."

"Thank you…"

"What time do you finish?"

"Normally, I finish at eight, but I have to leave early today, at three."

It was not my place to ask why she was leaving early, so I did not.

"I have to see my dentist. One of my false teeth needs replacing."

"Aren't you rather young to have false teeth?"

"I lost one of my front teeth. I had an accident. I walked into a fist, silly me."

"Walk away from him, Flora. Go to the police. They will deal with him, believe me."

"He's picking me up when I finish. He's driving me to the dentist's. He does everything for me. He even thinks for me." Tapping her temple, she said, "He's in here." She wiped her eyes with the tissue. "Even if I do walk away from him, and get him out of my life, he will always be in my head."

"One day, very soon, he will be nothing worse than a bad memory."

"Do you promise?"

"On my life, I promise."

"He has another place for me to go to…when this place closes."

"But you won't be going there."

"I won't be." Flora dabbed her eyes, which was a sign that they were drying and that the worst of the crying was over. "We all have demons, don't we?"

"Yes...and demons are never beaten easily. Perhaps they are never beaten. Perhaps the best that we can hope for is to hold them at bay and keep them there."

Flora pondered my words for what seemed like ages. "I would settle for that," she said, sounding more like a woman now. "Thank you..."

"What are you thanking me for?"

"For helping me..."

"I thank *you* for helping *me*."

"But I haven't helped you."

"Trust me, you have."

At the foot of the stairs, Suzie was waiting for me, dressed exactly as she had been the day before. She must have come back to the house when I was with Flora. She was giving me the look that a redoubtable head-mistress gives a boy when he turns up ten minutes late for assembly. I prepared myself for the challenge.

"Well, dress me in pink and call me Alice, if it isn't you again."

"I'm not sure that pink would suit you."

"It's the journalist again."

"I'm not a journalist."

"It's the policeman again."

"I'm not a policeman."

"You've been chaste with my girls."

"Have they said so?"

"They didn't have to."

"I paid."

"It would have suited me had you not come at all, either yesterday or today."

"I would not have come without good reason."

"I don't doubt that."

"I'm not a threat to you."

"You're meddling in my affairs. You're asking questions of my girls. That makes you a nuisance."

"I'm a friend of Philip's."

For a few moments, Suzie was unsure how to react, but I could see that my revelation had mollified her, pacified her, and made her less likely to have me followed. Even so, she did not suddenly turn into a pussy cat.

"And you thought you would sniff around my girls, trying to find out why he died and who killed him?"

Suzie did not need to know that I was a private detective, looking for a girl who, by some insane coincidence, had an intimate connection with my friend and her boss.

"That's what best friends do."

"Philip hanged himself."

"The police think otherwise."

"They're just keeping an open mind."

"Why is everyone sure that Philip took his own life?"

"People who know him are surprised that he didn't top himself sooner."

The woman was irritating enough with her precious talk of "my girls", but I found her use of careless slang deeply irksome, and would have found it so had she been talking about a stranger.

"I've known him all my life. How long have you known him?"

"I've known him fifteen years."

"They happen to be the fifteen years since he and I became estranged."

"I know all about Philip's choirboy past...but you can only guess what he became."

Suzie went to the door and showed me the world outside.

"I know *what* he became and *why* he became it."

"Good for you..." The woman held out her left hand as if to remind me that there was a big wide world outside waiting for me.

"I find your demeanour strangely hostile."

"I don't like the way you operate."

"Philip really did fall from grace, didn't he?"

"Are you a priest now?"

Finally, I accepted Suzie's invitation to reacquaint myself with the world outside. "Will I see you at the funeral?" I asked.

Suzie shook her head. "I doubt it."

"Why not?"

"People will wonder who I am."

"Let them wonder."

"Let them keep the illusion of who Philip was."

"People who knew Philip knew the *real* Philip."

The door was closed in my face.

Twenty-Five

The River Adur starts life as a leak in the ground somewhere near Cowfold. Almost unnoticed, swelling imperceptibly, it then winds its way through Downland valleys, and around small towns and sleepy villages, until it reaches the approach to Shoreham, where it bursts into life in torrents, burgeoning alarmingly and threatening to swamp all before it; swollen intolerably, and dammed by an isthmus on either side, it then effects a dramatic union with the sea.

I sat in my car on the edge of the western isthmus, with Shoreham Beach behind me, the harbour before me, and the sprawl that is the village away to my left. The tide was higher than I had ever seen it. Inside the harbour walls, little boats and yachts rose and fell, in peril, but in much less peril than the vessels beyond the walls, for they swayed and rocked precariously in the choppy sea. Ahead of me, almost lost in the mist and the swirling rain, chimneys rose above the industrial spread of Portslade. In the distance, just visible, stood the remains of the collapsed West Pier; a little further along the coast loomed the old Palace Pier, now known simply as Brighton Pier. Overhead, light aircraft droned as they flew in and out of Shoreham Airport.

Transformer, Lou Reed's second album, played on the stereo. I had already listened to six of the album's tracks, including *Perfect Day* and *Walk on the Wild Side*, and now I waited for *Satellite of Love*. The album marked Reed's first proper venture as a solo artist, his previous album having consisted largely of then-unreleased Velvet Underground songs. That said, some would argue that Lou Reed was the Velvets, for he had been their wordsmith and inspiration. I had listened to Reed's first album on my journey south that morning; one of its three new songs was *Berlin*, which became the title track for his third album, the one that vexed Kendal so much.

It was time that I read the letter again.

Friday 29th July, 2005

Dear Daniel,

Forgive me for being so bold as to contact you so many years after our last meeting. If memory serves me correctly, that meeting was somewhat strained, as it was bound to be when the two of us were – and, no doubt, still are – divided by a common love.

In a sense, every man or boy who has ever set eyes on Sylvia has loved her; for, as well you know, she is possessed of some quality, divine and diabolical in equal measure, which inspires – some might say, demands – devotion. Sylvia captivates. She makes unspoken promises. All too rarely, she demurs. Alas, she never rewards. Such is her nature. She cannot escape it. If she were a scorpion, she would sting even the kindly swan that takes her across the river. As I write, someone, somewhere, in Lancing or in Timbuctoo, will be asking himself the same old questions. Who was she? Where did she come from? Why did she captivate me so? Why, after all these years, can I not get her out of my mind? Many a man, Daniel, has lost his mind over Sylvia Blackman. Many a woman, too, I shouldn't wonder. Where the mind has gone, the heart has often followed.

Of the two of us, where Sylvia is concerned, you were the lucky one. Moreover, you were the clever one. Lucky, because she chose not to make you her project. Clever, because, knowing her power, you kept your distance. Believe me, Daniel, she was fascinated by you. Though you chose not to notice, she was always watching you. Even after you moved away, rare was the day when she failed to speak of you. Last time I saw her, fifteen years ago, she was still speaking of you. In you, I believe, she saw something of herself. A man of your otherworldly perspicacity will be quite able to see why she chose not to get too close. I envy you, Daniel. It is with great regret that I tell you that, as I write, if she is thinking of either of us then it is you. I have always envied you, my dear friend. How could you so effortlessly have been so unmistakably both of your class and so far removed from it? How was it that you dressed like an urchin and spoke like a king? Though I recognise that you never used it as such, your class was your advantage over me. There we were, two boys born in adjacent beds, only minutes apart, but different as chalk and cheese. In Sylvia's eyes, your being a child of Mountbatten Close enhanced your aura of otherness. In terms of background, she and I were simply too alike. I am most ashamed when

I tell you that I was relieved when you moved away and felt threatened whenever you returned. Sincerely, I hope that you can find the heart to forgive me. Sylvia and I can never be reconciled. But I hope that you and I can.

When Sylvia cast me aside, as I had long known she would, I was broken. My soul took flight, my mind was scrambled and my heart drained of all feeling. Sylvia had driven me. All that I did was for her. Every exam that I passed was passed for her. My every concert performance was performed for her. Every pound that I made in the City was made for her. What was it all for? When the love of my life spurned me, I had no reason to perform even life's mundane tasks, never mind achieve anything of note. From wanting to be a hero, someone whom Sylvia could admire, I became one who wished to die. Never strive to be someone for someone, Daniel. All that you do, do for yourself, because your love for yourself is less likely to be unrequited.

My friend, I have to tell you that my love for Sylvia was too pure to suffer rejection. From our first days together, as young children, I believed – should I say, felt? – that Sylvia and I were bonded by some force greater than sexual love. Believe me when I say that the idea of consummating our love never entered my head. I could no more have forged a carnal union with Sylvia than I could have defiled the Virgin Mary. When I asked Sylvia to be my wife, she said that, though she loved me, she did not love me in the way that I wanted her to. Though what she said was right – by which I mean that her words were accurate – she had little or no idea as to the nature of my love. As she saw it, my love was of the sort that might find expression in marriage and that might help a couple navigate their way along the challenging highways and byways of domestic life. Sylvia did not share my love as it was. She did not share my love as she thought it was. Our love, then, was doomed to fail. I asked for her hand in marriage – so old-fashioned am I that I asked her father for it first – because I loved her and could not imagine – more precisely, I could not bear to imagine – life without her by my side. When you showed me your painting of Sylvia, you will remember, I fled your flat, an act for which I am ashamed, not to say embarrassed. All I will say in my defence is that the painting was more than mere oil and canvas. It was flesh and blood. It was spirit. It was the very essence. With all the beauty and cruelty, neither of which qualities she ever meant to inflict, it was Sylvia. It was the girl whom I had always loved, whom I would always love, and who, just the day before, had spurned me.

My dear friend, I hope that you will not judge me too harshly when

I tell you that, such was my disillusionment with love purely of the heart, I embraced another kind of love: that which is called lust. It was as if all the natural urges that had been caged by my focus on purity had been released. The urges overwhelmed me and I had no desire to resist. This lust manifested itself as a wish to treat woman as I thought she deserved to be treated; as I thought she wished to be treated. So it was that I established two brothels, one in Portslade and another in Oxford. By way of an experiment, I kept two very different houses: the one in Portslade, seedy and run down; and the one in Oxford, decorative and classy. I wanted to see what sort of girl gravitated to each house. To which end I gave Suzie, the manageress of both houses, absolute freedom with regard to recruitment. To my eternal shame – please appreciate, my friend, that I am making a full and frank disclosure – I insisted on having sex with every girl that Suzie saw fit to take on board, my thinking having been that I would not buy a car, used or otherwise, without testing it. One girl, however, was spared the audition: a Hampstead beauty by the name of Miranda, also known as Dana. She and I had already become close: intimate, you might say. I rescued her from the clutches of the Great Dane. You will have heard of him, I'm sure. His girls dance on mini-stages raised above a dance floor surrounded by fish tanks. To say that he was not pleased by my poaching the girl is hugely to understate the case. If you know anything about the Great Dane then you will appreciate that my death wish might yet be fulfilled.

Miranda is the daughter of an eminent lawyer. Everything I touch seems to be respectable on the outside, but thoroughly corrupt within. Miranda, herself, with her blonde locks and heavenly smile, looks for all the world like an angel. Alas, she arrived in Oxford looking to sell herself as meat to a butcher. Who was waiting to be her agent in the market of flesh if it wasn't I? "The Great Dane," I hear you reply. He merely skinned her, Daniel. He stripped her. I put her in the window as the finished product: young and tender; more than irresistible for even the occasional eater of meat. One day, my friend, Miranda will walk away from me and the world that I inhabit. She will seek to get herself back; to be the person she was before she went astray. Though she might succeed to some degree – certainly, she will convince herself that she has succeeded – always, she will be reminded, by the monster lurking within, of the person from whom she has fled. We talk about reforming ourselves. But, once we have nurtured and nourished the bad seed within us, we remain rotten to the core. We talk about redemption. But only God has the power to redeem; and we can't be sure that He exists. I never saw God walking down the City Road.

If God doesn't exist – and there is more than an even chance that He doesn't – then why do we burden ourselves with morals? Why do we cling to notions of virtue? Is it because, as a certain German philosopher wrote, two-thousand years of Christianity have infected us with bad conscience? Because of this creed, one that has been drummed into us since the day we were born – wasn't Mister Cox an amalgam of Jeremiah and Saint Paul? – we cannot help but examine our every deed, not to say our every thought, as if we are being watched by some omniscient deity in the sky. Instead of being masters of our own destiny, we get down on our knees and beseech the Lord to help us. Instead of unthinkingly doing what comes natural to us, we use words like "corrupt" and "rotten" and hope that they will still us. We are feeble, Daniel, when we should be strong. We might as well live with our bones broken and our muscles wasted, such is our weakness. Instead of taking us into a world where all is possible, our minds tie us to a hidebound world, because they, too, are broken and wasted. If only we could root out bad conscience, my friend, think what we could achieve.

Earlier, I spoke of the purity of my love for Sylvia. You may think the notion a little godly from one who has just extolled the virtues of the godless life. Love, however, is an emotion with which we are born. It is not taught. We are not made to love so that the physically weak may continue to rule the strong. Knowing you as I do, I suspect that you would argue that what we call love is nothing more than an evolved mechanism by which the species is perpetuated. What I suspect also is that, in arguing so, you would be acting as devil's advocate. Because I divine that, whatever reason tells you, your heart suggests the presence of a god who loves you. I can say as much, Daniel, because I feel the same. What a thoroughgoing mess we're in, my friend. Is mankind condemned to settle nothing? How can he answer the question of God when his heart and his head are at war with each other? Reason denies. The heart affirms. We go with the heart because the heart gives us hope, and hope is the raft that might bring us salvation. Because, Daniel, even though we cannot say from what we wish to be saved, we cannot bear the thought of going to our death unsaved. We heed the promptings of the heart because the heart gives us love. We love through God and for God. God is love. Love is God. God is our only hope. Hope brings salvation. Perhaps reason affirms, after all. You see, my friend, how God thwarts my every attempt to rationalise Him away. I can only hope that, should the Lord strike me down someday soon, I will meet my Maker in a state of grace.

When I think of you, Daniel, I think of one who is ever in a state of grace. As boys, as we began to make our way in the world, you were serene, assured, moved by neither trial nor tribulation. In the face of life's myriad provocations, you refused so much as to blink. You seemed to be blessed with an inner certainty of your place in the world. You were rooted firmly in some place and in some thing. Perhaps, you were rooted in some one. Indeed, my friend, you were blessed. Someone, somewhere, was looking after you, enabling success at key stages in your life and ensuring that setbacks served only to enrich and strengthen you. Rest assured, every step that you take in this world is the fulfilment of some divine purpose. As for me, suffice it to say that I was never so privileged a person as appearances might have suggested I was. Nor was my personality so cohesive. My fall from grace – if, indeed, I was ever so blessed – was a natural consequence of my having been built on the shakiest of foundations. Impressive though my curriculum vitae might appear, I am a man of straw. I have never felt more worthless than I feel as I write these words.

As a first step on the path to rehabilitation, Daniel, I would like to see you again. You never know, some of the grace that has been bestowed upon you might infect me. May I suggest, then, that we convene in the Morse Bar of the Randolph Hotel, on Friday, August fifth, at ten o'clock? I will be there. I trust that you will be too. I propose that we drink to your success in winning Sylvia's heart. For you have done precisely that, Daniel, even if you don't know it. It could not have happened otherwise, because, in essence, you and Sylvia are two of a kind. There are precious few of your kind in this world of men. People like you may not know what you are, but you recognise a kindred spirit when you encounter one. Neither of you is a saint. But, then, nor were the Patriarchs. Nor was David.

Let us, David and Jonathan, after so much time apart, have a drink together. Let us drink to the avatars among us. Let us drink to the chosen few.

Yours truly,

Philip

At the top of the letter was a telephone number, written by hand in red ink. I reached for my mobile and dialled the number. My late friend's voice cut in straightaway. "You have reached the voicemail of one Philip Haygreen, whoever he is," the recording began. "If that is who I think it is then leave a message," it went on. "If that is not who I think it is then leave a message, anyway." Though stunned, I had to laugh. Replace Philip's name with mine, and the words formed the very same message that greeted callers to my phone. Philip must have called me. A week before, I had missed a call. The caller had left no message, so I dismissed the call as one from one of my few remaining creditors.

I put the pieces together. On the day before he died, Philip had phoned me. How he had obtained my number, I did not know. He had replicated the message on my voicemail in case, for whatever reason, we never spoke to each other again. Why, though, had he simply not left a message? Why had he been so cryptic? On the day of his death, he had delivered a letter to my block of flats, omitting to address the letter fully, probably because he did not know my full address. I could only guess how he had come to know where I lived. I sensed that my friend had been crying for help, and was flattered that he had turned to me, though, given the situation he was in, I doubted that I could have offered him much in the way of assistance. I would have urged him to go to the police, advice that he would have ignored.

The letter reminded me that once I had been an artist. That is to say, when I was twenty-five, I had taken up painting to relieve some of the stress of being a Metropolitan policeman. The only painting of mine that I had kept was the one that Philip had seen when he visited me, at my Hammersmith flat, the day after he had been spurned by Sylvia. Upon seeing the painting, Philip had broken down and wept.

I had painted Roseanne. But Philip had seen Sylvia.

Twenty-Six

Without quite knowing how and why, I found myself parked outside the Blackmans' house. As I had done as a boy, I stared at the house, fascinated and overawed, and imagined what was happening inside, and what was being said, by whom and to whom. Many years before, the house had been the base from which Sylvia strode with confidence into a world populated by people who could not help but revere her. Now it was a refuge for a broken woman, a place where she might lick her wounds and hide from the eyes of people who had long ago ceased to revere her. People said that she was reaping what she had sewn. They might have been right to say so. I wondered if the mob harboured a single soul prepared to step forward to plead her case. "My Lord, though the accused fully comprehends her power, she is powerless to contain it." Such a plea was called for in the name of justice, for Sylvia Blackman had never wilfully laid waste to a single soul. She had tried to love. The one man that she could have loved as a woman loves, as a woman should love, she had tried to love. Behind her failure to love, people had seen only malice, they had seen malice aforethought, indeed, as if she had murdered Philip's heart. The brutal slaying of Philip's heart had crowned her reputation as a Jezebel, as a bloodthirsty Salome, among women. The crowd knew Sylvia's heart, for it knew all that she had done, and the crowd was bound to judge. Had there been a Pontius Pilate to hand, the crowd would have had Sylvia crucified long ago; it would happily have seen the most notorious criminal released and Sylvia nailed to a cross in his place. It was Sylvia's fate to live among people who reviled her, because the only place where she could be was home. Society had no place for her. For her, truly, there was no place like home.

Without quite comprehending why, I found myself standing by the cherry-red portal of the Blackmans' house, poised to ring the bell. I stilled my hand when my attention was caught by words being sent down a telephone by a well-spoken woman.

"Her father's taken her to Oxford to see Philip's solicitor…Philip left her a house in his will…And another, in Portslade, of all the Godforsaken places…Sylvia's going to Portslade tomorrow. Of course, she's minded not to accept the bequest. After all, she was not exactly good to Philip, was she? I soon told her not to be so bloody noble. If Philip is daft enough to leave the houses to her…Exactly…And, anyway, why frustrate the will of the donor? It would be wrong to do so…What a dreadful business. I hope the police up there know what they're doing… Initially, they thought that Philip might have been murdered, but now they're sure that he killed himself. I must say, I can't think why anyone would want to kill Philip, though, of course, I don't know what he got himself into. It's hard to imagine Philip getting himself into anything, apart from a dinner suit…He was found hanging in his own house…I've just been advised of the coroner's verdict. Henry and Sylvia caught the tail-end of the inquest…I know…I, too, was surprised at how soon after Philip's death the inquest was held. It seems that it was clear-cut. It's all very murky…The funeral takes place next Wednesday, in Lancing, at Saint James the Less. Sylvia plans to go, though she won't be welcome."

Having listened long enough to someone singing from a *Daily Mail* hymn sheet, I turned to leave, only to be stopped in my tracks by Mrs Blackman, who had thrown open the door in a state of agitation.

"Can I help you?" she asked. "I saw you standing by the door."

The upper part of the door was decorated with segmented glass arranged in a half-circle; wishing not to intrude, I had desisted from peering through the glass into the hallway, but had been spotted in spite of my discretion.

I walked back towards the house. Mrs Blackman was a virtual clone of Mrs Haygreen, except that the former seemed to be making more of an effort to retain the most unlikely remnants of youth. Strangely, Sylvia's mother looked not dissimilar to Maureen. Perhaps I was predisposed to viewing all women of a certain age as near-identical specimens, in the same way that I saw each hooded youth, eyeballing me on every street corner, as having no personality distinct from that of the rest of his tribe.

"I came to see Sylvia," I said.

As my hair blew this way and that in the wind, Mrs Blackman asked questions of me with curious eyes, wondering, no doubt, if I were the latest cad to try to insinuate himself into the life of her troubled daughter.

"Do I know you?" she asked.

"Sylvia knows me."

"Are you a friend of hers?"

"I hope so."

"You *hope* so?"

"My relationship with Sylvia is difficult to describe."

Mrs Blackman looked at me in bemusement.

"She and I share something, but we're not sure what that something is, or even if that something exists."

The lady looked unsure whether she wished to call the police or an ambulance.

"Who are you?"

"My name is Daniel Winter."

The lady's face suggested a pang of recognition.

"Sylvia and I went to school together."

"Sylvia left school a long time ago."

"So did I."

"Are you Roseanne Winter's boy?"

"I am."

"I'm sorry about what happened."

"These things happen, though not often, thankfully."

"Did she ever come back?"

"She was never going to come back. There is no return from where she went."

"Where did she go?"

"'My mother and my brothers are those who hear the word of God and do it.'"

"I see."

192

Though Mrs Blackman had eyes, I was not convinced that she did see.

"She had another family," I said, my heart leaping as John the Baptist leapt in the womb of Elizabeth as she welcomed Mary to her home. "That other family called her…and she heeded the call."

"I see," the lady returned, not quite seeing.

"It could not have been otherwise."

From the Blackmans' house, I walked the short distance to the school, entering by the lower gate in Mill Road. The original North Lancing School, now the church hall, as ever, fortified as it was by legions of flint, gave the impression that it would be the last building in Lancing left standing after all others had turned to dust. Under what circumstances all things would turn to dust, I could not know. But turn to dust they would, as surely as they had begun as dust. The building, though resolute still, seemed past its best, as if it had lost something of its soul. It looked unsure of itself in this modern world. I wondered why. Was it because it was no longer used for the purpose for which it was built? I first stepped foot inside the place, as a fledgling cub scout of the Fifth Lancing pack, one-hundred years after it was built, and even then it had long since ceased to be a school. Perhaps it mourned the children it had schooled, most of whom, in peace or at war, had passed away. I recalled the photograph of Archie Holbourne. I had seen it in my book of *Old Lancing*. The photograph was taken on Empire Day, nineteen-hundred-and-eight, when Archie was twelve years old. He stood in the foreground, holding the Union flag by a pole that was twice the size of him. Behind him stood columns and rows of his peers, boys in tweed suits and girls in summer frocks, all of them saluting the King and thanking God for having matched them with His hour. Archie Holbourne died, a day before the Armistice, from a stray bullet fired by one from his own side, his death, then, tragic as it was, embellished by the absurd. The past was all around me. Why would it not have been, when, no sooner has a moment arrived, having waited for all time to come forth, than it joins the legions of its fellows in the past? All, then, is past. There is barely a present, never mind a future.

At the end of the passage, I turned right and made my way up the slope, at the top of which were some steps, until I reached the school.

There it was, unchanged in thirty years, except that the classrooms to the left had been knocked down, as had the old canteen, and a new unit had swallowed half of the playground. The swimming pool, opened by Mr Cox in nineteen-seventy, was still there. I walked over to it and peered over the fence. It was full, ready to be drained for the winter. Already, autumnal debris, leaves and the like, had fallen in and floated on the surface. There was something at the bottom. I tried to make out what it was. It was a branch or a stick of some kind. Though the nearest tree was some fifty yards away, I could just about imagine how leaves might have found their way to the pool, but I failed to see how a branch the size of a walking stick could have been prized from a tree and carried to the water. I guessed that a child had thrown it in. As the rain fell on the water, threatening to cause an overflow, concentric circles radiated outwards, collided with their neighbours and dissolved, only to be reborn no sooner had they passed away.

I walked along the top end of the pool to the main body of the school, to the room that had received me as a four-year-old. Inside, tiny chairs surrounded tiny tables. Beside each chair was a name written on a card. I read some of the names: Darren, Kyle, Hayley and Mae. There was no Philip, no Sylvia, and no Daniel. Such names, I thought, must have gone out of fashion. Paintings and drawings, all bearing the names of the artists, decorated the walls. What appeared to be the same sandpit that my class had used, back in sixty-nine, stood to the left, in the corner. To the right hung not a blackboard but a whiteboard, on which, in green ink, some in upper case and some in lower, were written letters of the alphabet.

Moments later, I found myself in the centre of the playground, looking around, rolling back the years, feeling for the past with the senses of the inner man. I looked for Philip. At last, I saw him. Dignified, as ever he was, he walked through crowds of rampaging children, who, in their clamour, made random, crazy patterns across the tarmac. I looked for clues: something in his eyes, in his demeanour, that prefigured a life lived fast and loose – in its latter stages, at least – and a death died slow and tight. My inner voice told me that the chain of cause-and-effect linked the eight-year-old boy that I saw with a forty-year-old man whom I had never seen, and he, in turn, with a beautiful girl some twenty years his junior, and that the girl, blonde and charged with danger, had everything to do with his death.

Thoughts of Philip Haygreen merged with those of Archie Holbourne. Archie's name was inscribed on the war memorial, down in South Street, by the parish hall. Every time I walked past it, and saw the words "To the glory of God" above the names, I wondered if the Almighty could not have diverted the stray bullet for the glory of Archie Holbourne. At the end of Philip's funeral, the dead man's soul would be commended to the Lord. If accepted, to the glory of God he would go. But what of the glory of Philip Haygreen would be left on earth?

It was two o'clock. It was raining. I was standing in the graveyard of Saint James the Less Parish Church, in North Lancing. Except for the deceased, I was alone. The grass round about was lush and overgrown. Birdsong filled the quiet air, so that the scene before me looked and sounded like the aftermath of a battle, which, in a sense, it was, for the field was strewn with bodies. People had battled with life, doing their best, only, in the end, to lose; they had battled with others, loved-ones or not, in a war of wills, in love as in war, and, regardless of any victories won, finished as dust. Each of the deceased had done some good, some bad, and much that was neither good nor bad. In the course of life, the good would have redeemed the bad, so that any judge disposed to show mercy, discerning the balance, might withhold punishment where he would not reward. God is so disposed, but His mercy must not be taken for granted, it must be sought, and it must be prayed for. Some people say as much.

I was about to enter the church, the church of my childhood, and get out of the rain, to suffer a bout of mawkishness, as I wallowed in lost innocence, and to pray. I stayed where I was, in the rain, because I told myself that I should not go back, not even for a visit driven by nostalgia, because my place, my house of prayer, was the Roman Catholic Church, the holy and apostolic Church. My soul belonged to the Church of Rome, the Bride of Christ, the Church from which, thanks to a misguided Tudor king, England had been divorced. I would attend Mass that evening, at the Oxford Oratory, the Roman Catholic Church of Saint Aloysius Gonzaga, and say my prayers then and there. I could not get there soon enough.

My sudden affinity with the Catholic Church was bound up with my feelings for Roseanne. I wondered how long the affinity would last. My soul was in kinship with Roseanne's, and her soul belonged to Rome, and always would belong to Rome, so, I reasoned, my soul, too, belonged to Rome. But for how long? Reason told me that my soul would belong to Rome evermore. That had to be the case. But that was absurd: not the metaphysical Absurd of Albert Camus, the philosophy of meaninglessness that had long given my life meaning, but, simply, absurd.

There were matters that I needed to discuss with Kendal, because she, though absurdly young, understood. Such matters related to the timing of Roseanne's formal consecration, and the steps that she had taken to have Laura and me cared for between her leaving and that same consecration. My Auntie Hillary was another with questions to answer. She was party to the conspiracy of silence. There was no doubting that.

Looking around, I wondered where Philip would be buried: there seemed to be no room. Some of the headstones were so old that their inscriptions had been worn away by the elements; lichen was everywhere; and gaping cracks and holes served as depressing evidence of man's capacity for neglect and indifference. A crow landed on one of the headstones. It looked around, in its element, at home, surrounded by ash and bones. It looked at me. Then it flew away, over the beech trees at the far end of the graveyard, squawking some message of foreboding to its kith and kin.

I walked down the gravel path, stones crunching underfoot, to the grave where the crow had been. Then I remembered that I had been there before. This was the resting place of one Maeve Nesfield, Philip's maternal grandmother. Born in nineteen-thirteen, she died in nineteen-ninety-three, a veteran of two world wars. Eighty years, I thought: what are they in the scheme of things? They form not so much as a drop in the boundless ocean that is eternity. For Maeve Nesfield, eighty years was the span of her life. She had been blessed with more happiness than most. I wondered whether Philip's maternal grandfather was alive. The Nesfields of Sompting Village were devoted to each other, so husband and wife would have been bound to be buried together. There was no sign of the husband, so he had to be alive, somewhere, yearning for his dear departed. It is unnatural for a parent to outlive a child, and downright perverse for a grandparent to outlive a grandchild.

There were so many souls to pray for and not enough hours in the day.

With that thought in mind, I began to make my way back to the car, which was parked by the Potter. Something ahead of me moved sharply. I looked up to see a figure wearing a red raincoat, the hood over the head, trotting along the gravel path towards the gate by West Lane. At the gate the figure stopped. It turned around and looked at me. It was a woman. Her eyes, some eighty yards distant, were as clear to me as if she were standing three feet away. They were the eyes of Sylvia. But the woman could not possibly have been Sylvia; and, anyway, never in a million years would the Sylvia that I knew have worn red.

I had never known an August afternoon to be so dark. Portslade-by-Sea is none too attractive in the best of lights, so the unseasonal gloom made for the most inhospitable of welcomes as I returned for my second visit of the day. Cars passed me with their headlights aglow, illuminating pedestrians as they went. People hurried to where they were going, for they knew that a storm was about to break.

When I drove into Middle Way, I took the only parking space available: a patch of wasteland fronting a tumbledown garage with dilapidated double doors. Around me, alleyways and paths seemed to fade into darkness, as if they had been lured into a trap by the mouths of some multi-headed Leviathan. Though I wanted to play some music, I kept my hands well away from the stereo, because I wished to remain alert, so that I would be ready when Flora emerged from the squalid dwelling in which she plied her sordid trade. I was there to greet her privately, though not in person. I was there because I was curious. My visit to the house – Philip's other house, in the other Middle Way – and my meeting Flora therein, formed a narrative, a chapter in a book, and I was keen to see how the chapter ended. A chapter in Flora's life was due to end, and I was there to see it end.

Not a second after three o'clock, Flora appeared at the door. Her promptitude was reassuring, as it signalled an urgency to leave behind an outgrown way of life. That Suzie came to the door to hug Flora also reassured me, for the parting was unmistakably valedictory. Flora was leaving her old self behind.

No sooner had Suzie closed the door than a man burst out of the car parked directly outside the house and met Flora halfway down the garden path. The man warrants no description. Suffice it to say that he was the kind of man to whom Alexis de Tocqueville's doctrine of American exceptionalism meant little or nothing. Though Flora put up stout resistance, she was no match for a man of such brutish proportions: within seconds, she had been dragged down the pathway and bundled into the man's awaiting car. The struggle that ensued lasted as long as it took the man's ample fist to connect with the girl's delicate face. When I saw the small object being waved at Flora, angrily, I wished that I had not given her my business card. I reflected on my time as a policeman. Every day, no matter how well I had performed my duties, I made a small mistake that would make my life harder and more than inconvenience someone else. My career as a private detective was going to follow a similar pattern, it seemed.

As I watched the man turn his car around, and take the coast road into Brighton, I dwelt on the thought that the last word about Flora, the girl from Whitehawk, might not have been written, after all.

Twenty-Seven

In the reading, from Ezekiel, much had been said about the rebellious house of Israel, about the burdens and responsibilities of prophecy, about watchmen, about moral guardians, about unrighteousness and iniquity, and about punishment and exile.

Words such as these weighed me down and, the longer and harder I thought about them, the greater was their weight upon me, for they were words that warned me that there were people around me better than I, people who, though inclined to rebel, shouldered the burdens and responsibilities of faith, who served as watchmen for themselves and their brethren, who placed their trust in appointed moral guardians, who fought against unrighteousness and iniquity, and who, even in their most complacent moments, guarded fiercely against the prospect of punishment and exile.

The Gospel reading had told us of Peter's declared recognition of Jesus as the Christ, at Caesarea Philippi, and of the Saviour's ensuing investment of authority in Peter as the foundation of the Church, the rock upon which the Faith would be built.

The passage in Matthew, Peter's confession of Jesus as the Christ, the Son of the Living God, shattered me every time I read it, breaking with its shuddering power my desperate need not to believe, but, even so, I had denied, many more times than Peter had, that I knew Jesus; worse, much worse, I had denied, countless times, that Jesus was who Peter said He was.

I had listened to the homily attentively as anyone among the faithful scattered around the church. The priest had spoken of love and told the congregation, which consisted of some fifty people, that it was the benchmark by which we would be judged. The ultimate question that we would be asked, he said, was: how much had we loved? I had reflected that love meant different things to different people, that it was impossible to define, never mind measure, and that, rather than wasting our time with love, we should aspire to a state of dignity at all times, for that was one ideal to which we could do justice.

After Communion – as a non-Catholic, I was not entitled to partake of it – as I awaited the Concluding Rites, sitting at the back of church, again, I had completed my meditation on Flora. Though I wanted to pray for her, I was not in the habit of praying. I hoped that someone, somewhere, was praying for her. I hoped that someone, somewhere, was praying for the man to whom Flora was beholden. Flora's oppressor might have been less deserving of anyone's prayers, but, doubtless, he was no less in need of them.

The church was empty. It was so quiet that I could almost hear the angels collecting the prayers just offered before taking them to God's altar in heaven. During the Eucharistic Prayer, the priest had said that the angels did as much. I walked down the aisle and imagined myself getting married. I genuflected before the Sanctuary. I felt that I had to genuflect. Then I took a seat in the front pew, on the right of the aisle, and waited for something to happen. I have no idea what I was expecting to happen, though an epiphany of some sort would have been nice, some revelation of Truth to lure my mind from its existential lair.

A figure emerged from the darkness enveloping the Lady Chapel. I was now well enough acquainted with his stoop and shuffling gait to know whose outline it was approaching me in the gloom. He sat beside me and looked ahead at the Sanctuary, a man with answers to most of the questions worth asking.

"May I talk to you about a friend of mine, Father?"

"Be my guest."

"He died five days ago. The circumstances of his death have been declared officially to be free of suspicion of foul play, which is to say that the official verdict of the inquest was that he took his own life. I know that Philip did not die by his own hands. He might have had a death wish, for he had grown to despise himself, but he did not take his own life.

"I don't want to talk about the way in which Philip met his end. Rather, I wish to speak with you about my friend's state of mind, about the health of his soul, at the hour of his death.

"For most of his life, Philip was a good Christian. At the very least, his was a Christian sensibility, even if his life was not governed entirely by his Church. His was a humble Anglican soul. He was godly without trying to be. He believed that the more fortunate in life, the privileged, had a duty to live by good example. He embodied that ideal without effort and without expectation of reward, either on earth or in heaven. He believed that with privilege came responsibility. That was the *real* Philip Haygreen.

"Philip's life changed when Sylvia Blackman rejected his proposal of marriage. Rather, he changed and his life changed with him. Embittered, he discarded his devotion to purity and chastity and embraced a life of dissolution and depravity. He enriched himself by exploiting vulnerable women. The object of his ideal love had spurned him, so he spurned ideal love in favour of the kind of love that only the Devil would encourage. The sordid world that he embraced contained the seeds of his destruction. He was a stranger in this new world of his, and, as a stranger, lost in a foreign land, he met his death.

"I believe that he died still a good man at heart. He left behind the good life only because he could not cope with a situation with which he had never expected to have to cope. His heart remained with Sylvia, his childhood sweetheart, the love of his life, the only woman he had ever loved and could ever love. Philip Haygreen loved Sylvia Blackman until the day he died. His final, dying thought would have been of her.

"Philip lived and died for Sylvia Blackman. He was good to her. He doted on her. He was devoted to her. He nursed her when she was sick. He saved her from herself. He saved her from the abyss. Alas, in saving Sylvia, he destroyed himself. Sylvia did not ask Philip to give himself so, nor, some might say, did she deserve the sacrifice, but Philip, without thought for his own wellbeing, gave himself so that another might live. That was the *real* Philip Haygreen.

"Philip was led astray by the Devil, you might say. True, he left himself exposed to Satan's cunning, but the Evil One, as ever, showed no mercy in exploiting the first sign of weakness in even a man as godly as Philip. Philip's godliness took the form of innate moral character, uprightness and sobriety, but, alas, it was not quite faith. His essential goodness, undermined by despair, was no match for the Devil. Philip was not quite sober enough, nor was he watchful enough, and his adversary, the Devil, prowling around like a roaring lion, seeking someone to devour, seized upon Philip and consumed him. The Devil covets souls that are close to God, as Philip's was, because they are the greatest prize. Would you not say so?"

"I most certainly would." My companion's gaze remained fixed on the Sanctuary. "When did you last see Philip?"

"Fifteen years ago…"

"That long?"

"We fell out over Sylvia."

"Are you still in contact with her?"

"Only telepathically…"

"Philip sounds like he was a tortured soul."

"He was, but only because of Sylvia, though she never meant to hurt him. She never meant to destroy him, either, but hurt him and destroy him she did."

"What has she done to you?"

"She haunts me."

"Would you like me to say Mass for Philip?"

"He wasn't a Catholic."

"That doesn't matter."

"That would be nice, thank you."

"I am celebrating Mass on Monday evening. I will dedicate that Mass to the repose of Philip's soul."

"That's kind of you, Father. I will be here."

"In the meantime, I will pray for you and for Sylvia, for peace of mind for you both."

"I appreciate that, Father, more than I can say."

"Well, dinner beckons. I can't be late for dinner, or Mrs Bentine, our cook, will hit me with her wooden spoon…and if word gets around that such things are going on in the Oratory House then the Catholic Church really will be in trouble."

If all else failed, the Catholic Church had the ultimate weapon, humour, amply at its disposal.

Twenty-Eight

"You're full of surprises, Kendal, as ever."

"Am I?"

"You have a thousand albums in my collection to choose from, and I come home and find you listening to this."

"I've had a weird day. I thought I might as well keep it weird."

"My day's been positively surreal."

"Drink your tea."

"Oh, sweetheart, you've made me some tea…"

Kendal and I were in our respective seats, at the kitchen table, listening to Brian Eno's first solo album, *Here Come The Warm Jets*, both dressed in black, looking and feeling like two people who were at a splendid party, but glad that it was coming to an end. Kendal looked tired, but content, as if she had just sat a strenuous examination, but knew that she had passed it with flying colours. I was simply happy that my prayers would not fall on deaf ears.

"The tea's good."

"Anyone can make a cup of tea, Daniel."

"My sister can't."

"Yeah, it was pretty rank."

"That's putting it mildly."

"She came, Daniel."

"Who did?"

"Sylvia…to the inquest…"

"So you said on the phone."

"But it was like you said, when you talked about the funeral." Kendal seemed enthralled by her own words. "When she entered the room, everyone there turned to look at her, even the coroner and the policeman in the witness box, and they kept looking at her, long after she'd sat down. The policeman in the witness box lost his train of thought completely. He even asked the coroner what the question was, and he'd been answering it for ten minutes."

"That's Sylvia for you."

"Guess who Sylvia looked at first."

"Mrs Haygreen…"

"Yes, and they just stared at each other for what seemed like ages. I could tell that they hate each other…or that Mrs Haygreen hates Sylvia, at least. But Mr Haygreen…well, he glanced at Sylvia, but that was all, as if she were just someone, a stranger, who'd walked in off the street."

"Mr Haygreen is one of the most phlegmatic characters you'll ever meet."

"Guess who Sylvia looked at next."

"You?"

Kendal nodded, her eyes ablaze with wonder. "She held me in a kind of…trance…and I think I did the same to her. We were waiting for the other to blink. Then we blinked, together."

"How did you know that she was Sylvia?"

"Because, Daniel, she…"

Kendal looked away, her face contorted by fear, for what she had seen was unknown to her, and she knew not how what she had seen had come about. When her eyes were upon me again, they were wide and radiant with hope, for now, more than ever before, she knew that a life lived in some realm beyond the apprehension of the people of this world could and would be hers, because now she knew that there were kindred spirits abroad, a collective that would bind and nurture her in communal solidarity.

"Because, Daniel, she looked just like me…"

At that moment, I was struck by terror at what I had done. I had brought Sylvia into Kendal's world. Kendal's life would never be the same again. Kendal was under her spell. I would look back on my next few words as those that sealed Kendal's fate, as those that locked her firmly into Sylvia's troubled and troublesome world.

"After dinner, we're going to watch a film."

"Which film?"

"*The Aviator's Wife...*" I replied. "It is the first of Eric Rohmer's *Comedies & Proverbs* cycle of films, though none of them is especially funny, nor do any of them contain anything you might call proverbial."

Kendal waited in vain for my words to register with her, for her mind was elsewhere, a long way away.

"But they are all profound," I added.

Kendal remained lost in a place where I could not reach her.

"After the film, I am going to show you a painting."

Such, absolutely, was the last thing that I should have shown her, but I too was under a spell. I was heeding the voice of the demon which persists in urging me to take a story to its limits, even when I know that the story can only end with yet more darkness being brought into this fallen world.

Twenty-Nine

As I shaved, I played *Love Not Money*, the best album made by Everything But The Girl. I placed the CD-player on the side, by the bath, balanced precariously, and kept glancing at the machine, in case it took a tumble. It was often placed in precisely the same position, and had never fallen into the bath yet, so my caution, likely as not, was unfounded. My circumspection, I suspected, had much to do with the fact that I, too, was balanced somewhat delicately, my case, such as it was, resting on a knife-edge, able to fall one way or the other, or, now that I thought of it, straight down, under the weight of its own absurdity, sliced in two, leaving me with a pair of cases neither of which would be solved, never mind reconciled the one with the other.

Kendal also had become the cause of no little angst, for she had retreated into her shell. I should have known that that would happen. I should never have shown her the painting. I had painted Roseanne. In the painting, Philip had seen Sylvia and broken down. In the painting, Kendal had seen herself and fled to her room. She had yet to emerge. Before going to bed, I had knocked on her door but not been answered. That morning, twice, with a tap on the door with a trembling hand, I had tried to rouse her from her torpor, only to be told, by silence, that the girl was not for talking.

Kendal had done her bit for the case, she could do no more, so I went on my way hoping that she would rest awhile and have recovered herself by evening.

"You look like you're expecting someone."

"I am," I replied, "and she's arrived."

"You look like you're expecting someone else."

"It's funny you should say that."

Carey gave me that look of puzzlement that people often give me.

Though it would be crass to say that I did not recognise Carey with her clothes on, she did not arrive at the Morse Bar of the Randolph Hotel, at the appointed hour, as quite the same person I had met two days before. On an overcast August day, she was a tad overdressed in a roll-neck sweater and maroon jacket made of tweed. Justice was fully served on her curves by a pair of tight-fitting jeans. I was surprised that she was not wearing a hat. She seemed the type that would wear one.

"I took the liberty of ordering you some coffee," I said.

"Thank you..." After pouring milk into her cup, she added two lumps of brown sugar; before the sugar had even begun to dissolve, she drank some coffee and gasped her relief in a manner that smacked of desperation.

"Cold up north, is it?" I asked.

"It was cold in Banbury first thing this morning."

"You must be baking now."

"I'm trying to project the right image."

It was unclear to me what image she wished to project: from the waist down, she was a young woman, with pronounced hips and thighs, exuding the sex appeal of nubile youth; above the black leather belt, with the job in hand foremost in my thoughts, she was too "Women's Institute" for my liking.

"What's in the envelope?"

I handed ten fifty-pound notes across the table.

Carey lifted the flap and peered inside. "Gosh!" she said.

"I'm sorry it's in cash," I joked. "I didn't think you'd accept a cheque."

Carey looked around the room to check that nobody was looking our way. "How dodgy does this look?" she said, under her breath.

I watched as she dropped the envelope into a handbag that had so many pockets and compartments that it could have housed an army of refugees.

"What do I have to do for this money?"

"Go and see someone..."

"Who?"

"The man they call the Great Dane…"

"Dane Goldman?"

I nodded.

"You want me to go to The Aquarium?"

"I do."

"And say what?"

"Ask to speak with the owner…"

"It would be easier to get an audience with the Queen. Dane Goldman isn't the most accessible of people, so I've heard."

"Say that you want to work for him."

"And if he won't see me?"

"If you act the part well enough then he will see you."

"What part do you want me to play?"

"You have to give the impression of being vulnerable."

"And if he's not taken in by my act?"

"The Great Dane is a man who likes to control women. At the same time, he likes to be their father."

"I doubt that he's going to come over all paternal on *me*."

"All you need to do is get a foot inside his lair."

Carey sighed. "Okay," she said. "I get an audience with him. How does that help you?"

"I'd like you to ask a few searching, but discreet, questions."

"About what?"

"This and that," I replied. "Get the measure of the man. Gain his confidence. You might be surprised by what he tells you."

"So, as well as wanting me to be vulnerable, you want me to be searching, but discreet?"

"If that's not too much trouble…"

"It's one hell of an act I'm going to have to put on."

"You're used to acting for twelve hours a day. I'm asking you to act for half an hour."

"What if he gets suspicious?"

"He won't."

"You have too much faith in my acting."

"I would nominate you for an Oscar, right here and now, if I could."

As if it were an elixir that would embolden her for the challenge ahead, she drank what remained of her coffee in three gulps. "May I ask why you are so interested in Dane Goldman?"

"He preys on girls. He exploits women. He kills people."

"And you want me to go and see this delightful man with nothing more than a handbag for protection?"

"I wouldn't mess with any woman carrying that thing," I returned, with a nod at the handbag.

Carey touched each of the golden hoops that hung from her ears. I wondered whether the gesture were an act of superstition. She might have been making sure that the rings were still there, so weightlessly did they seem to dangle from her lobes.

"Has this Dane character killed someone you know?"

"He has."

"Who?"

"My best friend…"

"Why?"

"Because he crossed him…"

"How?"

I took the photograph of the blonde from my pocket. I put it on the table. Every time I looked at the picture, I saw a new quality in the girl. No longer, then, did I behold mere beauty. As ever, the mouth bespoke a passion that smouldered on the brink of consummation. The lips, thick and a glossy red, invited one to kiss them even as they made to withdraw. The teeth, in their white brilliance, were strong and healthy. The skin, smooth as velvet, was a snapshot of fleeting youth. The nose was delicate as porcelain. The blonde locks, though they cascaded wildly, evinced a measure of control. Her blue eyes glinted like chips of ice on a frosty morning. It was the eyes that gave the face its character. Devoid of warmth, the girl had no compassion in her soul, not even for herself.

"Who's that?"

"That is one Miranda Ward-Homer."

"Who's she?"

"You might know her as Dana."

"*Our* Dana?"

"*Your* Dana…"

"You know where to find her."

"I plan to catch up with her this evening."

"That's the job done then."

"I need proof that I've found her," I said. "To get proof, I need to see her."

"That makes sense."

"I can't see her in the house, because Suzie wouldn't let me in, so I'll have to intercept her when she leaves."

"What if she leaves early?"

"I must hope that she doesn't."

"The place closes on Sunday. The house is being sold, following the owner's death, and Suzie wants to pack it all in."

"So, today is my last chance to speak with Dana."

"So it would seem."

"When did you find out about the owner's death?"

"On Monday…"

"You didn't mention his death on Wednesday."

"You were prying, not without good reason, but I didn't want to tell you too much. Anyway, I assumed you knew. You would be a useless private detective if you hadn't known."

"The owner of the house in Middle Way was my best friend. He was virtually my twin brother."

"Oh, I…" Carey thought hard about what to say. "Dana worked for Dane Goldman, who killed your friend, because your friend poached Dana from him."

"What other conclusion can one draw?"

"That was rather daring of him."

"Philip had long been a stranger to me…and to himself, I dare say."

"Perhaps Philip knew Dana before he poached her."

"He must have…but how their paths ever crossed shall remain a mystery to me."

"What a tangled web…"

"You couldn't make it up."

"Am I right in thinking that Dana's – Miranda's – father is paying you to find her?"

"You are."

"He must be worried sick."

"I get the impression that father and daughter have never been close. He wants only to know that she is alive and well. He didn't approach me himself. He sent an associate, a Mr Hardcastle, and very sinister he was too."

"The plot thickens."

"It's not a book. It's not a film. It's real life."

"You will have to tell me more."

"I will, after you've seen our friend."

"What will you do whilst I'm dicing with death?"

"I will sit here, drinking tea."

"Don't worry on my account, will you?"

"Though I might have a beer, as it's getting late…"

"Don't let me keep you…"

"Come on," I said. "I'll walk you to the taxi rank."

"Can you spare the time?"

Though I was enjoying the banter, we had a job to do. As we left the opulent setting that is the Randolph Hotel, I watched people watching us go, and wondered if any of the eyes that I saw were watching us with more than a passing interest.

"Observe the juxtaposition of the Gothic and the Classical," I declared, imitating a tour guide, as we walked down Beaumont Street towards Gloucester Green. I was referring to the Gothic splendour of the Randolph and the Classical majesty that is the Ashmolean Museum. "I bet you don't get that in Banbury."

"You can run down the place all you like, mister, because I'm not from Banbury."

"But you live in Banbury."

"My home is Reading. I moved to Banbury when I got the job at the travel agent at Birmingham International Airport."

"Birmingham is some way from Banbury."

"Banbury is close enough to Birmingham and not too far from Reading."

As we turned left into Gloucester Street, I compared Flora and Dana and Carey, and concluded that they were three very different people who happened to have been drawn to the same profession, and one which people assume attracts a particular type of person.

"Isn't working in Banbury rather awkward?"

"No…"

"You might meet someone you know."

"I don't know anyone in Banbury, except the loan shark, and I doubt that he frequents Bubbles."

"Bubbles?"

"Silly, isn't it?"

"It's more than silly."

"Can I ask you something?"

"Go ahead."

"How do you know that Dane Goldman will be at The Aquarium when I get there?"

"I took steps to ensure that he would."

"Where shall I meet you afterwards?"

"I shall join you towards the end of your interview."

"What?"

I showed Carey the warrant card.

Carey laughed. "What is that?" She emphasised each of the three words, speaking slowly, as if it occupied a one-word sentence.

"It's a warrant card."

"It's unreal."

"Of course it's unreal. Do you think there's anyone on the planet with a name like that?"

"It has your photo on it."

"It wouldn't be much of a warrant card without my photo on it."

"Where did you get it?"

"Someone I know is a brilliant forger."

"Isn't it illegal to impersonate a policeman?"

"It's illegal to keep a brothel."

We stopped outside The Goose. Gloucester Green was populated by more pigeons than people, the presence of the market notwithstanding. Morning mist was clinging to the square like barnacles on a wave-breaker. The eerie silence pervading the place put me in mind of the fog-shrouded squares of Venice in Nicolas Roeg's film of nineteen-seventy-three, *Don't Look Now*.

"How come you're prepared to pay so much money for the little information that I'm likely to come back with?"

"Whatever you tell me, it will be priceless."

"I sense that there's someone else involved in this murky affair."

"Like who?"

"A woman…and, whoever she is, she means a lot to you."

"Unfortunately, she's tainted, and will be tainted further by her involvement in this sordid business."

"Do you and this woman have a future together?"

"I'm doomed forever to be the Pip to her Estella."

"Life's full of these little tragedies."

"So it is," I laughed.

We made our way to the front of the line of taxis, which skirted the top of Gloucester Green like a giant black snake basking in the shade.

"The Aquarium, please," I told the driver, "on the Cowley Road…"

"I know where The Aquarium is, my friend."

"That's the trouble with waiting," Carey said. "It makes you grumpy." She boarded the carriage in as ladylike a manner as is possible when climbing into such contraptions. She tapped on the window before she wound it down. "Well?" she asked.

"Well, what?"

"What do I pay with?"

"I've just given you five-hundred quid."

"Nice try…"

I found ten pounds and handed the note to Carey. "That should cover it."

"It had better."

"Here's my card. I've always wanted to say that."

Carey took the card and studied it. "Is this another fabrication?"

"I wish it were. I'm tired of being a private eye…and this is my first case."

The car left the rank in what appeared to be fourth gear, throwing Carey back against the seat as it went.

Bus drivers were not so obnoxious, after all.

"You all right there, boss?" the market trader asked as I surveyed the junk that decorated his stall.

"I'm fine," I replied. "Why do you ask?"

"You're crying."

"I'm not crying."

"Water's pouring from your eyes."

"My eyes water from time to time. I've no idea why."

"You want to get those eyes seen to. You might have something nasty."

"A year ago, all at once, I had viral conjunctivitis, bacterial conjunctivitis and ulcers on the inside of my eyelids. At the time, I was reading *Story Of The Eye*, by Georges Bataille, and had just seen the Stanley Kubrick film *Eyes Wide Shut*…and Snow Patrol's album *Eyes Open* was just about to come out. The Fates certainly know how to make a man suffer."

"You must have been a sight for sore eyes." So reduced to hysteria, the market trader rendered himself still of the market but temporarily unable to trade.

"I looked like something out of *The Evil Dead*," I replied. "Children were laughing at me."

"They say things come in threes." Again, the man was unable to contain his mirth.

I smiled as I recalled sitting in an aeroplane, bound for Krakow, winking, in an effort to prevent my healing eyes from sticking, and observing the looks given me by the hostesses as they went about their business.

"Why don't you treat yourself to one of these?" the trader asked.

"What is it?"

"Never mind what it is." The man fondled the object lovingly. "Just feel the quality."

"I'm sure it's full of quality," I said. "But I'd still like to know what it is."

"It's whatever you want it to be. Have you no imagination?"

"I'm coming back this way later," I lied. "I'll pick it up then."

"I might have sold it."

"I'll take the chance."

Thirty

With tears flowing down my cheeks – how I cursed this inexplicable phenomenon – I reflected on another mystery that I was keen to have explained. Accordingly, I wondered if it were a tradition in Oxford for undergraduates to decorate the walls of their colleges with graffiti. A new scrawl had appeared on the outside wall of Exeter College. "Don't trust the mainstream media" was the proclamation. "Don't trust people who write on walls" someone had written, with the same indelibility, below. On the front wall of New College, someone had sprayed, in red, "God is dead". "No, I'm not" had been sprayed, in white, below. Was the ghost of Nietzsche stalking the precincts of Oxford? It was more likely that Richard Dawkins, the world's most vociferous atheist, was having a conversation with himself and taking out his madness on the walls of New College. Alas, for posterity, the exchange had been erased with an instrument that must have been industrial in scale. An attempt had been made to wipe away the message that was written on the front wall of Keble College, the venerable home of *The Light Of The World*. "Life is not a paragraph" was etched into the fabric of the red bricks. "No", I felt like writing below, "it's a bloody sentence".

I walked along Saint Clement's Street. From George Street, I had ambled down Queen Street, a busy thoroughfare of shops and people through which buses passed like a camel through the half-blocked eye of a needle. Then, to pass the time, I had taken my shadow down Turl and Holywell Streets, followed by Queen's Lane, before reaching the High. As I approached The Plain, the sun had broken through both the clouds and the myriad leafy trees that guarded Magdalen Bridge. I came to the Cowley Road by Jeune Street. I flinched as sunlight flashed at me from the windscreen of a passing car. I cursed the sun. As always, it was bringing out the worst in people: naked torsos, tattoos, flabby midriffs, and buttocks no part of which should ever see the light of day.

By the Ultimate Picture Palace, I stood at one of the gateways to Oxford's little piece of Bohemia. It was the part of the city where pimps and prostitutes, users and dealers, those inclined to the occult, men and women of an overtly homosexual persuasion, people from here, there, and, it seemed, everywhere, made their home. In this enclave, the homeless would put down roots. To some, the street was vibrant. To others, it was a mess. One man thought it the place to be. Another cared to pretend that it did not exist. The first man might see the Cowley Road as an invitation to indulge his Everyman. The second might view it as a river, a torrent, that, were it given half the chance – were it not faced down by the bastion of Christendom that is Magdalen's bell-tower – would flood the city of God and the mind.

"Behold the glories of East Oxford," I said as I surveyed the spectacle before me.

Betjeman blamed the mess on William Morris the Second, and on all the books in the Bodleian that had failed to guide, and on the first-class minds of the Gown that had served only to blight the Town. I sniffed the air. Through the stench of gas and oil and dustbins and freshly-squeezed orange juice and croissants and coffee and Bombay mix and mozzarella and bagels and the weed came that pure smell of salt from the sea, of grass from the Downs, and of bacon and eggs being cooked in the Mermaid. Into my heart had blown, from yon far country, an air that killed. I chided myself for being so sentimental. I looked at the poster advertising the film being shown. I had grown used to coincidences that grabbed me by the neck and shook me until my teeth chattered. Daphne du Maurier had set the story in a great Italian city, the churches and waterways of which glowed and sparkled in the tragic heat of summer. But Nicolas Roeg had been so inspired in placing the celluloid version of *Don't Look Now* in a Venice whose spires and domes were soaked in rain and whose death-ridden canals were stalked by the fog of winter.

"It's that year again," I sighed. "Nineteen-seventy-three…"

The man at the door looked like he would break a bone or two if words of encouragement were whispered in his ear. He was smart in a black designer suit. The suit was so expensive that I was not surprised that he could afford to regard me as if I were something that the cat had dragged in and changed its mind about.

"No unauthorised personnel," he grunted with a disappointing lack of poetry.

"I've been authorised."

"Who by?"

I showed the man my warrant card. "This..." I said.

When the man moved to take the card from me, I withdrew it so that it hung an inch from my face. The man read what was written on the card. He smiled. I had seen more welcoming smiles.

"I don't think so," he said.

"Do you think I like being called Maximilian Doublesnake?"

The man pondered my question. I could tell that he was not used to thinking.

"If I were going to impersonate a police officer, do you think I'd chose a name like that?"

The man was in agony now. The thinking was killing him.

"It's hardly the most credible name, is it?"

After one final thought, the one that might have had him reaching for the painkillers, the man asked me what I wanted.

"I'd like a word with your boss."

"He's busy."

"I'll wait."

"It could be a long wait."

"I've not much on, except a murder, but that can wait."

The man was too confused to think. He looked at me. Rather than looking me in the eye, he focussed on a point between my eyes. I wondered if a boil had appeared there without my noticing.

"Aren't you going to invite me in?"

Having thought enough for one day, the man stepped aside. An immense boulder had been rolled away from the mouth of a cave. Into the dark unknown, I stepped. My steps echoed in the empty corridor.

"What are you doing?" the man shouted. He had followed me after I turned right into a yet darker, and yet emptier, corridor.

I stopped walking. I turned to face the man. "First, a grunt, and now a bark," I replied. "Your vocal range would put Pavarotti to shame."

"Huh?"

"I'm looking around."

"Don't you need a search warrant for that?"

"I'm not searching," I said. "I'm just looking."

Having resumed my journey into the unknown, I stopped by a door halfway down the corridor. I looked up the corridor. The man might have been there. It was too dark to see. I turned the handle. I pushed the door. It was a little stiff. I entered a strange world. All around me was glass. I was standing inside a big square made of glass, around the sides of which were booths made of glass. The walls were made of glass. There were glass tanks round about containing fish of every conceivable size and shape. Some of the creatures were so large and colourful that I wondered if they were fish at all. The floor was made of glass. The ceiling was made of glass. To be precise, the ceiling was an enormous square mirror. In each corner of the room was a bed. Inside the square in which I stood was another square, again, with a bed in each corner. Inside that square was another with a bed in each corner. In the middle of each side of the two inner squares was an archway. In the middle of the whole arrangement – in the centre of the innermost square, that is – was a gigantic bed raised on a platform, to which access was gained, on all four sides, via three massive steps. The light was dim, though bright enough for me to wonder at what I was seeing. In all my years as a policeman, I had never seen anything quite so outlandish. I wondered how such a place could exist within earshot of the bells of Magdalen College. I wondered if what went on amid all this glass was remotely legal. Hearing heavy footsteps approaching me from the corridor from which I had come, I went right and then left. I left the festival of glass by another door and found myself in another dark corridor. The noise behind me was getting louder, so I walked to the end of the corridor, before turning left into yet another dark corridor. I heard voices coming from the other side of yet another door. There was no mistaking the woman's voice.

"Stop larking about, Sab," a man said.

"Don't you like it when I dance, Jimmy?"

"I love it when you dance, babe, but we have a job to do."

"Where are we going this time?"

"Same place as last time…"

"Shotover Hill?"

"Where else?"

"I liked being your lover up there."

"You're going to have to pretend to be my girl again."

"I *am* your girl, Jimmy."

"Let's go, honey."

"Last time we went up there, you dropped the gear and there was nobody there."

"They were there, all right."

"I didn't see them."

"That was the idea."

"I know. I'm teasing you."

"We drop the gear at twelve."

"That doesn't give us long to amuse ourselves on the Hill."

"It gives us long enough."

I had to act quickly when I heard the steps of the lovers coming my way. Quietly as I could, I stepped down the corridor and into another dark corridor. I might have gone down the corridor before. I was lost. As I pressed my back against the wall, I prayed that Jimmy and Sabrina would go left up the corridor and not right. Though Jimmy scared me enough, I was more afraid of being seen by Sabrina. Jimmy would have been merely curious as to why I was lurking in the corridors of his patron's lair, though his curiosity might well have been expressed with narrowed eyes and clenched fists. Sabrina had the power to blow my cover and promote me to the top of the Great Dane's list of jobs to be done. To my great relief, they turned left. They did not hear my heart thumping. As the sound of their footsteps faded, my heart made its peace with my ribcage. A door opened and closed. Then I heard distant voices. Jimmy, Sabrina and the bouncer were passing the time of day. They were not joking. Having nowhere to go but left, I went to the end of the corridor. I stopped at a door. I knocked on the door.

"Enter…"

I obeyed.

The Great Dane was sitting at his desk, looking thoughtful. Running a club like The Aquarium, he must have had much to think about, like how to maintain a discerning clientele by keeping the ever-curious rabble at bay. People who come to my club, he seemed to be thinking, must have a certain breadth of mind. They must have a healthy contempt for the mores of a hidebound commonality. They must indulge the pleasures of the flesh with a certain perverse decorum, with a manic detachment, with a faceless intimacy, and with a restrained, near-cerebral savagery. They must be the sort of people who offer their gentleness to the world laced with malice.

"You must be the policeman that I've been told about."

The door closed behind me. Looking around, I beheld more fish. I wondered if any fish were left in the tropics. So many were the bubbles, from the mouths of fish and the pumps attached to the tanks, that I was entranced for a moment by their short lives and little deaths, as, from the depths of the tanks, too fragile for the world in which they found themselves, they floated upwards like regiments of doomed poets in the heat of battle.

"I'm sorry to interrupt you," I said, trying to sound as if I carried some authority. "I'd like a word with Miss Seymour here."

"How did you know she was here?"

"An officer saw her enter these premises. She witnessed an incident this morning. We need to ask her some questions."

"Haven't I answered all your questions, Inspector?" Far from looking threatened by the Great Dane's presence, Carey seemed to be having the time of her life and revelling in the role she was playing.

"One or two more questions need to be asked, Miss Seymour."

"I'm at your service, Inspector."

"Have you been amusing yourself in my club, Inspector?"

The man was irritating me with his condescending tone. It was high time that I asserted my authority. It was time that he knew what I knew.

"I was just *hanging* around," I said. "Now I could *murder* a drink."

The Great Dane regarded me with intent. His eyes threatened me. Behind his eyes lurked an evil scheme the seed of which had been planted by my recklessness. I never learned. He no more believed that I was a policeman than he believed that I was Mary Poppins. He knew who I was.

"Take Miss Seymour," he said at last. "She was just leaving, anyway."

"Was the interview successful?" I asked.

"That's between Miss Seymour and me, *Inspector*?"

I did not care for the man's stress on that last word, for it contained the promise of violence. So enraged was I by what he had done to Philip, though, that I was past caring what he thought of me and what designs he had on me. Overtaken by pride, then – in myself, in Philip, and in our shared home – I made one final allusion to what I knew about Dane Goldman's murderous exploits.

"You could do worse than Miss Seymour here," I said. "She would give your club a much-needed *fillip*."

During the ensuing five seconds, during which time the man pondered my words, I studied the characters flanking him. I had not noticed them before. I tried to work out whether they were seated or standing. They appeared to be standing. Their legs were short as they come. Identical in their ugliness, they had to be twins. When they were born, the midwife must have departed from convention and slapped the mother.

"Imagine the scenario, *Detective Inspector Maximilian Doublesnake*," the Great Dane intoned.

"What scenario would that be?"

"Imagine that I discover, following discreet enquiries, that you are not who you say you are." The man was playing the sort of game that only gangsters play. He turned to Carey. "Imagine, if you will, Miss Seymour, that I discover – again, following discreet enquiries – that you have come to my club under false pretences."

Carey looked at me. I looked at her. I was surprised to see that she looked neither scared nor angry. Though she carried five-hundred pounds' worth of courage in her handbag, she had every right to harbour fear and anger, given the situation in which I had placed her.

"Are you suggesting that Miss Seymour and I are in league for some purpose?"

Thoughtfully, the Great Dane stared at me. He stared at me long and hard and with ever-increasing thoughtfulness. When he had stared long and hard and thoughtfully enough, he asked me what I thought of his club.

"It has a lot of glass," I replied, "but not so much class."

The man was silent again. To my relief, he soon grew tired of silence.

"You must go, Miss Seymour," he said. "Take your friend with you."

Carey Seymour and I needed no further encouragement to take our leave.

"You bastard!"

"Actually, being born in wedlock is one of my few accomplishments."

"You cut it rather fine."

"You two seemed to be getting on all right."

"He was indulging me. He even seemed to know my real name."

"Did he call you by your name?"

"He alluded to it."

"How?"

"He asked me if I liked coconut."

"What is your real name?"

"Charlotte Bounty…"

We were walking up the long corridor which led to the front entrance. The door was open. Three figures stood in the doorway, chatting.

"Oh, no," Carey said, "it's that bonehead again."

"I know the two people with him…and I'm not looking forward to the next few seconds."

Jimmy did not like the look that Sabrina gave me. He liked still less the look that I gave Sabrina.

"What's going on?" he asked Sabrina.

"What are you talking about?" his girlfriend replied.

"Do you two know each other?"

"No…"

"Yes, you do…and something's going on. I can tell. And you've been acting weird lately, ignoring me…and going places."

"Get a grip of yourself, Jimmy," Sabrina said.

Jimmy turned on me. "What's been going on?"

"I thought you taxi-drivers knew everything."

Jimmy's coming for me was checked by the bouncer.

"Speak to your boss, Jimmy," I said. "He will tell you what's been going on."

"*I'll* tell Jimmy what's been going on," Sabrina said, "and I will tell him gladly."

"You'd better go, my friend," the bouncer told me.

"Consider me gone."

"Who was that girl?" Carey asked me once we were ensconced in a taxi and heading back into town.

"Sabrina Connor…"

"I'm none the wiser."

"I've been seeing her."

"Now it makes sense."

"She's been checking me out, spying on me for the Big Dog, though, for some strange reason, Jimmy was kept in the dark about it."

"Did Sabrina ever mention Jimmy?"

"She told me that they were finished as a couple."

"The plot gets thicker and thicker."

"I'm sorry that I dragged you into it."

"Don't be sorry. I'm enjoying the adventure."

"Tell me that when the Great Dane finds out where you live and pays you a visit."

"How would he find out where I live?"

"He seems to know everything about everyone."

"Will he be knocking on your door?"

"I'm expecting him to pop round for tea any day now."

"What will you do?"

"I'll pray."

Carey laughed. "Did you ever suspect what Sabrina was up to?"

I nodded. "Last time we saw each other, she gave herself away."

"She let the mask slip then?"

"She won't be applying to join MI6 anytime soon, that's for sure."

"You could do with a bit more discretion yourself."

We journeyed up the High Street in silence. Language students were everywhere. Their clustering and the ubiquitous rucksacks gave them away. I wanted to start a game of "guess the nationality" with my fellow passenger, but I sensed that she was no longer in the mood for games. We were in Saint Aldate's, passing Christ Church, before either of us spoke again.

"So, what did the Great Dane tell you?"

"Not much..."

"He must have told you something."

"The only thing of substance that he told me was that my working for him was inconceivable."

"Why is it inconceivable?"

"Because, he said, he approaches girls, they do not approach him..."

"We knew that already, but it was still worth hearing."

"Who were those jokers in the office with us?"

"I'm glad you saw them. I did wonder if I was seeing things."

"How grotesque were they?"

"They are God's creatures, so we shouldn't mock."

"They were dwarves...and, my God, they were twins!"

"Can't dwarves be twins?"

"It's not a combination that you encounter often, is it?"

"A dwarf is as likely to be a twin as any other type of person, wouldn't you say?"

"The dwarves just stood there," Carey went on. "The Great Dane didn't acknowledge them, never mind introduce them to me."

"Why are you surprised?" I asked.

"Men like him normally have a bit of class," Carey replied, "even if it is only for show."

"How much class do you think he showed before he had my friend hanged from a banister?"

Carey was not speaking without compassion when she urged me to go to the police. I was not speaking without due respect for officers of the law when I replied that I was not going to let a gang of plodding detectives ruin an investigation that had reached a most delicate stage. In any case, the police had already made up their minds.

The driver having negotiated the tricky – some say, crazy – collection of traffic lights in Hythe Bridge Street, we arrived at the station. We got out of the car. I winced as I paid the driver, for the day was proving to be alarmingly expensive. The taxi gone, Carey and I found ourselves at the foot of the steps outside the station's main entrance.

"I should make the twelve-fifteen."

"Thanks for your help today."

"I'm not sure how helpful I've been."

"You've been *most* helpful."

Carey reached into her handbag and lifted out the bundle of notes that I'd given her in the Randolph. She handed the notes to me.

"What are you doing?"

"I'm giving you your money back."

"Why?"

"Philip was your friend. Dana – Miranda – was one of his girls. She is one of *our* girls. She's in danger. You're in danger. I'm in danger. We're all in this together. As such, I can't take your money."

"I can claim it as expenses."

"Take the money back."

I took the envelope from Carey's hand and looked around to see who was looking. It is impossible not to feel self-conscious when someone is handing you an envelope stuffed with money.

"What about the money that you would have earned today?"

"I wouldn't have made much. The sex industry in Banbury is absolutely flat on its back."

"Never mind the sex industry. There's a place in comedy for you."

"You could be my agent."

"As you have been mine…"

"Will you let me know how the story ends?"

"I will call you tomorrow."

"You won't forget?"

"I won't forget."

Carey leaned forward and kissed me on the cheek. It was a kiss for which I had not paid, so it felt real.

"Until tomorrow…" she whispered.

As I watched Carey go up the steps and make her way to the entrance, my eyes started to water again. Anyone watching would have assumed that I had just said goodbye to a loved one.

If only I could find love, I thought, I could re-join the human race.

Thirty-One

I could not decide which of my two favourite episodes of *The Sweeney* to watch, *Abducted* or *Big Brother*, so I took from the shelf series two of *Minder* and played the first episode, entitled *National Pelmet*, which was first broadcast, on Independent Television, on the eleventh of September, nineteen-eighty, when I was fifteen years old. I remembered the excitement that I had felt as the second series of *Minder* beckoned, twenty-five years back. I appreciated the quality of the writing when I was a boy, but I marvelled at it as a man.

George Cole's Arthur Daley, then, was treating Terry to a day at the races. Arthur was intent on expanding his network of contacts. Seduced by the trappings of wealth, his mind was lost in a fog of misplaced ambition. Everywhere and everyone was an opportunity to make a pitch.

"Smell that affluence, Terrence," Arthur says, having breathed in some aromatic country air. "You don't get that at Hackney dog track."

"It's dung," Terry replies. "You're standing in it."

Arthur looks down at his feet, sees that Terry isn't joking, and grimaces.

Writing does not come any better than that.

After watching *Minder*, I decided to read the final chapter of the book that I had been reading. I was about to pick up *The Long Goodbye*, the last of Raymond Chandler's Philip Marlowe novels, when my mobile rang. I had read all of Chandler's other Marlowe books, so felt a sense of achievement at being on the point of completing the canon of works. I had long been a devotee of detective fiction; now, as one myself, I was immersed in the private-detective genre. I had read Arthur Conan Doyle's Sherlock Holmes stories countless times. I had read all of Robert B. Parker's Sunny Randall mysteries. I had read Charles Bukowski's *Pulp*, a beautifully cynical tale of a private eye who solves his cases by sitting them out. I would have to try that.

"Laura?"

"You left me a message, asking me to call you."

"We need to talk."

"It's about Mum, isn't it?"

"It is."

"You've found her?"

"*She's* found *us*," I said. "Or, rather, she found *you*."

"What do you mean?"

I was bracing myself for a long and arduous chat with Laura, a chat that she deserved, when the doorbell rang.

"There's someone at the door." I thought it was Kendal, returning after a bout of soul-searching. "I have to go."

"Let them wait! How long have we been waiting for news of our mother?" Laura was in tears.

"Can you hear that frantic ringing?" I had cause to doubt that it was Kendal calling. "There's some maniac at my door."

"Will you call me back as soon as you can?"

"Of course I will."

The emotionally-charged conversation with Laura over, for the moment, I went to the door. I opened it. Standing before me were the Great Dane and his two miniature henchmen. The big man put his foot over the threshold to stop me closing the door, though, had I closed it, he would only have kicked it in, or else caught up with me another time. I had to face the music. I wanted to face the music. Again, my recklessness had set in train events that would have to run their course.

Had the Great Dane barged past me, he would have been acting with undue politeness. Instead, he barged into me and bounced me down the hallway. When I found myself in the lounge, just about on my feet, I feared the worst, but was bent on taking my punishment defiantly and with my dignity intact. The Great Dane entered the room, flanked by his little army. Not three hours before, I had caught up with the man in his inner sanctum. I had beheld him reposing on his throne. He had looked big then. He looked bigger now. He was wide as I was high. To make the situation more desperate for me, not an ounce of fat adorned his person.

A little cellulite would have given me a glimmer of hope.

"Do not be afraid," I said. "I mean you no harm." My hope that a splash of humour would take the heat out of the situation was wholly misplaced.

"Sit down, Mr Winter," my adversary commanded.

"I won't be invited to sit down in my own flat, thank you."

Before I knew what had happened, I was sitting down, having been helped onto the armchair by my guest, who had me locked in such a position that I could hardly blink, never mind move.

"I don't want to have to fight you in my best slippers," I said, forcing the words out, such was the Great Dane's hold on my neck.

The Diddy Men approached me in a pincer movement, pulling up their sleeves in unison as they came.

"That's very good," I croaked at the twins. "I'm sure that there's a circus somewhere that will take you in."

"You're in no position to speak with such a liberal tongue, Mr Winter," the Great Dane submitted.

"On the contrary," I returned, "my position is so hopeless that I might as well say what I like."

"You've given yourself more than enough rope with which to hang yourself, Mr Winter."

The man was being unnecessarily aggressive, for his aftershave alone was capable of committing grievous bodily harm. The pendant hanging from the giant's neck gleamed golden against his skin. It was obvious what the "D" stood for. It might have stood for much else besides. It was an inch from my eyes.

"It's a shame that I couldn't provide you with a staircase." Trying to talk was doing my throat no good. I sounded like a constipated frog.

As the grip on my neck tightened, I heard the familiar trill of my neighbour's voice. I had never been so glad to hear it. I tried to reply. Maureen entered the room. Thankfully, the Diddy Men had forgotten to close the front door behind them, so consumed were they by the desire to break a neck.

"Is that you under there, Daniel?"

"Afternoon, Maureen…" I said, the big dog's grip having loosened slightly.

"Is everything all right?"

"My friend here was just showing me one of his best moves."

"I've brought the *Oxford Mail* for you."

"Thanks," I replied. "Leave it on the table."

"I'm disinclined to go until these gentlemen have departed."

"Stick around, then, and you might witness a murder."

The Great Dane released his grip and threw me back against the chair with such force that I nearly toppled over and landed on my back. The man was asking for a slap.

"This isn't over," he hissed.

"I say!" Maureen exclaimed.

The man left the room in a pulsating concert of rippling muscles and a cloud of aftershave. The little men followed, but only after they had stood before Maureen, gazing at her with what looked like erotic intent, forcing her to pull her cardigan across her body to conceal her cleavage.

"You played a blinder there, Maureen," I gasped, clutching my throat.

"I think that man had an entire bottle of cologne splashed over him."

"The entire *city* of Cologne, more like…"

"What a dreadful business."

"I reckon you've pulled, Maureen," I choked. "Those two jokers took a shining to you."

"That's a grotesque notion, Daniel."

"You're right." I coughed like a man who had just smoked ninety cigarettes. "It doesn't bear thinking about."

"Who were those men?"

"Just a bunch of actors from the local troupe…"

"They didn't look like actors to me."

"They're good actors."

"Will they be coming back?"

"Now they know that you're here to protect me, they won't."

Thirty-Two

With only a few hours to go before my appointment with Miranda, I was in desperate need of a drink, if only to loosen my compressed larynx. Though breathing had become easier, speaking was no easy task. I had not realised how close I was to being strangled or to having my neck broken. I realised now.

"What happened to your voice?" Barry asked as he poured my drink.

"I lost it."

"Don't tell me," the landlord said as he placed a pint of bitter on the bar and regarded my sore neck, "you've been at your favourite hobby again."

"Which favourite hobby would that be?"

"Bondage…"

"Judo, more like…"

Barry took the money and placed it in the till. "Listen, I'm hosting a pub quiz next week, and want to put a few questions together."

"That shouldn't be hard."

"I thought of a really good question: who was the last Brighton player to play for England?"

"Gary Stevens, John Gregory…" I began.

"Whilst playing for Brighton…"

"Steve Foster…"

"Which year?"

"Nineteen-eighty-two…"

Barry laughed like a schoolboy. "Twenty-three years…" he said in a derisive tone.

"I can count on one hand the number of West Bromwich Albion players who have played for England," I countered, mindful that I was on shaky ground.

"Let's see," Barry said. "There's the great Jeff Astle…"

"Great by West Brom's standards…"

"Then there's Laurie Cunningham, Cyril Regis, Bryan Robson, Derek Statham…"

"Like I said, one hand…"

"I have customers to serve," Barry said. "I'll be back with some more names, don't you worry." He looked to his right with a smile. "In the meantime, enjoy your drink with Mandy."

Having followed Barry's line of vision, I saw the old man approaching me. The same shabby clothes hung from his creaking frame with the same desperation to escape, the same stubbly intimations of old age populated his craggy chin, and the same oil slick held in check what remained of his hair. Ominously, he appeared to be accompanied by the usual band of kangaroos from the western hemisphere.

"Hello, young Daniel!"

"Good evening, Mandy…"

"How's that young lady of yours?" His half-empty glass of beer shaking in his hand, Mandy climbed the stool by the bar as if it were a scaffold. When he was on the stool, he looked as if he were about to fall off it.

"Sabrina and I are finished," I replied. "It wasn't true love, after all."

Mandy wondered which of the many girls with whom he thought he had seen me was Sabrina. "What happened?"

"She nearly bloody strangled me, didn't she?" I stroked my neck. "She had to go."

With all the clarity of a blind man with conjunctivitis, Mandy peered at my neck in disbelief. "*She* did *that*?"

"I tell you, Mandy, whoever said that hell hath no fury like a woman scorned was guilty of gross underestimation."

"What did you say to her to make her do that?"

"I simply told her that she needed to lose some weight."

"And all hell broke loose?"

"The full wrath of hellfire and damnation was unleashed upon me."

"I bet you didn't stand a chance."

"Talk about David and Goliath…"

Mandy drained his glass in three gulps, then put the glass on the bar as if to suggest that it was my round. "I'm truly sorry, Daniel," he said. "I thought you had that one in the bag."

It occurred to me to ask Mandy if he hadn't meant "pouch", instead of "bag", but I was loath to encourage him. We had been talking for a couple of minutes, and a kangaroo from the western hemisphere had yet to spring forth, so it was a matter of time before one did. I wondered what form the next marsupial would take. In past encounters, Mandy had invoked the kangaroo jumping for joy, the one hopping mad, the one making a gigantic leap of faith, the one with a spring in its step, and the one skipping lunch. No, I remembered, I gave him that last one. He had promised to use it on some unsuspecting victim. Not wishing to have a recycled lunch-skipping kangaroo from the western hemisphere inflicted on me, I hoped that he had used it and got it off his chest.

"It's a desperately sad story, young Daniel." Like the drunkard he was, Mandy was slurring his words, but only slightly, since the night was young and he was in the early stages of inebriation. "It's enough to make every kangaroo in the western hemisphere say 'ouch'."

For the next ten seconds, I was put in mind of the film *Groundhog Day*. Even Nietzsche's doctrine of eternal recurrence reared its ugly head.

"Or should I say 'pouch'?"

Mandy considered his quip. He burst into uproarious laughter. The inside of his mouth was exposed, forcing me to subject it to a moment's unwitting inspection. It resembled one of the gutted houses on the Wood Farm housing estate. When he slapped me on the back, I lost a mouthful of ale and nearly fell off my stool.

Around a table nearby sat three old boys without dominoes. "Keep the noise down, Mandy," one of the men said. "We're trying to sleep over here." The man lost his cigarette when it fell from his mouth into his beer. That did not stop him retrieving the cigarette and trying to relight it.

"That's a good one!" Mandy roared. "Don't you think?"

"Your best ever..."

"Can I confess something to you, Daniel?" The man's tone had changed in a moment.

"So long as it's clean..."

"I'm running out of kangaroos."

"Would they be kangaroos of the western hemisphere," I enquired, "or kangaroos in general?"

"Kangaroos from the western hemisphere are the only ones I know."

"You'll find plenty of kangaroos in the eastern hemisphere," I said. "Give them a go."

"Do you think it'll work?"

"You can but try."

"Kangaroos in the western hemisphere are extinct, anyway."

"Are they?"

"When did you last see a kangaroo in Oxford?"

"Yes," I said, "kangaroos are conspicuous by their absence on the Banbury Road."

"And the Woodstock Road," the old man said. "Don't forget the Woodstock Road."

"Colin Suggett!" Barry yelled at me.

"Don't give me that!" I yelled back. "Colin Suggett never played for England!" I wasn't sure that he had played for West Bromwich Albion.

With nearly a pint of ale inside me, I felt bold enough to call my sister back, so I took my drink from the bar and went outside.

Thirty-Three

Though I would not have convinced a policeman that I was sober enough to drive, I risked moving the Jensen the few yards from its usual resting place to a point in Middle Way where I could see movement to and from the brothel. I had been sitting there for over an hour, drinking tea from a flask and listening to *Live At The Witch Trials*, the first album by The Fall. Disc One of the latest version of the album consisted of the original eleven tracks, together with those forming the *Bingo-Master's Break-Out* EP and sides A and B of The Fall's second single. Disc Two offered a couple of John Peel sessions and *Liverpool 78*, a live album that sounds like it was recorded in someone's bathroom, but which is of great historical interest for the band's dwindling band of followers. I had been a fan of The Fall since the release of *Witch Trials*, in seventy-eight, and was looking forward to the imminent release of their twenty-fifth studio album. *Last Orders* had just played, so I was about to replace the first disc with the second, when people appeared at the door of the house.

Only women could make such a performance of saying goodbye. Where men would shake hands and express their mutual regard with economy, women would kiss every cheek in sight, throwing their arms about as they did so, and scatter felicitations until the season changed. Finally, as autumn approached, three women stepped out of the house and onto the path. One of them was Dana, also known as Miranda Ward-Homer. Awestruck by blonde hair and a figure that must have been fashioned by a sculptor visited by divine inspiration, I watched. Having seen the girl only in a photograph, and having watched a film in my mind of her charged affair with Philip, I felt as if I were seeing a famous person in the flesh for the first time. With as much effort as the three women had put into their valedictory performance, I tried not to move a muscle. Indeed, I tried not to breathe.

Once Suzie had gone back to the house and closed the door behind her, Dana and her friend walked to the end of the path. They stopped in their tracks and started to talk again. Then they began to say goodbye to each other. I braced myself for an extended vigil.

After the girls had been talking for two or three minutes – about what, I could not tell, for they spoke quietly – a taxi appeared. Its lights threatened to expose me, so I hid my face and crouched a little. Another performance followed, this one mercifully shorter, before the brunette got in the car and was driven away towards South Parade. Dana waved at her departing friend. Then she set off in the direction of Squitchey Lane. Having allowed enough time to elapse to forestall suspicion, but not so much time that I risked losing Dana's track, I set off after her, umbrella in hand.

When I had walked no more than fifty yards, I saw that Dana had put up a small umbrella and was walking at speed. Then she stopped. Though I carried on walking, I hid behind my umbrella. Dana began walking again. I followed. The two of us seemed to have Summertown to ourselves.

In Squitchey Lane, our isolation was accentuated. Our footsteps echoed in the damp air. Synchronised, as they were, our steps resounded unnervingly. Conscious of how unsettling the sound of footsteps must have been for Dana – they were disconcerting enough for me, and I was the stalker – I adjusted my steps so that they followed hers. Alas, the quieter one-two-three-four sounded more alarming than the louder one-two-one-two, so I adjusted my step again so that we were synchronised once more.

Incredibly, Banbury Road saw us no less alone in the night. I wondered where everyone was. Had a ten-o'clock curfew for all denizens of North Oxford been declared? As we strode towards Cutteslowe, I prayed that Dana would not take me on too long a journey. I had a programme to watch at eleven. To my consternation, Dana stopped walking. She looked over her shoulder at me. There I was, some fifty yards behind her, but getting nearer, big umbrella in pursuit of small umbrella, man after woman. Though she was a woman fit to grace any Raymond Chandler novel, she did not take too kindly to being followed. As I wondered whether she might not be waiting for me to pass her, an eventuality that would have undermined my clumsily executed plan, fatally, Dana turned on her not-inconsiderable heels and quickened her pace. I tried to think of something other than what I was doing, my reasoning being that if I detached myself, somehow, from the situation in hand then my breathing down the girl's neck would not be so conspicuous. So it was that I saw myself playing Scrabble with Kendal and placing two letters on the board. "What's a gnhops?" the girls asks in disbelief. "It's what a one-legged gnome does," I reply. When that incident occurred, I had managed to replicate a scene from the *Big Brother* episode of *The Sweeney*. I laughed to myself, but loud enough to permit a woman walking forty yards ahead to hear me. Putting myself in that woman's shoes, I saw a strange man in pursuit of me. He was dressed all in black and carried a black umbrella. He had compounded his threatening behaviour by laughing to himself like a madman. It was time to get away from him.

To my relief – she was not walking me all the way to Kidlington, after all – Dana turned right into Wentworth Road. A minute later, I did the same. Past Southdale, Cavendish and Jackson Roads she went. I went with her, getting closer with every step. Into Aldridge Road she went. I was ten yards behind her now. Aldridge Road, not the most salubrious of council estates, was the last place to which I expected to follow her. I wondered where she was taking me. She stopped outside number twenty-four. The scene before me had me squinting in disbelief. The garden was strewn with so much debris that it made a landfill site resemble a bowling green. The grass had been cut, though God only knew how long ago. The window frames were stretched and had split in all directions. Though it was too dark to see the panes in detail, I had the impression that they last saw soap and water on the day that the grass last saw a lawnmower. Whoever had stripped the front door of its colour had not hung around to repaint it. To my amazement, an old pram, tatty and soiled, stood in the long grass. It was so old that one might call it a perambulator. Surely, the glorious Miranda Ward-Homer, she of Hampstead provenance, could not be about to enter a house such as this. Immersed in disbelief, as I was, I failed to notice that Dana had indeed entered the house.

A girl in Gothic-type costume answered the door. She looked at me as if my calling round were a daily occurrence.

"Miranda's been expecting you," she said.

The door was held open, so I stepped inside. The house was not unlike the one in Portslade, the one that Sylvia had been lucky enough to inherit. It looked seedier still in the dark.

"Top of the stairs, turn right…" the girl said.

"Thanks…" I replied.

The creaking wooden hill was overlaid by one of those carpets that cover only the middle part of the stairs, leaving the sides bare and exposed. I had never seen the point of such partial furnishing. The wood underfoot was so rotten that I doubted my facility to reach the summit without putting my foot through it. The walls around me had once been adorned with paper, but were now shorn of decoration, cracked and rutted. The lights hung starkly from the ceiling like dead rats hanging from their tails, and flies buzzed around them like children in sweetshops. Compared with this place, the house in Portslade was a palace fit for a queen. The rich girl had picked a perfect place to hide.

Miranda was looking out of the bedroom window through a gap in the blind. With aimless eyes, she peered into the gloom. As if she hadn't heard me enter, a minute passed before she turned to face me. I had seen some sights in my time, but never so beautiful and refined a girl in so miserable a setting.

"So, you're the hapless individual being paid to find me…"

"Not so hapless…" I replied. "I've found you."

"I knew my father had put someone onto me."

"He wouldn't be much of a father if he didn't look for his missing daughter."

"He has been the missing father."

"I know what it's like to have an absent parent."

"He was present in person, but missing here." Miranda pressed a hand against her broken heart.

"It's not too late to make amends."

"He was too busy to come looking for me himself, he paid a private detective to look for me…and, even then, through that lapdog Hardcastle."

"That's more than some fathers would have done."

The girl dismissed my words with a shake of her head. "For the past

240

week or so, I have felt someone breathing down my neck."

"Would that someone be me, or Dane Goldman?"

"Dane Goldman is always breathing down my neck."

"I know the feeling."

"If you've made an enemy of that man then you will spend the rest of your days looking over your shoulder."

"He's already paid me a less-than-friendly visit."

"So how come you're still breathing?"

"I have a minder. She's called Maureen."

Miranda shook her head again, this time with the hint of a smile. "You know Philip, don't you?"

"How do you know that?"

"There's a part of him that lives in you. I can sense it. You must have known him a long time."

"Since the day we were born…"

"Are you brothers?"

"Not quite…"

"It's strange. I…"

"I know how you're feeling."

"Do you?"

"You're feeling drawn to me, close to me, because of my connection with Philip."

"Yes…"

"Philip loved you."

"Ours was a strange kind of love."

"It takes all sorts…"

"Come with me to Paris."

"When are you going?"

"I leave early tomorrow morning."

"I could do with a holiday, but…"

"This won't be a holiday."

"You're not coming back?"

"Why would I come back?"

When Miranda stepped towards the cluttered dressing-table, I went to her. Up close, I looked for blemishes that I might have missed from a distance. I searched in vain. In heels, she was taller than I. Over black see-through lingerie, she wore a matching garment that resembled a frockcoat. Her skin was milky-white and her hair a glory to her in cascading blonde. I gave her my card.

"Will you visit me?" she asked.

"Gladly…"

"We have much to tell each other."

"I will tell you the whole story."

"So will I…"

"I'll come to Paris…soon."

"You won't tell anyone where I've gone?"

"You have my word."

Still shrouded in a mystique that could not be fathomed, the girl who had led me on a mystery tour reached for something that lay on the dressing-table beside her. She picked up that something and handed it to me. It was a colour photograph of her standing in front of the Leaning Tower of Pisa.

"Show this to Mr Hardcastle," she said. "He will accept it as proof that I'm alive and well."

"He might ask where you are."

"He won't."

"I will call him tonight and arrange a meeting between him and me."

Miranda stared at my card longingly, as if it bore Philip's living countenance. "Philip talked about you, Daniel, often."

"Did he ever mention Sylvia Blackman?"

Remembering our mutual friend fondly, the girl smiled tenderly. "He tried not to talk about her."

"Perhaps you'll meet her someday."

"I hope so."

Miranda put her arms around me and held me. She began to cry. My eyes began to water. Though I pitied the girl, I discerned her inner strength. Wherever she went, though broken in spirit, she would survive and prosper. She would go to Paris and live like Anaïs Nin. She would live her life in the Delta of Venus.

"It's all my fault," she sobbed.

"Philip did not die because of you."

"He did."

"Though she's done no wrong, Sylvia is the source of all Philip's troubles," I said. "Because of *her*, Philip is dead."

Thirty-Four

"How did you know I was here?"

"The Jericho Café is the place to be. Besides, I looked in all your other haunts, and you were nowhere to be seen."

"Where have you been?"

"I went home."

"Why?"

"Mum said that she was going to report you to Social Services. I didn't want you to go through that. I hate her."

"Don't be too hard on her. She knows not what she does."

"She knows exactly what she does."

"You'll be old enough to leave home soon."

"I won't wait until then."

"I miss having you around."

"I miss being around."

"You can visit anytime."

"I will."

"I'm sorry for freaking you out with that painting."

"I can't talk about that, Daniel. That painting did something to me. I looked at it and saw myself, my soul, and I hated what I saw. I had to be by myself for a while, to think about who and what I am, and what lurks within."

"Can I get you anything?"

"No, thanks, I've just eaten. What's that?"

"Mashed potato, with diced chicken and strips of bacon, with pesto sauce on the side…"

"It looks nice."

"It's what I always have when I come here."

"Have you been to see her?"

"Who?"

"Your mum…"

"No, but I will go and see her. She's not going anywhere, is she?"

"I guess not."

"So much has happened. Has it all been a dream?"

"It was the first of many adventures."

"That I will ever get to see Roseanne is a miracle."

"It must be so weird…after all this time…"

"I cannot tell you how weird it is."

"Has your sister been to see her?"

"She's going to the convent tomorrow."

"Can I visit her, you know, when you go?"

"Sure…"

"When did she become a Catholic? And when did she become a nun?"

"She could have become a Catholic anytime. She couldn't have become a nun until Laura and I were no longer dependent on her."

"But you weren't dependent on her. Your aunt and uncle brought you up."

"Until we had become adults, then, and were no longer of a dependent age…"

"You think that your Auntie Hillary knows something, don't you?"

"She and Roseanne conspired. Auntie Hillary allowed – encouraged – Roseanne to leave. She was childless, so jumped at the chance to bring us up. Roseanne left happy in the knowledge that we would be well cared for."

"Will you talk to Hillary about it?"

"You bet I will."

"What will you say to your mum when you see her?"

"She will ask me how I've been, like people do."

"What will you say?"

"I will tell her that I've been just…sailing by."

"What will she say to that?"

"We're from a seaside town. She will be expecting a nautical metaphor."

"I wish Mum would go sailing by…or, even better, sailing off into the sunset."

"You'd miss her if she went."

"Don't bet on it."

"You're cynical beyond your years."

"Have you any more news?"

"You know I have."

"Let's hear it then."

"I'll tell you in the pub."

"Which pub are we going to?"

"The Jude…"

"You know how to show a girl a good time, Daniel."

"I need to drown my sorrows: Albion lost. I had a ticket for the game at Derby as well."

"They drew one-all."

"How do you know?"

"I checked the score before I came out."

"Are you winding me up?"

"I promise you, the game finished one-one."

"That definitely calls for a drink."

"Can I have one?"

"If anyone deserves to drink illegally, it's you."

"What about the law?"

"Bollocks to it."